HOW TO DATE A
DRAGON

ASHLYN CHASE

sourcebooks
casablanca

Published by Sourcebooks Casablanca, an imprint of Sourcebooks, Inc.
P.O. Box 4410, Naperville, Illinois 60567-4410
(630) 961-3900
Fax: (630) 961-2168
www.sourcebooks.com

Printed and bound in the United States of America
RRD 20 19 18 17 16 15 14

To my niece Nancy. She may (hopefully) never read this book, because her auntie writing about love and sex might give her the "ickies."

But she helped brainstorm this series when she was a mere twelve years old and deserves more than a hug and a pizza.

I wouldn't be surprised if she becomes a writer when she grows up. The kid's got talent and imagination.

Chapter 1

"I'M NEVER ATTENDING A DESTINATION WEDDING AGAIN."

Bliss Russo dragged her garment bag and carry-on up the ramp to her Boston apartment building. Her purse had fallen off her shoulder ten minutes ago and dangled from her wrist. She needed the other hand to hold her cell phone to her ear so she could bitch to her friend Claudia.

"Oh, poor you. Someone made you go to Hawaii." Claudia chuckled. "The bastards."

"Seriously... do you know how long the flight is? Or I should say flights. First there's the leg from Boston to L.A., then L.A. to Honolulu, and finally Honolulu to Maui. Two days later, I go from Maui to Honolulu. Then Honolulu to L.A. Then L.A. to Boston. Plus I had to follow Hawaiian wedding tradition—at least what the bride's parents assured us was the tradition—and party all night. I haven't slept for days."

"You're exaggerating."

"No, I'm not. Unless you count the five-minute nap I took at LAX. I was so exhausted, I woke up on the chair next to me when the guy I had apparently fallen asleep on got up and left."

"Sorry. Okay, you're right. It was a lousy, miserable thing to make you do. So where are you now?"

"Almost home. In fact, I'll probably lose you in the elevator. Give me a few days to sleep and I'll call you back."

"Call by Thursday if you can, and let me know if you want to go out Saturday night."

Bliss jostled the door open, and one of the residents held it while she maneuvered her luggage through. "I shouldn't. I worked a little harder and got a few days ahead so I could go to this damn wedding in the first place, but I really can't afford to take any more time off. The competition will crush me."

"That's what you get for landing in the finals of your dream reality show. What is it? America's Next Great Greeting Card Designer?"

"It's not called America's Next... oh, forget it. I'm at the elevator now and I'm too tired to care. I'll call you."

"Okay, sugar. Sweet dreams."

"Thanks." Bliss hung up and dropped her phone into the bowels of her purse. She yanked and stuffed her luggage into the tiny elevator, which she rode to the second floor. Eventually, she dragged everything to her door, rattled the key in her lock, and brought it all into her bedroom. Passing out on top of her bed fully dressed seemed like the only good idea she was capable of having, so she donned a sleep mask, did a face-plant, and stayed that way.

─────

Hours later—or maybe days—Bliss awoke to a deafening blare. Still disoriented, she had no idea what the hell the noise was or, for that matter, if it was night or day. She tore off the sleep mask and still couldn't tell what was going on. But what was that smell?

Oh. My. God. Smoke! That ear-piercing screech is the friggin' fire alarm.

Bliss tried to remember what to do. *Oh yeah, crouch down low and get the fuck out of Dodge.* Thank the good Lord she lived on the second floor, because she couldn't use the stupid elevator.

Bliss remembered just in time to put her hand to the door before opening it. It didn't feel as though there were an inferno on the other side. Staying low, she opened the door. The smoke was so thick she could barely see. She held her breath and charged toward the end of the hall.

Suddenly, her head hit something firm and she fell backward. "Oomph." The sharp intake of breath resulted in a coughing fit.

Looking up to see what she had hit, she realized she had just head-butted a firefighter's ass.

He swiveled and mumbled through his mask. "Really? I'm here to save you, and you spank me?"

Despite her earlier panic, Bliss felt a whole lot safer and started to giggle. *Oh no. My computer!* "Wait, I have to go back…"

"No. You need to get out of here, now." The firefighter lifted her like she weighed nothing—an amazing feat in itself—then carried her the wrong way down the rest of the hallway, through the fire door, and down the stairs.

"Wait!" She grasped him around the neck and tried to see his face through watering eyes.

His mask, helmet, and shield covered almost his whole head, but she caught a glimpse of gold eyes and a shock of hair, wheat-colored with yellow streaks, angled across his forehead. She thought it odd that the city would let firefighters dye their hair like rock musicians.

As soon as they'd made it to the street, she could see better and noticed his eyes were actually green and almond shaped. She must have imagined the gold color. He set her down near the waiting ambulance and pulled off his mask.

What a hottie! But I don't have time for that now. She staggered slightly as she tried to head back toward the door.

He grabbed her arm to steady her. "Hey," he shouted to one of the paramedics. "Give her some oxygen."

"No, I'm fine. I don't need any medical attention." *Thanks to the gorgeous hunk with the weird hair.*

"Please… let them check you out."

"I'd rather let *you* check me out." She covered her mouth and grinned. "Sorry. It must be the smoke inhalation.

He laughed. "Seriously? First you grab my ass, and now you're hitting on me?"

"I didn't 'grab your ass.' For your information, I ran face-first into your… behind."

"Oh. Well, pardon me for being in the way."

His smile almost stopped her heart—or was it the lack of oxygen? Regardless, she *had to* rip herself away from him and get her computer out of the building before it melted. No matter how hard she pulled, he didn't budge.

"You need to go back in there for my computer. Apartment twenty-five, halfway down the hall."

He took off his gloves. "Look, I'm sorry, miss, but if I went back in there now, my chief would have my hide."

"But my whole life is on that computer. I'm in the finale of a huge TV competition."

He didn't seem impressed, so she tried again.

"It's my greeting card business and all my newest designs are there. This show would pay for a whole ad campaign and give me fifty grand if I win." Realizing she sounded like a babbling idiot, she pressed on. "I've worked so hard to make it this far. If I lose my work, I'll never catch up. I'll wind up presenting a half-assed portfolio, and not only can I forget about winning, but it could ruin me!"

———— ⁓ ————

Drake couldn't believe what he was hearing. His weakness might be beautiful brunettes, but did she honestly expect him to risk his life for an object that could be replaced? Could she not see smoke pouring out of the building? Sure, he could probably manage it, being fireproof and all, but after the chewing out he got the last time…

"Don't you keep a backup file online?"

"No. I don't trust the Internet," she said with the saddest expression in her beautiful brown eyes. "There are too many hackers out there, and this greeting card competition is outrageously competitive. Pleeeease!"

All this hoopla for a piece of paper that reads, "Roses are red. Violets are blue?" The brunette didn't appear to be insane, no matter how stupid this reality show sounded. There were crazier things on TV.

His chief had already warned Drake about risking his neck and told him to knock off taking stupid chances. He'd lucked out the last time. The mayor, a big dog lover, heard that Drake had gone back into a two-alarm blaze to rescue a greyhound. Then Mr. Mayor made the chief disregard any thought of suspending Drake by giving him a medal. But that sort of luck wouldn't hold, especially if this insubordination was about an inanimate object.

Drake reached out and physically turned the woman

around so she could see the inferno behind her. The feel
of her soft, warm skin sent an unexpected jolt of aware-
ness through him.

Her hands flew to cover her mouth, and the same sad,
desperate sound all fire victims made as they witnessed
the destruction and loss of something precious eked out.
The tears forming in her eyes did him in.

If he weren't fireproof, running back into that building would toast him like a marshmallow, but being a
dragon, he knew he could do it.

"Ah, hell." Before anyone could stop him, he dashed
in the side entrance. He could always say he thought he
heard a call for help.

"Stop. Oh, crap," was what he really heard.
Apparently the brunette had changed her mind, but he
was committed now.

Second floor, halfway down the hall, he repeated to
himself until he found it. She had left her door open.
Fortunate for him, not so much for her apartment.
Smoke and flames were everywhere. He felt the familiar tingle just under his skin that signaled an impending
shift. *Fan-fucking-tastic*. Skin became scales. Fingers
became claws. His neck elongated, and out popped his
tail, creating an unsightly bulge in the back of his loose
coveralls. His wings were cramped and folded up under
his jacket, but it couldn't be helped.

His sight was greatly improved in his alternate form,
and he spotted the Mac on her glass tabletop. The flames
hadn't reached it yet, so he did his best to grab it with his
eagle-like talons and carry it against his chest.

Lumbering down the hall, he wondered where, and
if, he'd be able to shift back before anyone saw him.

Maybe it's cooler in the basement—but what if I get trapped down there?

Instead of heading down another level, he opened the emergency door just enough to toss the laptop onto the grass outside. The outside air was so much cooler that he thought he might be able to shift back right there.

Concentrating on his human form, he inhaled the fresh air and sensed his head and body shrinking and compacting. He glanced down and saw his human hands again. His back felt enormously better without squished wings digging into it.

Ah… I made it undetected.

Or had he? The brunette was standing a few feet away, wide-eyed and open mouthed—hugging her computer.

"What the…"

The handsome firefighter, who had appeared like some kind of dinosaur in the smoke only a moment earlier, stepped out of the building and stretched as if trying to work a kink out of his spine. He whipped off his mask and stared at her.

Bliss scrubbed her eye socket with the heel of her hand. *My eyes must have been playing tricks on me.* There was no other possible explanation. Between her jet-lagged brain and smoke-filled vision, her mind's eye had concocted a reptilian form that was really her hero firefighter.

Oh, fuck it. "Thank you!" *He deserves a reward.* She rushed up to him and cupped the back of his head, dragging him down until she mashed her lips to his in the mother of all adoring kisses. He wrapped his arms around her back and pulled her against him, returning her kiss. She fit his body as if they'd been made for each other. The fire he'd just rescued her from had nothing on the heat in his kiss.

Unfortunately for both of them, the chief came striding around the corner along with the paramedics. The paramedics led her away while her hottie fireman received the dressing-down of a lifetime, complete with explicit and crude language.

"Please don't be mad at him," Bliss called over her shoulder. "It's my fault. I asked him to go back in." But it was too late. A paramedic slapped an oxygen mask over her face as she heard the chief sputter the words "suspended" and "get the hell out of my sight" to her hot hero. She tried to wrestle off the damn mask, but by the time she did, he was gone.

Upon their return to the fire station, the guys whistled at a curvaceous blond waiting for them with a camera. Drake vaguely remembered the chief saying something about their posing for a calendar.

"Terrific," he muttered.

The chief spotted her and groaned. Then he pointed at Drake. "He goes first."

As they hung up their jackets, the chief strode to his office.

"Drake, buddy," Benjamin said, "I'd hang around and watch, but I gotta shower." He slapped Drake on the back and jogged up the stairs with the rest of them.

Drake glanced down at his filthy hands as the blond sashayed over to him.

"Hey there, handsome," she said.

"Look, I hate to make you wait, but I should shower before you take any pictures. We just…"

She finger-walked her way up his chest. "Oh, I know. You were out fighting fires and saving people. I think that's sexy as hell. Don't change a thing. Except, take your shirt off."

Drake stifled a groan. He was tired and about to be suspended. This was the last thing he wanted to do right now.

Figuring he was in enough trouble for defying the chief's orders, he whipped off his white undershirt, faced the blond female photographer as if she were a firing squad, and asked, "How do you want me?"

She chuckled and raised one eyebrow.

"Uh… What should I be doing?" he asked.

From the look in her eyes and the way she licked her lips, the answer was X-rated. Maybe they shouldn't have sent a woman to shoot the annual firefighters' calendar. At this rate it would be December before she finished taking the pictures.

"I don't want to be rude, but I really don't feel like doing this right now." When she didn't respond, he waved a hand in front of her eyes. "Hello," he said to break through the woman's vacant stare.

"Your hair… I've never seen yellow streaks like that. They're like primary colors."

"Yeah, it's unusual, and before you ask, it's natural. My whole family has them." *It would be so much easier if I could just come out and say it's how dragons know each other by clan.* But, of course, he could not. Dragons were governed by the same rule every paranormal faction had to live by—namely not to reveal their existence to humans. To do so would cause widespread panic, witch hunts, and they'd probably wind up as government lab rats.

"Oh, um…" At last she seemed to remember her professionalism. "Pick up that hose and stand a quarter-turn to the right."

Drake did as he was asked and she clicked her shutter release.

"Um, you might want to hold it higher."

Drake realized he was holding the nozzle right in front of his junk as if it were a limp phallus. He dropped it and grabbed an ax instead, resting it on his shoulder.

"Oh, yeah. That pose really shows off your muscles." She moved and clicked. Moved and clicked some more.

"Act like you're having fun. Smile," she said.

Drake rolled his eyes. "Fighting fires isn't exactly a laugh a second."

"Maybe if you think about something pleasant, it'll produce the look I'm going for."

Let's see… something pleasant. Unfortunately, he couldn't come up with much of anything at the moment. He had just lost the last friendly dragon he knew—his mother—a few weeks ago and still didn't feel like his old jovial self. Plus he was in trouble with the chief. He'd never work his way up the ladder at this rate, and the job was his life. Maybe his buddies were right. He needed a hobby.

"You're still looking awfully serious. Here, let me try something."

"Christ," he muttered.

She set down the camera and strolled up to him. Unbuttoning her blouse enough to expose lush cleavage, she said in a low, sultry voice, "Think of the fun we can have after I finish the shoot."

He raised his eyebrows. *Think of the horror when you find out I'm a dragon.*

"No, that's still not the expression I want. What's the matter? Are you having a bad day?"

"You could say that."

"Anything I can do?"

"Nope." He'd have to take his punishment just like any other firefighter who did what he'd done, regardless of his inability to burn. He should be grateful for the chance to delay facing the chief, but to be honest, he just wanted to get it over with.

As Drake was thinking about what to tell him, Chief Tate strolled out where they were shooting.

"Are you almost done here?" the chief asked.

The photographer backed away and quickly buttoned her blouse. "Ah, yes. I'd like one more pose…"

"I'll wait." Chief Tate stuffed his hands in his pockets and rocked back and forth on his heels.

Shit, I'm in bigger trouble than I thought. Drake decided to have some fun with the shoot after all. He set down the ax, moved beside the chief, and threw his arm around Tate's shoulder. "Here. Take one of me and the chief. I'll pay you for it."

"Huh?" Chief Tate leaned away and frowned at Drake. "What the hell for?"

"A memento. If I'm about to be fired, I'd like a picture of my old boss for my scrapbook."

Chief Tate reared back and laughed. "I'm not going to fire your ass, Cameron. I probably should for taking such a dumb chance. This isn't like the time the mayor heard about you saving a damn dog and was impressed. You won't be getting a commendation for this one."

The photographer grinned. "Wow. A commendation from the mayor! Now there's something to smile about."

The chief snorted. "Yeah, I told him to take off the word 'bravery' and make it a citation for stupidity."

Shrugging one shoulder, Drake said, "It figures." At least it didn't sound like he was getting canned. That was a relief.

Chief Tate addressed the woman without looking at her. "Don't encourage him. He risked his life for a damn pet. Cameron, you're just lucky the mayor's a big dog lover."

The photographer got even more excited, if that were possible. "Oh, he is. I've photographed him, and he has pictures of his greyhounds right on his desk."

"Is that right?" The chief didn't sound impressed, despite his words. "Look, as soon as you finish up here, Cameron, come to my office."

"Sure thing, chief."

The photographer cozied up to Drake. She held out a card. "If you had a shirt on, I'd tuck this in your pocket."

He took the card and glanced at it.

Suzanne Bloom
Blooming Great Photography
617-555-8349

He smiled and she said, "Freeze." Backing up a couple feet, she snapped a few more pictures. "There. Now I have what I want."

Yeah, your phone number in my hand.

—◆—

"I've got to do something to make this right, Claudia." Bliss sat at her friend's breakfast bar, running her fingers over the smooth granite.

Claudia took a sip of her coffee. "Look, he saved your business and possibly your place in the competition. Why don't you make him a card?"

"A Hall-Snark card? What would it say? *I'm sorry I got you suspended, but you looked great in suspenders?*"

Claudia grimaced. "Ah, no. I'm sure you can do better than that."

Bliss slumped over and rested her cheek on the cool stone. "My computer didn't survive, by the way. Well, I mean, the hardware did, but I think the rest is fubar."

"Fubar? What's that?"

She leaned back and sighed. "Sorry. It's something my brother Ricky, the ex-marine, says. It means fucked up beyond all recognition."

Claudia chuckled and opened the laptop in question. She hit the power button and a light came on. "Are you sure? It looks okay."

"I tried to boot it up several times, and all I can get out of it is, 'Operating system not found.'"

"Don't give up yet. There's something called forensic data recovery. You'd be surprised what the FBI can get off computers that were supposedly destroyed."

"I doubt the FBI would consider a reality TV show about a greeting card competition worthy of their time or equipment." Bliss cupped her chin and rested her elbow on the counter. "I don't know what I was thinking. He could have died. I don't even know his name…" She lifted her head and sat up straight. "Wait. The back of his jacket said Cameron."

Claudia set a tall glass of ice water in front of Bliss. "There you go. Is that his first name or last?"

Bliss sighed. "I don't know."

"What did the other guys' jackets look like? First names or last?"

Bliss rested her chin on both palms and her elbows on the counter. "I don't know. I only had eyes for him—as they say."

Claudia chuckled. "Oh, yeah. You've got it bad."

Bliss took a long swallow of her ice water. Her parched throat welcomed the cool liquid. "You want to know the worst thing about all this?"

"What?"

"Forget that my home and all my belongings except my precious laptop are toast. I have to go back to Winthrop and live with my annoying parents for who knows how long. If I don't win the contest, it could be forever." She groaned.

Claudia rubbed her friend's back. "I wish I could let you move in here, but my place is just too damn small. We'd get on each other's nerves, and our friendship is more important than anything to me."

"I know. I feel the same way. But I do have to go home. I lost my glasses in the fire. I think I have a spare pair in my old bedroom. Some of my old clothes might still be there, and I'll need them, if they fit. Stupidly, I didn't get renter's insurance, and now I have zero money and no time for shopping."

"So, have you told your parents yet?"

Bliss took a deep breath and let it out slowly. "No, but

I have to soon, before they see it on the news. They'll have a fit."

"Not because you need a place to stay, I hope."

"No, that's not it." She snorted. "They're always hoping us kids will come home for dinner… or a month. No, they'll be upset because one of their precious spawn had a brush with death. And they're going to try to get me married off and living in the suburbs."

"Oh, boy. I don't envy you, but at least your parents aren't stuck on the idea of your marrying a rich guy."

"Seriously? Yours are like that? Do they know what you do?"

Claudia laughed. "They know I work on Beacon Hill, but they don't know I manage a bar. If they did, they'd have a fit. I'm supposed to be rubbing elbows with Boston's elite."

"What do they think you do?"

"All they know is that I got my MBA and I manage a small independent company on Charles Street. Technically, that's true, so if you ever see them, don't mention the bar. Actually, the less said about my job, the better."

"You completed your business degree? I thought you still had another semester to go."

"I finished it in December."

"Congrats. So, are you looking for a better job?"

"Nope."

Her friend confused her sometimes, but Bliss had other things to think about right now. "Unfortunately, if I go back home, I can look forward to a lot of arranged, so-called accidental meetings with eligible young men. My parents will want him to be Italian so they can have a whole passel of *paisano* grandkids."

"With a name like Cameron, it sounds like your hero might be Irish," Claudia said.

"Or Scottish. I think I remember seeing a Cameron clan wearing their tartan kilts at that Highland Games thing we went to."

"Oh, yeah. Who could forget those sexy kilts?" Claudia waggled her eyebrows. "So… what does your guy look like?"

"Tall, about six feet. Rugged, great firm ass, green eyes, and hair that's hard to describe. It's not blond or red. It's kind of sandy or light brown with actual yellow streaks. Not highlights like you see on other people. I'm talking about a primary color in half- or quarter-inch stripes."

"Interesting… What else?"

"He has a side part and it's long in the front—right to his eyebrows. It kind of angles across his forehead. All shaggy and sexy." She sighed.

"He sounds like a hunk."

"Yeah, and if you ever see him, keep your mitts off. He's mine."

"I wouldn't dream of horning in on your territory. You might bite."

Bliss smiled, at last. "Or tell you to bite *me*."

The more Bliss thought about it, the more she liked the idea of making a card for the handsome firefighter. It *wouldn't* be one of her trademark Hall-Snark cards. Those were blunt, irreverently honest or flippant, and bordering on rude, but she could come up with something on the fly.

Let's see… what could I make and drop off at the fire station before I relocate?

"Claudia, can I borrow your computer, printer, and some card stock?"

"Sure. You can use my photos too if you want."

"You're sweet, but I have a design in my head that I can draw. I'd make the whole thing with a pen, but my handwriting is terrible and I want him to be able to read it." *Jesus. I'm lucky I can still draw breath, never mind cards, thanks again to Cameron Something or Something Cameron.* "Just drawing the artwork will be quicker, and there's no way you have a picture of what I want."

"Okay, I'll give you the necessary stuff and turn on the printer. As for card stock, I happen to have some with matching envelopes. It's plain white. Is that okay?"

"That's perfect."

—◆—

Drake plopped into his desk chair and powered up his computer.

"Well, I have plenty of time on my hands. Let's see what kind of trouble I can get into here," he muttered to himself.

Holding the lovely brunette had reminded him of something he'd been meaning to investigate. Dating websites. That had been on Drake's to-do list for a while. He craved some kind of company, specifically of the female variety, and loneliness had been setting in big time. The death of his last known relative had made him feel adrift in an aloof sea.

Unfortunately, his mother would never see her fondest wish come true. She had always wanted him to find a nice female dragon, settle down, and continue the species.

He was the last of his line now, and finding another clan had proven nearly impossible. There was an Asian clan in San Francisco, but they had made it clear East Coast dragons weren't welcome. *Thanks again, Uncle Mob Boss*.

His uncle had missed the family fortune and power so much, he'd decided to recreate it quickly in any way he could. Loan sharking, running guns, selling drugs to kids. Drake had not only walked away from one fortune, but two. The lair where his family had kept their treasure had caved in at about the same time they had to flee Britain. He wondered if his uncle had something to do with that. *If he couldn't take it with him...*

When Drake discovered how his uncle "earned" his new money, he refused to have anything to do with the older dragon. His elder didn't appreciate being judged but gave Drake a chance to reconsider and join the "family business." Drake's principles won out and he packed his bags.

He had originally moved to Boston because he'd heard about a female dragon and a paranormal bar here. Even though the dragon was a prostitute, he was willing to give it a go. He'd do just about anything to honor his dear mother's wishes. Unfortunately, by the time he acted on the information and found Boston Uncommon, the female had gone home to San Francisco. The guys at the bar said something about all being forgiven and Lily being in her family's embrace again. Nice for Lily. Not so much for him... and the species.

The only problem with a human hookup was that sometimes during sex, if he overheated before he finished "blowing off steam," so to speak, his eyes glowed and his skin toughened into hard scales. He could even develop claws, all of which signified a shift he might not be able to stop. A couple of close calls with former female companions had told him he'd have to find someone who could accept him *and* his secret.

He was fairly sure the young woman whose life and business he had saved saw his alternate form, yet she didn't faint or scream. Perhaps it was the *heat* of the moment, but he thought he sensed a willing connection, and when he glanced at her finger, he didn't see a wedding ring.

Maybe I can find a dragon-tolerant human after all. If only I knew where she went…

If only the chief hadn't had such a need to rip him a new one right then and there, he'd have pursued her. Now she was gone.

He typed in his password to access the dating site and tried to think of some cryptic way to describe himself and what he was looking for that would attract another dragon—or someone who was dragon-tolerant.

Why, oh why didn't dragons have their own dating site? He snorted to himself and a slight curl of smoke exited his nostrils. *Because we're almost extinct, dumbass.* At least that's what he'd been led to believe.

If dragons were open about their alternate identities, he might be able to find more, but "coming out of the cave" was forbidden. Humans would fear them. Fear leads to hate, and hate leads to discrimination—or worse, annihilation. No. He was stuck. There *must* be other dragons out there but he had been unable to find them, because each had learned the sad truth about being different.

He sighed and scanned a few profiles. *Okay, Cameron. Think. There's got to be a way to find a like-minded individual*. His father had found his mother, and that was before the Internet. She worked in a store specializing in all things Celtic—mostly Scottish and Irish woolens, jewelry with symbolic thistles or Celtic knot designs, some imported foods, and books about Ireland and the United Kingdom.

His paternal grandparents had moved to Nova Scotia from Scotland when his father was a wee lad. He smiled, thinking about how his grandparents spoke. His maternal great-grandparents had come from Ireland a century ago. His great-grandfather on his father's side was *supposedly* the "last dragon." During the Middle Ages, his family had been rich and powerful, but after that debacle, the dragon clans went into hiding. Returning to living in caves, they'd given up everything to protect what was left of their dwindling species.

His father visited New Brunswick one summer, and according to family history, he and his mother had a whirlwind romance. They married the following winter and Drake was born a year later. Surely his mother's and father's families weren't the only dragons to immigrate and intermarry.

There was no "dragon community" he was aware of. How nice it would be to have the Dragon-American club, like the Polish-Americans or French-Americans and many other ethnic subgroups.

Wishing wouldn't produce results, so he settled in for the great hunt. Thank goodness the site had a free trial. If things kept going the way they were, he might be fired and then he'd need his money while he looked for another job. *Ha. Fired while being fireproof. If only they knew…*

Bliss had made the card, drawing it by hand. She designed the inside text with Claudia's basic Word program and printed it using Claudia's color ink-jet printer. Thinking about how much she'd have to spend to replace everything was giving her indigestion, but there was no other way to stay in the race. She needed to buy a decent laptop and good quality software at a rock-bottom price that same day. The printer could wait a bit, but she'd need one soon to proof her own work—and the rules of the competition required that she receive no outside help.

The most important contract of her career hung on her ability to produce all her designs in three weeks. Unfortunately, she didn't have a few thousand dollars for forensic data retrieval, so she'd have to recreate every one of them from scratch.

She couldn't even afford a hotel for more than a night or two, so she called her mother, who alternately sobbed and yelled into the phone. As predicted, her mother wanted her to move home and never leave again. *Yeah. Good luck with that, Mom. I may be poor and desperate, but I'm not suicidal.*

Her next stop was the fire station. Maybe that would be a kinder experience.

She approached the open bay, hoping *Cameron* was still there.

A dark-haired firefighter she barely remembered seeing earlier caught sight of her, grinned, and strolled over. The name *Benjamin* was stitched onto his dark blue uniform shirt. *No help as far as knowing if they display their first or last names.*

"Hello, beautiful. Can I help you?"

"I was wondering if Cameron is around."

His expression grew serious. "Ah, no. He isn't. Is there something *I* can do for you? Get your cat out of a tree or something?"

She couldn't help but smile, then she quickly schooled her expression. "Well, you can give him this when you see him." She handed Benjamin the card she'd made.

He glanced down at the envelope as he took it. "What's this?"

"Just a thank-you note. He went above and beyond for me today."

"Oh!" Sudden recognition dawned in his eyes. "You're the chick who got him to run into that apartment building for some computer or something. Yeah, he's in a shitload of trouble for that little stunt."

She frowned. Apparently word got around. "Yeah. I'm afraid that's me. There's also an apology in there." She nodded toward the card.

"It better be a doozy. He's been suspended for a week."

"Damn," she muttered. Suddenly she had an idea. "May I speak to your chief?"

The guy had the audacity to laugh. "Are you sure you want to do that? He's not in a very receptive mood right now. Maybe you should come back tomorrow."

"I won't be around then. I have to go stay with my parents for a while. He's not the only one who's miserable."

Benjamin chuckled. "Okay. I'll get this to Cameron, but I'd suggest you forget about talking to the chief. There's nothing he hates more than wives or girlfriends trying to change his mind about something."

"Does that happen a lot?"

"Not really, but when it does, the guy pays for it."

"Oh. In that case, forget it. Thanks for getting the card to him." She strode off before anyone else saw her.

Drake Cameron had taken his lumps like a man and had let the chief reprimand him without getting defensive. There would be no commendation this time, just a seven-day suspension.

Having distracted himself with the Internet for as long as he could, he felt the need for solace, so he headed to the bar his buddies frequented. Even when one of them did something stupid, they were supportive after the chief finished with them. The paranormal bar he went to would be supportive too, but sometimes he needed his human brotherhood.

As soon as he strolled in, he spotted Ralph Benjamin and Mike Kelly at the bar. They waved him over.

"I'm glad you came in. You saved me a trip," Benjamin said.

"A trip where?"

"Your place. That crazy chick who got you suspended came by and dropped something off for you."

"Yeah?" His heart leaped. *Maybe I haven't lost her after all!* He had saved some hot women before, but none of them came to the firehouse bearing gifts. It was usually the blue-haired grannies who brought in home-made cookies or pies.

Ralph reached into his pocket and pulled out an envelope.

Oh. Just a friggin' card. I guess she doesn't bake. He opened it and focused on the bright design. It was a fire-breathing dragon. *Holy shit. Is she psychic or did she really see me through the smoke?* Either way, she didn't seem terrified. Maybe she was worth getting suspended for.

With some trepidation, he opened it. A smile spread across his face as he read: "I know it's your job and I'm sure you're not braggin', but I felt like a knob as you slew my dragon. You saved my ass and I'll never forget it. I ran into yours and I don't regret it. I'm sorry I sent you into harm's way. You're *so* my hero and I hope you're okay." It was signed, "Sincerely, Bliss." Beneath that it said, "Please pardon the terrible rhyme. It was the best I could do with limited time."

He tucked the card and envelope into his shirt pocket.

"She said it was an apology."

"Yeah, it was." *And maybe a little more.* The hope of finding a woman who could handle his dragon identity sprang to life like an ember coaxed back into a burning flame.

"Did she say where she was staying?"

"Said she had to move back in with her parents."

"Where do they live?"

"Don't know."

"Did she mention their names?"

"Nope."

Damn. "Did she say anything else?"

"She wanted to speak to the chief and take the blame for what you did, but I told her it wouldn't help. She just rushed off after that."

"Did you see where she went?"

"Sorry, no."

<hr />

Finally back to work, Drake had promised the chief that he'd stop taking stupid chances. The one-week suspension had seemed like a month. He grabbed a cup of coffee in the fire station's kitchen and leaned against the counter.

"That's been there since this morning," Mike said.

"That's one good thing about staying home for a few days. Decent coffee."

"So how's the computer dating thing going?" Ralph asked.

Drake was beginning to regret ever telling the guys how he'd spent his time off. "It was a stupid idea. Nothing came of it."

"Why not? Were you asking for a Victoria's Secret model who's a brain surgeon in her spare time?"

Drake chuckled. "No. Nothing like that." *It'd be easier to find a neurosurgeon lingerie model than a female dragon.*

He could picture the brunette as a model. She was tall, though not as tall as he was. He hadn't seen her in heels, only bare feet, but she might be close to his six feet if she wore four-inch stilettos.

He couldn't believe he'd caught himself thinking about her for the umpteenth time. *If only I could find her.* But it seemed hopeless.

His family had lost the ability to breathe fire, which was a good thing. Otherwise, he'd have been tempted to let out a fiery blast of frustration.

"I'm going to check the dating site again, just in case." He ambled off to the firehouse's activity room with the guys wishing him good luck.

A few minutes later, Drake gaped at the computer monitor. He couldn't believe his Internet dating search had paid off. The response he'd just received was obviously from a female dragon.

Hallelujah! There is *hope for the dragon species*.

Fathering children was something he really wanted to do someday, and because that was only possible with another dragon, he had to at least look into it. This was the whole reason he'd moved to paranormal-rich Boston. If there was a single female dragon anywhere…

Suddenly, he thought of Bliss. He'd been willing to give up the dragon search when he met her. More accurately, he'd change his search from a female dragon to a female he could fall in love with, one who wouldn't run from him in terror. A human couldn't bear his children, but if that wasn't important to her, perhaps…

He still didn't know if she had actually seen his alternate form, and he was driving himself nuts trying to figure out a way to ask her… without asking her. *If* he ever saw her again.

Maybe this was a sign he should keep his options open a bit longer—at least long enough to meet the lady dragon. *Don't think beyond the immediate task at hand, Cameron…for once*.

Ignoring his ambivalence, he began typing his answer.

"I'd like to meet you. There's a place called the Green Shamrock near Quincy Market. Do you know it?"

A few minutes later, she emailed him with her answer. "Yeh, I can meet you dayuh tomorrah. Whah time?"

Wow, she seems anxious… and barely literate. Drake chastised himself. Maybe she was just a terrible speller.

If all dragons had such a difficult time finding other single dragons, it made sense that she wouldn't want to wait—and he shouldn't either.

He typed, "I'll be there at four o'clock. How will I know you?" And just to be doubly sure he was talking to another dragon, he said, "What are your distinguishing marks?"

"Mi family has chaka black hair wit a streak ah silvah growin out ah da widah's peak."

That was his confirmation. She mentioned her family's marking. All dragon families had some visible way to identify their clan. Silver growing out of pure black, only in their widow's peaks, sounded odd enough for a dragon's markings.

On the line right below that, she asked, "An yas?"

Something didn't feel quite right. His fingers tingled and shook slightly as he typed, "Sandy hair with yellow streaks. Side part."

Am I about to make a mistake?

Some dragons, himself included, had a type of sixth sense alerting them to danger.

He thought about Bliss and figured he must be feeling a twinge of ambivalence. What possible danger could a blind date entail? *Ugh. Don't answer that, Drake.*

Without questioning himself further, he hit "send."

She responded with a quick, "See ya den."

And he typed, "See you tomorrow."

He was just stepping away from the computer when Benjamin appeared in the doorway. "Lunch is ready, Drake. Any luck on the dating front?"

"Uh, maybe." He hadn't mentioned his desire to find Bliss. The guys would probably think he was nuts to get involved with the woman responsible for sending him back into a burning building for her computer—and getting him suspended.

"Hey, that's great. Maybe we won't have to worry about our sisters after all." Benjamin returned to the kitchen without further comment.

That's what Drake liked about the guys he worked with. They could joke around and leave an opening if a buddy wanted to share his personal life. The others would listen and maybe sympathize or offer an opinion, but no one pushed or prodded. Drake wasn't about to volunteer any information. Not yet.

He was very glad the female dragon wanted to meet him tomorrow. A little more than twenty-four hours suddenly felt like a long time.

"No, no, no! Not her! Anyone but her!"

Mother Nature stared into the bright sky, gathered two fistfuls of her long, white hair next to her ears, and squeezed. "Gahhh!"

Apollo abandoned his poker game and joined her near the window. The entire top floor of the office building was covered in a glass bubble, so essentially the entire perimeter was a giant window that allowed the Supernatural Council an unobstructed view of Boston.

"What's wrong, Grandma?"

"I told you never to call me that," she hissed through gritted teeth.

"Sorry, Gaia. It's just that you gave birth to Zeus, who's my father, so therefore…"

She glared at him and a violent wind ripped through the room, blowing cards off the table and rippling everyone's long, white gowns.

"Sorry, Goddess. Forgive me."

She sighed. "I'll forgive you this time, but only because you're my favorite."

The other gods gaped at them, several with raised eyebrows.

"Oh, relax," she called out. "You're all my favorites." Then she rolled her eyes.

They looked away, although some of them still appeared tweaked. A moment later, the cards were magically back in their hands and they resumed their game.

"So what's wrong? How can I help?"

"That fucking Caribbean dragon, Zina," Mother Nature muttered. "What's she doing up here?"

Apollo shrugged. "You probably have a better idea than I do since I don't know who you're talking about."

Gaia pointed her long finger at a motorcyclist cruising down Storrow Drive. "That bitch right there. Thanks to a voodoo priestess, she's run amok for two centuries and there's nothing I can do to stop her."

"What's she doing that you need to stop?"

Gaia threw her hands in the air and whirled away from the glass. "Everything. That creature does whatever she damn well pleases and cares nothing about the consequences. I understand she has a lair where she keeps sex slaves. She finds men vacationing alone, and suddenly they're never heard from again."

"Why haven't we been supplicated? Beseeched? Prayed to for help?"

Gaia chortled. "Come on… Do you really expect men to complain about being sex slaves?"

Apollo shrugged.

"But that's not all. Humans have almost spotted her in dragon form, either through her carelessness or because she's tempting fate on purpose. It's happening more and more frequently."

"Why would she do that?"

"I swear she's goading me. She's a spoiled brat, and the last time I caught her flying, I paid her a little visit. I thought she understood my stern warning. After that, I decided to take a nice walk on the beach and she zipped past me, singing, "Neener, neener, neener.""

"Don't let her get to you."

"Oh, sure. Be the bigger goddess, right? Ignore her, right?"

"Exactly."

"I *can't!*" Mother Nature shouted so loudly the gods jumped and dropped their cards. "She's coming into her fertile cycle. If she mates with another dragon, I'll have to deal with more of them." Mother Nature crossed her arms and muttered under her breath, "I was almost rid of them too."

"Why do you want to get rid of them?"

"I don't make mistakes, but sometimes… Never mind."

"So, what should we do?"

"We shouldn't do anything, yet. There are barely any dragons left, so chances of her finding one are slim. But just in case, contact the Balogs and ask them to keep an eye on that bar where the paranormals hang out. If she shows up there, we'll need to know right away."

Chapter 2

BLISS SAT AT THE FAMILY DINING TABLE, TRYING TO concentrate on her work despite constant interruptions. For some reason, her mother could not understand that talking while Bliss was trying to think was the same as interrupting.

"Is it so terrible to be back home? You've done nothing but mope for days."

Her mother stirred the pasta sauce bubbling on the stove. The tangy tomatoes mixed with garlic and spices smelled like home. Under other circumstances, it would be wonderful. If Bliss were in her own apartment, she would have simply opened a jar. *Try to be nice*.

"I'm sorry, Ma. It's not bad. It's just…"

"Just what?"

Bliss sighed. "I don't know. I feel like a nine-year-old when I'm back home, letting you cook for me, sleeping in my old bedroom."

Her mother wiped her hands on her apron. "If you were married, I'd let you have the guest room."

"And give up the opportunity to sleep in a bunk bed again?" Bliss slapped a hand over her heart in a dramatic gesture. "Perish the thought."

"Yeah, yeah, Miss Sarcastic. Look, we don't know how long you'll be here. It could be months or years, and what if your married brothers and their lovely wives come to visit?"

Bliss tried not to groan out loud. "Why would they stay over? They live less than a mile away."

"You never know. Besides, your sister and her husband could decide to visit from India at any time. I'm sure it wouldn't be a short stay. The thing is, you should be married and in your own home by now. If you were married, you could forget about that silly competition. I'm sure your husband would support you no matter what happened in life. It's good to have someone you can count on, and Daddy and I won't be here forever. The older you get, the more I worry. I was married by the time I was twenty."

"You were pregnant with Ricky."

"No I wasn't. Your brother was born early. And for your information, your father and I had been engaged for two years, so we were ready to settle down. We just waited until he graduated from the tech. You're nearly twenty-eight! What are you waiting for?"

It was the same old argument. Bliss didn't know why they continued with the charade. Her brother would have had to be about four months early to make the timeline work. She usually let it go, but maybe if she pursued it, her mother would be the one to shut up and let her get back to work.

"Why did Nonna and Nonno rush the wedding plans?"

"There was no rush. I just wanted a June wedding. If you want to talk about a rush, your grandmother was married at the age of eighteen after a two-week engagement."

"And look how well that worked out. The two of them bickered each other into early graves."

Her mother crossed herself and faced Bliss head-on.

"That's just how they communicated. They loved each other dearly. Why do you think they had six children?"

Bliss smirked. "I don't know… lack of birth control?"

Her mother tossed her hands in the air. "You have an answer for everything. Always did."

"Speaking of which, I should get back to work. I need to put into words all the things people are too afraid to say."

"That business of yours is what scares the men away. Honestly, the vicious things you write in those cards… it's dreadful. And now, because of that stupid TV show, everyone will know about it."

"Hopefully. My cards are funny and people love them. If I get the kind of exposure I think we're going to get, I should sell tons."

"I'll never understand that. If anyone gave me one of your cards, I'd be very upset."

You don't know how close you've come to getting one. Her mother would also never know how many snarky cards she'd inspired. There was just too much rich material to ignore. "I really do need to get working."

As Bliss strolled toward the adjoining dining room, her mother said, "Why don't you work at the desk in your room? It was always where you did your homework."

"Because I like my legs at a ninety-degree angle and under the surface I'm working on. If I sat at my old desk, my butt would be below my knees and they'd bump up against the side of the desk. Why are you keeping that old thing anyway?"

"You never know… Maybe I'll have a grandchild someday after all."

"Emilio and Ricky are married. Why don't you bug them about having kids?"

"Who says I haven't?"

Bliss chuckled. "I love my brothers, but thank God it's not just me."

Her mother crossed her arms. "Aren't you worried about your biological clock?"

Hell no. The alarm isn't going off and won't for years. "Ma, I don't want to marry the wrong man just to have kids."

"Has it never occurred to you that you might marry the right man? Honestly, you're such a pessimist."

"I am not. I just have a pessimistic life."

"Oh, really? What's so bad about your life?"

"For one thing, I cannot work in this house, and I have a deadline to meet."

"Deadline, shmedline... Why are they giving you a deadline? Are there greeting card emergencies?"

"Mom. I'm finally hopeful of landing big contracts. Remember how it was in the beginning? Me helping my big sister take cards to craft fairs and small gift shops? How many did she sell?"

"I have no idea."

"Not a hell of a lot. If she didn't have a friend in advertising, she might never have gotten the business off the ground. Now that she's entrusted it to me, I want to make it an even bigger success."

"If success was so important to her, then she wouldn't have left the business and moved to India. I'm sure she'd understand if you wanted to quit and get a *real* job. Maybe you'd meet someone if you worked in an office."

Bliss actually bit her tongue and counted to ten.

"And this contract is important, I take it." Her mother prattled on as if Bliss hadn't said any of the angry, sarcastic things streaming through her brain. *Oh, that's right…for once I managed not to.*

"Yes, Mama. It's a make-it-or-break-it moment. If I deliver the designs I envisioned in the finale, I could win, and Hall-Snark cards will be in all the large chain stores."

"And if you don't?"

"It's back to the craft fairs."

"Is that so bad? You could do it as a hobby if you were married."

Bliss wanted to knock her head against the table—repeatedly.

———∞———

Drake waited outside the Shamrock to meet the female dragon. He leaned casually against the large window made up of several smaller panes, feeling anything but casual. Cool, calm, collected—nope. All of those positive traits had deserted him.

Mating with a human would never produce the children he wanted to have someday. Not just wanted… he needed to have them to save the species. He would do his best to find a female dragon, settle down, and propagate like mad. Only another dragon could do that.

He checked his watch again. Four o'clock on the dot. He saw no one who looked as confident as a lady dragon with dark hair and a silver streak down the middle walking toward him.

A motorcycle roared up to the curb, and the black-leather-clad rider pulled off his helmet. Correction. *Her* helmet. Long, matted, dark dreadlocks fell over her pierced eyebrow, past her pierced nose and pierced lip to her shoulders, and horrors, a shock of silver hair flowed from her widow's peak.

"Zina?"

"Dat me. And ya be Drake, naa?"

"Uh-huh." Too late to deny it. Somehow, it had never occurred to him that the lady dragon might be a dragon lady. A tough biker chick with a crazy accent.

Bliss popped into his mind again. She seemed like a direct contrast to this, and he didn't even know Zina yet. He doubted this chick could measure up to beautiful, funny, intelligent Bliss and, well… he really needed to give Zina a chance before he made rash judgments. It was important because she was a dragon. Maybe the only single female dragon he'd ever find.

She dismounted her bike and chained it to a nearby tree. Then she planted her hands on her hips and said, "So, are ya gonna to buy me bagjuice, or wha?"

Bagjuice? Drake would have preferred the "or what" but she had come from somewhere far away to meet him, so buying her a drink was the least he could do. She had a heavy island accent, but he could make out what she was trying to say… barely. With the Rasta hair and accent, he'd guess she was from Jamaica. *There's something I can open a conversation with.*

"We goin?"

He made himself smile. "Of course. After you." He gestured toward the Shamrock's front door.

"Me bet you wanna see me backside."

"Er… or I could just want to be a gentleman."

She shrugged. "Mehbe, but me rather ya seein me backside. Is strong as rock." She smacked her ass and swished it into the bar.

What could he say to that? Nothing. *Say nothing, Drake*.

She picked a table and sat on the side closest to the door. Damn. If he wanted to flee, he'd have to pass her and she'd probably grab his arm. Dragons, even in human form, had excellent reflexes.

She eyed him as he sat down. "So, mon. Do ya do da workout?"

"What? Do I work out? I'm having a hard time understanding you sometimes."

Her lips thinned. "Ya wan me do speaky-spoky?"

He had no idea what she'd just said, so he thought he'd better skip it and carry on. "In answer to your question, sometimes I work out. There's exercise equipment at the station. If I'm bored or haven't had any runs for a while, I'll lift weights or…" Why did her eyes just narrow?

"Station? Ya a cop?"

"No. Firefighter."

"Whew. Aright." She seemed to relax.

"I take it you don't like cops?"

"Nah, me no like dem."

She didn't offer any further explanation, but he could guess she'd been on the wrong side of the law at some point. He honestly didn't care enough to pursue the subject, so he let it drop. Suddenly, he wondered why mating with another dragon mattered so much. The thought of doing what he had to do with this woman was completely distasteful.

He'd be polite, have a drink with her, then be on his way and never look for a female dragon again. He wanted Bliss more than ever.

As their conversation wore on, he found himself

unable to interpret what she was saying on several occasions. Apparently she was renting a condo just outside the city in a nice neighborhood. She wanted to find a "bupps," whatever that was, and she valued her "kulcha."

"So, why did you ask if I worked out? Do you belong to a gym?"

"Me buildin gots one. Ya go dere sometime?"

Uh-oh. Change the subject, quick. "You have beautiful eyes." *Why the hell did I say that? Now she'll think I like her.*

She leaned back and looked smug. "Ya wanna cock it up? Me be ya baby mudda?"

Oh, crap. He figured this might be a good time to use the language barrier to his advantage. "I'm really sorry, Zina. I'm afraid I'm just having too hard a time understanding you. It was nice to meet you, though. I'll pay for our drinks on the way out." He rose and tried to walk past her.

Her hand shot out, clamped around his wrist, and squeezed. "I see. Perhaps you'd prefer I speak the King's English with a Brrritish accent?"

"What the…" *Why the hell did she use the island accent if she—* *Oh, no. Does she have multiple personalities?* Drake twisted his wrist, trying to extricate himself from her grasp, but she held on tight.

"I can talk like you do too, Mr. All-American."

He gave up the struggle, his curiosity getting the better of him. "Okaaay. If you were perfectly capable of eliminating your accent, why did you make it so hard for me to understand you?"

"It was fun."

"Fun?"

"Yeah, fun. You should have seen your face." She finally let go of him.

Drake rubbed his wrist. "Hmmm... Well, I really do have to leave."

Before he took a step, she enunciated, "Sit. Back. Down."

He folded his arms and stood his ground. "I can't. There's somewhere I need to be."

"Where?"

"My annual firefighter's physical," he said, without missing a beat. It wasn't until next month, but she didn't have to know that.

She stared at him a moment, then wrote a phone number on her cocktail napkin and shoved it at him. "Here. Call me when you can take a joke."

"What if that never happens?"

"Call me anyway."

Drake folded the napkin and stuffed it in his pocket.

She leaned back in her chair with a satisfied smile, as if she knew her will would be obeyed. And just to rub in the point of her being a female dragon, her eyes shimmered gold.

I'm sorry, Mother. I just can't do it. Even you wouldn't want me to marry this bat-shit crazy dragon to continue the species.

"I'm going to check greeting card companies. Maybe I can find the brunette there."

He had told the guys about the Internet producing a disastrous blind date. They encouraged him to keep trying, but what he really needed to do was delete his profile completely. He ambled toward the community room that housed the computers.

"I hope you find her," Ralph said. "We've run out of friends to introduce you to. And none of us would let you near our sisters."

"Good thing," Drake called over his shoulder, "if they're as ugly as you mucks."

"Ha. You wish," Mike said. "Irish girls are the prettiest in the world—or at least in Boston. Brazil might have a few chicks worth lookin' at."

While Mike and Ralph debated the best places to find good-looking women, Drake settled himself in front of the PC and typed in his user name and password. *I'll delete my profile right after checking my last lead.* He searched for "greeting card companies." Bliss was the woman he wanted, if only he could find her.

Up came a list of them. He scanned and scanned and scanned some more. *Holy shit. There must be a hundred of them.* And those were just the *A*'s.

He slammed the lid shut. The card she'd made didn't have a logo or company name on the back. Apparently, she'd whipped it up on the fly, so he had no idea which card company to call. The TV show wasn't airing yet, and he couldn't get any information on the candidates. You'd think they were protecting the next high-tech product from corporate spies.

All he knew was her first name and that she owned the struggling company. *Maybe I could get her last name from the condo association.*

Since everyone in the small building had been

displaced, he doubted that possibility. Even if he did locate someone, the idea that they'd just hand over personal information about one of the residents to a total stranger was remote. He literally sagged in defeat.

With nothing else to do unless the fire alarm blared, he went to the online version of the daily newspaper. He checked the back issues until he found the one from the day after the fire. Maybe an article in the local news about the structure burning would provide a clue.

Fortunately, it must have been a slow news day and the paper had a photograph of the mayhem. There he was on the side lawn, kissing—or rather, being kissed by—the beautiful but elusive Bliss. Her back was to the camera, so he couldn't even show her picture around the neighborhood. *Damn.*

But the timeliness of the photo brought up another question. Could it be arson? Where did the picture come from? Was it provided by a citizen with a camera phone or a local reporter with a cameraman? If the latter, how did they get there so quickly? Did someone tip them off? Drake didn't remember seeing anyone. Bystanders were kept at a distance. The picture may have been taken with a telephoto lens, but the angle suggested the photographer was nearby.

An arson investigator would have been assigned to the case. Even if it wasn't arson, a fire investigator would try to determine the fire's cause and point of origin. *Maybe I could talk to him. You never know what kind of clues might wind up in the rubble.*

Drake knew he was reaching, but one of his double-edged traits was his tenacity. He wouldn't give up the search for her easily.

—๛—

"Claudia, my mother is driving me crazy," Bliss stood on the porch and whispered loudly into the phone.

"Ugh. What is she doing?"

Bliss let out a long sigh. "One minute she's treating me like a kid, and the next she's begging me to get married. Aren't there laws against marrying off little kids?"

"It sounds like you need a night on the town."

"Oh, yes, please!"

Bliss's mother opened the front door. "What are you doing out here, Blissy?"

"Argh. I told you not to call me that anymore."

Her mother shrugged. "It's your nickname, isn't it?"

Bliss pinched the bridge of her nose. "Ma, I'm on the phone."

"I can see that. Who are you talking to?"

Bliss thrust the phone into her mother's hand. "Here. Why don't you ask her?"

Her mother made a sound of disgust and pushed the phone back toward Bliss. "I don't want to interrupt. I was just curious."

"It's not your future son-in-law, okay?" Bliss took back the phone and waited while her mother returned to the house and shut the door.

Whispering frantically to Claudia, she said, "Do you see what I mean?"

"Oh, Lord. You need more than a night out. You need to go shopping for a new apartment."

"No kidding. Have you heard of any?"

"I'm asking around but so far the only places I've heard about are too expensive."

"I guess I'll have to empty my savings and pay a Realtor to find a decent place I can afford. It was good of you to look, but I can't stay here much longer."

"How did you hear about your last place?" Claudia asked.

"My printer told me about it. Her neighbor was going to China and needed to sublet."

"So you just kind of fell into it. It could happen that way again…" Claudia didn't sound as confident as her words.

"I'm afraid I'll wind up committing murder if I stay here. If I look at it that way, the Realtor will be a bargain."

"True. So when are you coming into the city again? I'll make dinner reservations at that place we wanted to try on Prince Street."

"How about now?"

Claudia laughed. "Oh, brother. You're really desperate."

"Did you not hear my interfering mother? At least I got a new greeting card out of it."

"Cool. Let me hear it!"

"Mother, dearest, I know you mean well, but knock off the nagging—it's a guilt trip to hell."

"It's not your best, but you're probably off your game right now."

"Probably?"

"I know. I sympathize."

"What do you know about it? Your parents live in Florida."

"Thank goodness. So, let's pick a night when you can come into the city and stay at my place overnight."

"I may never leave…"

"Threatening me won't help your cause."

"Sorry. Listen, I'll call a Realtor." Bliss shifted from foot to foot. "Then I'll call you back when I have some appointments and we can get together the night before, if I can stay with you."

"Of course. Maybe you can look up the hottie fireman you were telling me about."

After a sad pause, Bliss said, "He's tall, blond, heroic, and did I mention absolutely gorgeous? What would he want with a broad like me?"

"Stop it. Using the word 'broad' makes you sound like you're from the nineteen-thirties."

"Great. My mother thinks I'm a kid one minute and an old maid the next. Now you think I'm a grandmother from the nineteen-thirties. I'm getting a little messed up."

Claudia sighed. "Don't worry. We'll sort you out."

"I hope so. Well, I should go and call a Realtor."

"Okay. Oh, and Bliss?"

"Yeah?"

"Don't be too hard on your mother. She just wants what she thinks is best for you."

"Well, homicide isn't best for either of us. Unless a nice homicide detective shows up. Then I'm sure her spirit will forgive me."

"Maybe I'll have better luck with the *B*'s," Drake muttered. "After all, her name is Bliss." He drifted off into a fantasy of how blissful it would be to make love to her.

He had called every greeting card company beginning with A and had to stop to recharge his phone. He felt like a dork asking for Bliss each time and being told he had a wrong number, or worse. Some people treated him like a pervert! But if that was the only way to find her, he'd keep it up until he reached the last Z or his phone died permanently.

As he was about to check his battery again, the alarm went off and the firehouse sprang to life. The guys put on their gear and used the pole to get to the garage quickly.

"Any luck?" Benjamin asked.

"No, but I've just started." No one had to know he'd made sixty calls already.

Drake was glad for the distraction. He could drive himself a little crazy when he became obsessed with something or, in this case, someone. He really had to learn to let go.

He jumped up into the ladder truck and leaned out the window. Before long, they were rolling out onto the road.

They were heading to Boylston Street. Not far from the area where Bliss had lived before the fire. *Maybe she still has friends in the neighborhood and…* He shook his head hard, as if to sweep her out of his mind. *Knock it off, Cameron. Chances are slim that she's still nearby. She said she was going to be living with her parents and they could be anywhere.*

When they rolled up to the school building, nothing seemed amiss except for the smoke alarm going off inside and dozens of people standing around on the sidewalk.

The chief ordered the public back, clearing the area.

Drake grabbed an ax and led his comrades inside. No smoke on the first floor. They continued up the stairs and did a sweep of the second, then the third. So far, nothing. Must have been a false alarm. It happened, especially in schools. Probably a student didn't want to take an exam until he or she had more time to study.

Little bastards. Why can't they give up a night of partying and study like they're supposed to?

When the building had been thoroughly checked and the alarm turned off, he trudged out onto the sidewalk. Suddenly, in the crowd across the street, he thought he caught a glimpse of her. *It couldn't be. It's probably just…*

A couple with a stroller moved and he got a better look. *Holy shit. It is her!*

He charged across the street and grabbed the surprised, elusive woman by the arms. "Bliss. That's your name, isn't it?"

"Yeah." She was staring at him as if she had just seen a ghost.

"I've been…" *Whoa. Play it cool, Cameron.* "I was hoping to run into you again. Thanks for the creative card. Where are you staying?"

The chief yelled over at him, and Drake held up one hand as if to say, give me a minute.

"With my parents. I'm going crazy there and came back to look at apartments today. Is this neighborhood prone to fires? If so, I'd better look elsewhere."

"No! I mean, no, it's plenty safe."

She smiled and something inside him melted. The chief yelled at him again and started walking over.

"Listen, before I go, can you give me your number? I'd like to ask you out sometime." He started to back away.

"Sure." She grinned and rattled off her cell phone number.

The chief yelled out, "Hey, Cameron!"

"Wait! Is Cameron your first or last name?" Bliss asked.

"Last. My first name's Drake." He glanced in the chief's direction. "Uh, I'd better run."

Benjamin called after the chief. "Give him a minute, boss. That's the girl he's been looking for."

The chief threw his hands in the air. "Seriously? Everything is supposed to stop so Drake can talk to a pretty girl."

"Better than having him talk to your daughter, chief," Mike yelled out.

The chief snorted. "As if I'd let that happen." Then he focused on Drake and said, "Get her number and come on."

Chapter 3

DRAKE HAD CALLED! BLISS WAS STILL FLOATING, BUT butterflies were getting the best of her as she got ready for their date. To avoid subjecting him to the scrutiny of her parents, she'd asked him to pick her up at Claudia's apartment. Otherwise, her mother would have asked all kinds of embarrassing questions to see if he was good marriage material, and her father would have simply scowled and brooded because no man was good enough for his little girl. *Yeah. His twenty-seven-year-old little girl.*

"Why am I so nervous?" Bliss asked. "It's not like this is my first date. Maybe I shouldn't be doing this right now. The card competition—"

"Can wait for one evening. You need this."

"I know, but look..." She extended her trembling hand. "I'm practically shaking."

Claudia stepped back and admired her handiwork. "You're nervous because you really like this guy. If you didn't care, you'd be your usual flippant self."

"You're probably right." Bliss glanced down at her outfit again. "Are you sure I look okay?"

"You look beautiful. Come here." Claudia dragged her over to the closet and opened the door. A full-length mirror hung on the inside.

"Oh," Bliss murmured. She swiveled from side to side to take in the full effect. The crimson dress hugged her curves and fit perfectly. Claudia had done Bliss's hair in soft waves. It looked shiny and touchable. Her black pumps accentuated her long legs. "I think you performed a miracle."

"I had good material to work with." Claudia smiled and went to hug her.

"No. Don't touch me. I'm afraid the whole thing will fall apart if I move."

Claudia laughed. "You have to. Would he be willing to come in here and watch you stand like a statue?"

"I suppose not."

"Right. Now we just have to find some kind of outerwear for you. It's spring, but it still gets chilly at night."

"You mean I have to cover everything up with a jacket or sweater? Wouldn't that ruin the effect?"

"No. How about a pashmina? You can drape it over your arm or around your neck until you need it. Then it just wraps around your shoulders. They're thin but deceptively warm."

"I know what a pashmina is, and that might work. It won't add bulk. God knows, I don't need any more meat on my bones."

"Stop it. You're fine." Claudia reached into her closet and withdrew a black cashmere shawl with a subtle silky sheen.

"My mother's pasta has added at least five pounds to my hips."

"You're nuts. You don't look fat. Here." Claudia thrust the shawl at her.

"Thanks." Bliss folded the shawl and draped it over her arm. "Do I need a necklace, or are the earrings enough?"

"You don't want to look like you knocked yourself out getting ready, even if you did. Besides, if you're *not* wearing one, maybe he'll take the hint and get you one for a gift sometime."

"You must be dating much more observant guys than I am."

"No, but I can dream. Hey, I just had an idea for another card you can make," Claudia said.

"What's that?"

"Something for first dates."

Bliss laughed. "I can see it now. It can be a sympathy-type card."

"I was thinking more of a good-luck card, but whatever. You're the creative one."

"You're pretty creative too. That ad idea you put together for me was awesome. I loved the evil smile on the model's face."

"You would. Did it work as the introduction to your portfolio?"

"I haven't had a chance to finish it yet, but yeah, it will. With the fire and trying to stay as far away from my parents as I can and still live there…"

"I understand. Hopefully you can find your own place soon."

The phone rang and Bliss stiffened. It might be Claudia's concierge alerting her to the presence of a certain hottie in her lobby.

Claudia strode into her living room and answered it. Bliss followed her, and by the short conversation, she knew Drake was here and waiting for her.

Smiling, Claudia hung up the phone. "It's go time. Have fun tonight."

Bliss took a deep breath. "If I can just keep myself from fawning all over him, I should be all right."

Claudia laughed. "When have you ever fawned over anybody?"

"You're right. I should probably worry more about insulting him and pushing him away."

"Is that why you do it?"

Bliss gasped. "Hell, no. I just do it to be funny. I'm always surprised when people actually take offense."

"Well, behave yourself. You don't want to push this one away."

"And now I'm nervous again."

As soon as the waiter finished taking their orders, Bliss gazed at Drake with her big, brown eyes. "I'm curious about something."

"What's that?" *Uh-oh. Is she going to bring up what she saw through the smoke?*

"Something your firefighting buddy Benjamin said."

"Oh, no. What did he say?"

"He didn't say anything bad about you or anything. I just heard him yell over to the chief, 'That's the girl he's been looking for.'"

Busted. Drake grinned. "I couldn't stop thinking about you." He reached across the intimate table for two and took her hand. "That clever card... No one has given me anything like that before."

"Really? I should imagine you've had any number of girlfriends in the past." She flipped her hair over her shoulder in a sexy, flirty gesture. "None of them ever gave you a card?"

She has no idea how hard it is for a dragon to date. "Not made especially for me. I probably received a card on my birthday but nothing memorable like that."

Bliss smiled. "Well, I'm glad I did something memorable."

"I would have remembered you anyway."

"Why? I'm sure I'm not the only single woman you've carried out of a burning building."

"You're the most beautiful."

Bliss's olive complexion deepened with a slight flush of red and she dropped her gaze to her lap.

"I hope one little compliment didn't embarrass you. I might want to give you more sometime."

She chuckled. "No. I'm not embarrassed. Just not used to it."

"Seriously? You must have been dating morons. I'm told women need to hear how beautiful they are every now and then."

She was quiet for a moment. "How do you do it every day?"

"Do what?" Drake asked.

"Run into burning buildings. I've had nightmares about being trapped in another one ever since the fire."

"Ah, you're changing the subject." Drake chuckled. "Well, first of all, it doesn't happen every day."

"Thank goodness. But why doesn't it bother you? You seemed perfectly comfortable in the middle of it. You were even joking with me."

He shrugged one shoulder. "I had protective gear. You didn't."

"It wasn't just that," Bliss said.

"I'm used to it, I guess. Although I've heard that lots

of guys have dreams of fires and being trapped, especially in the beginning of their careers."

She was quiet for a moment. "Is there anything that can be done about it?"

"Are you asking if there's something you can do about *your* nightmares?"

"Maybe. I imagine it will fade, but now I jump whenever I hear a siren. The other day when I was looking at apartments and heard the fire alarm… even though I was in a different building altogether, I *had to* get outside. I never followed up on the apartment, either. It was too close to that stupid school."

"I think that's natural. Do you have claustrophobia?"

"No. At least I didn't. Don't tell me I'm going to develop it now."

He leaned back in his chair. "Probably not. I just wondered if you had it and that might have contributed to your need to get outside."

"I think it had more to do with how close together buildings are in this city. When one lights up, I'll bet a whole block could go."

"Not if we get there quickly enough. That's part of the job… to keep fires from spreading."

She was quiet for another moment. "What's the safest type of building to live in?"

"You mean like brick or concrete, as opposed to wood?"

"Yeah."

"Well, naturally wood is more flammable than brick or concrete. But your best bet is to have neighbors who don't smoke or cook or let their children play with matches."

Bliss rolled her eyes. "Oh sure. That's practical."

He grinned again. Bliss was beginning to love that grin. Drake certainly was a charmer. *Even if he isn't my future husband, he'd be great to practice on.*

At that moment, she thought she saw his eyes glow. They were a golden color but had been green a moment before.

"Are—are you all right?"

He leaned away from her and straightened. "What do you mean?"

"Your eyes. They took on this gold glow for a second."

He hesitated a moment, then chuckled. "It must have been the reflection of the candlelight."

"Oh. Of course." She felt like an idiot. *Get it together, Bliss. You don't want him to think you've lost your mind, even if you have.*

Thankfully, he didn't seem to think it was worth dwelling on. "So, how's your house hunt going? Any other prospects?"

"I may have found a place on Michelangelo Street. I'm just waiting for my application to be approved."

"That's a great neighborhood. I love the North End."

"At least it's Italian. Mama will be happy. A lot of younger people are moving there now, so I'll be happy too."

"We'll have to try out some of the restaurants in the area."

Yay! Second date talk. "I'd like that." She couldn't help smiling.

"So, tell me about the apartment."

"It's small. Tiny, really."

"A studio?"

"No. One bedroom. I don't think I could handle a bed in my living space."

"I have a studio. The high ceilings make it feel bigger, and during the day I have more square footage because I built a Murphy bed in the corner."

"That's the thing that folds up into the wall, right?"

"Exactly. And I built a desk into the underside so when I flip it up to put the bed away, I can simply unhook the desk and it folds down."

"You sound pretty handy."

"I like to work with my hands."

I hope you do more than build furniture with them.

"Let me see." She turned his hand over so she was looking at his palm. *Large, rough, oh yeah. I'll bet those would feel good skimming all over me.*

Putting on a fake Slavic accent, she said, "Let Madame Zola read you. Ah, I see you have a long lifeline."

He laughed. "You have no idea."

Drake had walked Bliss back to Claudia's place. He accompanied her up the elevator, and then the inevitable, awkward first-date moment arrived. *To kiss or not to kiss.*

It was not their first kiss. She had gotten that out of the way when Drake emerged from her burning apartment building after rescuing her laptop. She hadn't even thought about what she was doing. She'd just dragged his head down and planted her lips on his.

This time, all she did was open her mouth to tell him what a good time she'd had, and he pulled the same move. He dove for her lips, and at the same time he crushed her against his chest. Then he cupped her head and held her in place.

As if I might object and pull away. Ha!

Not about to protest, Bliss threw her arms around his neck and kissed him back just as enthusiastically. Drake's tongue met and swirled with hers. Her mind had emptied itself of every thought. All she wanted to do was feel... until suddenly, her lips were on fire!

Bliss pulled away and sucked in a cool breath. She touched her lower lip and it tingled with heat. Drake's chest was rising and falling, and he seemed to be panting.

"Good Lord, I've heard of hot kisses but that was something else," Bliss said.

"I know. I felt it too." Drake shifted uncomfortably, and Bliss wondered if he had something against hot, passionate kisses. Come to think of it, she'd thought "hot" was just a metaphor. Now she wondered about other words describing passion. Smoldering. Scorching. Sizzling. Searing. Every word romance novels used to convey desire seemed to begin with the letter *S*.

"I—uh, I'd better get home. Got an early day tomorrow."

What just happened?

"But let me know when you're moving," he continued. "I'd be glad to help."

Whew. He's not blowing me off. In fact, offering to help someone move is the definition of a true friend, isn't it? "Thanks. I might do that." *Yeah, I'll definitely do that.*

Bliss had another true friend. As soon as she walked into Claudia's apartment, the willowy woman rushed out of her bedroom and hugged her.

"Guess what?"

Bliss had expected her to ask about the date, but apparently Claudia had exciting news of her own. "Jeez, did you win the lottery?"

"No, but you did!"

"Huh? He's a great guy, but what are you telling me? Is he a Kennedy who changed his name or something?"

Claudia waved away her question. "No, I'm not talking about your date. I'll get to that later. Listen, your mother called and said the apartment in the North End fell through."

"Aw, shit. How is that like winning the lottery? Except for *her?*"

"I'm sorry. Listen, there's more. You got turned down because you don't have a job. They found out about your business going up in smoke and didn't think you could afford the rent while rebuilding your whole portfolio for the competition."

"Damn! I can't get a job right now. If I don't deliver the designs for the final taping in three weeks, I'll lose and then I really won't be able to afford rent, or anything else. Will you please get to the part about the lottery? Or do you just have a very skewed version of good news?"

"Listen, listen!" Claudia was practically jumping up and down. "I knew you'd be bummed out, so I called my boss and asked if he could use a part-timer in exchange for the apartment over the bar. The waitress who left last fall moved in with her boyfriend. Well, he's her husband now, but in any case, there's a room for you, if you want it. He rents the apartment to his employees at a drastically reduced rate. He usually requires the person to be a full-timer, but I pleaded your case."

"And he said yes?"

"Yes! Don't you see? I solved all your problems. A part-time job gives you money to live on, time to work on your other project, a wicked cheap rent in an awesome place, and me as your manager. It's a win-win-win-win."

Bliss smirked. She wanted to tease her friend about having her as a boss... badly, but Claudia had done her a solid. She deserved better than a smart-ass remark.

"Thank you. I—um. I've never worked in a bar before. Does that bother you?"

"Hell, no. It's easy. You'll pick it up in no time."

"Aren't you worried about my so-called people skills?"

Claudia chuckled. "Not as soon as you realize that good service equals good tips. Now, do you want the job or not?"

"I want it! When can I move in?"

"Anytime. You'll have a roommate. She's the bartender, but it's a two-bedroom apartment and quite roomy for the area. You won't get in each other's way at all."

"Eww... a roommate. I don't know, Claudie. It's not that I don't play well with others, it's that so many others are jackholes."

Claudia dropped her face into her hands, and Bliss thought she muttered, "Oh, crap. What have I done?" She lifted her face and glared. "Angie's no jackhole, and we *need* her. If you can't behave yourself, the deal's off."

"Don't worry. I'll be good. Anything is better than living in my childhood bedroom while my mother demands I fill it with babies."

Chapter 4

BLISS CHARGED DOWN THE STAIRS AND STOPPED BRIEFLY to say, "Get away from the window, Ma, or I won't open the door."

Her mother backed toward the kitchen, slowly.

Bliss could argue all day, but she'd have to give her parents a look at Drake or they'd think she was hiding some weird anomaly like crooked teeth or a big nose that could be passed on to their possible future grandchildren.

He knocked. Hoping for the best, Bliss opened the front door.

"Hi there, beautiful. It's a great day to move."

It was true. The sun shone in the clear blue sky, and the humidity was low. As an added bonus, Bliss hadn't committed matricide yet.

"Come in, Drake."

Mrs. Russo strolled over, and before she could berate her for not introducing them, Bliss said, "Drake, this is my mother, Malinda Russo."

"What a beautiful name. It suits you," he said.

Her mother tittered—actually tittered—and extended her hand. He shook it and held on for an extra moment. "I can see where Bliss gets her beauty."

Good going, Drake. Now she'll be adamant I make you her son-in-law. "There's not much stuff to load into your truck. Just a few castoffs and a suitcase. We can be on our way in about fifteen minutes."

"What's the rush, Blissful? He just got here. He's probably thirsty after the long drive."

Crap. Now he knows what my stupid nickname is. "It's not that long a drive, Ma, and I'm anxious to get going so I can settle in."

"Oh, all right." Her mother did the disappointed sigh better than a Jewish mother. "If you must, I guess you must."

Bliss rolled her eyes so Drake could see her but her mom couldn't.

"Maybe another time," he said.

"Oh, yes. I'd love to have you over for Sunday dinner... as a thank-you for helping Blissy move. I make lasagna better than you'll get in the city— including the North End."

"That sounds wonderful," Drake said, and gave Malinda Russo his killer grin.

Bliss thought her mother would faint.

"I'll show you the basement. That's where the old furniture is."

"It's not that old, Blissful."

Bliss slapped her own forehead. "Will you please stop calling me by the nicknames I hate?"

Her mother looked hurt, then angry, and stomped out of the room, muttering, "Everyone thought they were cute when you were little."

Damn. Now I'm the bad guy.

"Let's get to that furniture," Drake said. "It won't move itself."

Drake to the rescue... again. "Yes, let's."

She led him to the cellar door and they tromped down the stairs. Once they were in the basement he spun her toward him and said, "Don't worry about your nick-name. I get 'blissy' just looking at you." Before she could protest, he kissed her.

She practically melted in his arms. When he released her, she grasped the back of the sleeper sofa to steady herself.

"Wow. You do that so well."

He smiled and touched her cheek. "You're pretty good at it yourself." Pointing toward the sofa, he asked, "Is that going?"

"Huh? Oh, yeah. That'll be my bed until I get a real one. Then I'll put it in the guest room."

"You have a guest room?"

Bliss chuckled. "No, but that's what my friends and I call the living room if guests come. I was sleeping in Claudia's guest room last weekend."

"Gotcha. I suppose I should have a 'guest room.'" He made air quotes. "But I don't have guests."

"Oh." She didn't know if that was good news or bad. Did he make it a rule never to let anyone sleep over—or was he telling her she was his only girlfriend?

"I live in a studio for now. I had to find something quickly when I got to Boston, but I'll be on the lookout for something bigger as soon as the lease is up."

"Ah. That's right." She moved to one end of the couch. "Well, this thing is damn heavy. If we need more muscle, I can ask my dad to come down."

"Nah, it shouldn't be a problem." Drake picked up the sofa in the middle and hoisted the whole thing over his head.

"Holy cow," Bliss exclaimed. "How did you... I mean, whoa. Don't give yourself a hernia. I can help."

"No need. I've got it."

Shit. I figured he was strong enough to carry people out of burning buildings, but lifting ridiculously heavy seventies furniture over his head? "I'll guide you then." She hurried to the end of the sofa that was closest to the stairs. "Follow my legs."

"Gladly," he said with a hint of mischief in his voice.

Drake unloaded the last of her belongings while Bliss kept an eye on his truck. She'd told him again how amazed she was by his strength. Maybe he should have played it low key. No need to make her suspicious if she wasn't already, but he couldn't help showing off a little bit.

She handed him the extra key to her apartment so he could park in a legal spot and then come up to her place. He gave her a peck on the lips before he got in—and noticed her look of surprise that quickly turned into a smile.

I guess she's not used to public displays of affection. Apparently, showing up the guys in her past wouldn't be hard.

He found a parking spot just around the corner and strode back to her building. If things went well, maybe she'd be moving her belongings again someday... into a place of their own. *Christ, Drake, jumping the gun much?*

Still, it would be great to have a special woman who knew and accepted what he was. Barring any nasty surprises, he'd never have to explain it to anyone again.

He took the steps to the second floor two at a time.

He wasn't even winded from the exertion of moving and then walking quickly back to her place. Anticipation had him focusing on other things. Pleasanter things.

He knocked to give her fair warning, despite having the key, then used it and walked in. "Did I put things where you wanted them?"

"Yup. You read the boxes well," she teased.

"Thank you for making it fairly idiot-proof with the labels. I just wasn't sure if you wanted the couch in your bedroom or out here in the 'guest room' until you got another bed."

"You guessed right by putting it in the bedroom. I can deal with moving it out when the time comes. I'll just have to try extra hard not to ruin the hardwood floors if I have to drag it from one room to another."

"That's what I thought. But, if you ever need to move your stuff around again…"

"Don't worry. I'll ask." She grinned.

"I was going to say, ask someone else."

Her grin disappeared and her eyes rounded.

He laughed. "I was kidding."

"Oh! Well, I wouldn't blame you if you meant it. They made damn heavy furniture in the sixties and seventies."

"Is that when your parents bought everything?"

"Probably. It's old enough to be replaced, but not old enough to be antique. I think it qualifies as junk."

"Hey, if it gets the job done…"

He thought he caught a glint in her eye.

"I might need some help testing its functionality. Want to see if the bed is comfortable?"

He was surprised by her invitation but no less pleased. She did find nice ways of thanking him.

"Are you sure? I thought you had a roommate."

"She's working at the bar downstairs."

"I mean, of course I'd love to, but don't feel like you need—"

"Believe me, *I need*." She grabbed his shirt and dragged his mouth to hers, delivering a long, silencing kiss.

He let his hands roam over her body, eventually cupping her ass and giving it a squeeze.

She broke the kiss and said in a husky voice, "I'm glad I labeled the box with the sheets in it."

He chuckled and followed her into the bedroom where she found the box marked "Linens, etc." He tossed the couch cushions aside and opened the hide-a-bed. These things were rarely comfortable, but this one didn't look too bad. At least the mattress appeared thick enough to cushion the metal bar.

She practically ran back to the bed with an armful of sheets. *Wow. She seems as sex-starved as I am.*

Regardless of the fact that he'd have to stop at heavy petting, it was refreshing to find a woman who liked sex and didn't mind initiating it. Now he just had to hope he didn't get so hot and bothered that he'd start to shift. It could happen. He hadn't *blown off steam* in a while.

Bliss unfurled the bottom sheet across the bed and he caught it. The two of them made quick work of covering the bare mattress and rolled to the middle of it still wearing their clothes.

"Yup. Seems plenty comfortable—"

He didn't even get to say "to me," because she had him in a desperate clutch and was delivering another hot kiss. *Wow.*

She popped open the button on her jeans. "We have way too many layers between us."

Drake rolled up to a sitting position and unlaced his boots. Kicking them off, he grabbed the hem of his T-shirt. Before he could yank it up, he noticed Bliss had already stripped down to her underwear... and stopped.

"Do you have a condom?"

"No, but I'm clean and I can't get you pregnant." She hesitated. He figured he'd lighten the moment. "If we were playing strip poker, you'd lose."

"Not necessarily," she said. "I'm a pretty good poker player." Her wink seemed to say she'd enjoy a game of strip poker at some point.

He unzipped and whipped off his jeans. "We'll have to try it sometime."

She grinned and whispered, "Oh, yeah."

I love it when Bliss smiles. I hope I can make her smile a lot more.

He suddenly realized what she was smiling at—his big, rock-hard erection, and her expression was turning into a leer.

"Wow. I thought you'd be well endowed, but, well..."

"Well what?"

"Well, dayum!"

Drake couldn't help it. He let out a hearty laugh.

Suddenly she lost her grin. "I'm afraid I'll have to stop you before..."

"Before?"

"You know. The good part. No condom, no penetration."

"I understand completely. I have other tricks up my sleeve, though."

Bliss shoved against his chest and Drake flopped onto his back.

At that moment, a door opened and closed. It sounded as if someone had just entered the apartment.

"Shit," Bliss muttered.

"Hello?" a female voice called out. "Is anyone here?"

Drake and Bliss jumped off the bed and pulled on their jeans and T-shirts as fast as they could.

"Just a minute," Bliss yelled.

"That must be your roommate. I thought you said she was working," he said in a loud whisper.

"Maybe she's on her break and came up to introduce herself. Who knows?"

"I guess we'll find out."

Bliss checked to be sure Drake was decent and then opened the door. She strode out to the living room and saw an attractive young woman with blond highlighted hair puttering in the open kitchen.

She came out to the living area, drying her hands on a towel. "Hi. I'm Angie, and you must be Bliss. Claudia told me you'd be moving in today." Then she turned toward Drake and sent him a jaunty smile. "Hey, Drake. What are you doing here?"

Bliss glanced from one to the other. "You know each other?"

Drake shuffled his feet and focused on the floor. "I'm what you'd call a semi-regular at the bar downstairs."

"And I'm one of the bartenders," Angie said. "He usually occupies a stool right at the bar, so we chitchat during lulls."

Bliss wondered if a "semi-regular" was anything to be worried about. Was he semi-regularly drunk? Did they call out his name when he walked in the door? But it was too soon for such a personal question. She'd find out eventually, especially since she'd be working there starting tomorrow.

"So, Angie, I'm glad you came upstairs and introduced yourself," Bliss said. "Are you on your break?"

"No, my shift is done for the day. Full-timers work six-hour shifts. Today, I worked eleven to five. Most of the time, I work five to eleven."

"The bar is only open until eleven o'clock at night?"

"Yeah. Didn't Claudia tell you? I don't know why Anthony insists that everyone be out before midnight, but I'm not about to question my good luck."

"Hmmm…" Bliss wondered about that too. "Is that unusual? I thought most bars were open until at least one or two o'clock in the morning."

Angie shrugged. "We're just a neighborhood bar. Most late-nighters go to the trendy clubs. Anthony might have tried the later hours and found it wasn't worth it, but I really don't know."

Bliss could always ask Claudia, if she cared enough. For now she'd adopt Angie's attitude and just call it good luck.

"The only downside," Angie was saying, "is that we don't get breaks. There are labor laws on the books that say employees who work more than six hours must have a meal break. Personally, I'd rather go home than go on a useless break."

"I won't be working full time."

"Really?" Angie tipped her head. "Huh. Claudia

doesn't usually hire part-timers and let them live here. And even though all of us are *technically* working part-time at six hours a day, five days a week, she doesn't insult us by calling us part-timers. Oh! Not that there's anything wrong with that. I didn't mean…"

"No offense taken." Bliss figured Claudia was doing her a favor, but the others didn't need to know that. It might be a good idea to keep her friendship with the boss on the down-low, unless Claudia hadn't already mentioned it. "So does Claudia do all the hiring?"

"Yeah, as far as I know. Anthony seems to trust her completely. I've never seen him show up during the day, and that's when Claudia is in charge. Most interviews happen during the afternoon. She's the only one who works eight hours at a stretch, as far as I know. She spends a lot of time in the office, so maybe she considers that her meal break. Must be nice, having a two- or three-hour meal break every day."

Nope. Looks like Claudia didn't mention we're friends. That might be handy in case her friend needed to know what went on behind the scenes. *Nah. Stay out of bar politics, Bliss. You have more important things to focus on.* She probably wouldn't be working there long enough to care.

As long as she could redo most of her designs before the producers and camera crew showed up to film the segment where they checked in on all the finalists, she'd be okay. She did *not* want that happening at her parents' house. Other shows did that, and she'd always seen happy families who were supportive of their son's or daughter's ambitions. The last thing she needed was her mother calling the competition foolish.

Chapter 5

CLAUDIA HAD TAKEN BLISS INTO THE OFFICE AND given her a uniform. Black skirt, black apron, and white blouse. Bliss changed behind a folding screen. The uniform fit well enough, although she would have liked it tapered a bit to show a more feminine hourglass figure. Maybe she could find a tailor. Then she remembered she needed her money to rebuild her *real* job. If she didn't win the competition and the fifty-thousand dollars that came with it, she'd be screwed.

When she strolled around the partition, she asked, "Aren't uniforms sort of old school?"

Claudia smiled indulgently. "Wait until you meet Anthony. Talk about old school…"

"The owner? Why? Is he like a million years old?"

Claudia laughed and tied Bliss's apron tighter. "Not at all. He's young and ridiculously good looking, but he has this old-world charm. Very formal manners, a slight European accent, but he won't tell you exactly where he comes from, so don't bother asking."

"Okay…" Bliss glanced in the mirror and realized that when Claudia cinched the apron tighter, she gave her a nice nipped-in waist. Problem solved.

"Look, I'm just mentioning it because he can be a bit intimidating to new staff members. Don't worry about it, though. He's a sweetheart when you get to know him." She sighed.

"Do I detect a crush on the boss?"

Claudia's expression suddenly turned serious, and she shoved an order pad toward Bliss. "Maybe. But don't say anything or even hint at that. He doesn't date his employees, and he has a psycho girlfriend who you don't want to piss off."

Bliss took the order pad and continued to study her friend's face. "I've never seen you like this, Claudia. Is there something else going on?"

"No, just… just keep whatever I tell you confidential, okay? I'm giving you more information than I'd give an employee I didn't know. Anthony's a good guy, but Ruxandra—his girlfriend—is a piece of work. Steer clear of her. And stay as far away from Anthony as you can when she's around. If she gets the wrong idea…" Claudia shivered.

"Seriously? She's so jealous that you're afraid of her?"

"Not… not really. Anthony keeps her in check."

"Sounds like a wonderful relationship," Bliss said, rolling her eyes.

"Regardless, it's none of our business. I just wanted you to be aware of the dynamics."

Bliss scanned the order pad, which didn't look too complicated. "Okay. Fine. Consider me fully aware. So, I guess I'd better get out there and start my first shift."

"Yeah. I'll introduce you to the other employees, and the regulars will probably introduce themselves. How are you at handling sexual harassment?"

Bliss laughed. "You're kidding, right? You've seen my cards, haven't you?"

"Whoa. I'd rather you not insult the customers if you can help it."

"Don't worry. I can deflect, distract, or disconcert. I won't insult anyone, at least not directly." She gave her friend a teasing grin. "Kidding. What do you think is the best approach?"

"Go with your gut, unless that involves punching someone out. If a customer gets fresh and won't stop, find me or Anthony. We'll take care of it."

Bliss waved away the very idea that she couldn't handle any situation herself. "Don't worry about me. I'll be fine."

"Okay then. Let's go."

Claudia grasped her shoulders and turned her toward the door. Bliss marched forward stiffly, wondering why she was suddenly nervous. Waitressing was no big deal, right? She was probably just experiencing a little fear of the unknown. *Don't be ridiculous, Bliss. This isn't rocket science.*

Claudia opened the door and let Bliss pass through it first.

A guy sitting at the bar turned and whistled the minute he saw her, then announced to anyone within earshot, "Look, guys, fresh meat. A pretty one too."

Bliss muttered, "Fabulous. They don't waste any time, do they?"

Claudia strode directly over to the guy with the buzz cut, who grinned at her even when she slapped him up the backside of his head! "Kurt, behave yourself. Just because we have a new staff member doesn't mean you have to test her. I'm going to introduce her to the employees first. Then you can introduce yourself, *if* you can be civil."

"I'm always civil. After all, I was a marine."

Claudia groaned. "That's no guarantee you'll behave in a bar."

He chuckled. "Don't worry. I won't tease her... much."

His buddy Tory piped up. "I'll probably be nicer to her. I focus all my teasing on Angie."

Bliss planted her hand on her hip. "Give it all you've got, guys. I can take it, but be warned, I can dish it out too."

Kurt laughed. "I like her already. Good hire, Claudia."

Claudia rolled her eyes, then glanced at Bliss. "Kurt thinks he works here or owns the place or something, but he orders drinks so there's not much we can do about him." She winked at Kurt, so Bliss figured the comment was just good-natured ribbing. "Let's go meet the real staff." Claudia stepped in front of her and strode over to where the two bartenders were working.

"Bliss, this is Malcolm, and you know Angie, of course."

Malcolm extended his hand and Bliss shook it.

"Bliss, is it? That's a cool name."

"Thanks. My mother would be delighted to hear that, but I won't tell her. She doesn't need to be encouraged."

Malcolm grinned. "Well, if I ever see her, I won't mention it. Welcome to Boston Uncommon."

"Thank you, on both counts."

Claudia seemed pleased and hooked her hand around Bliss's arm. "Let's go meet the other waitresses."

"Lead the way."

They didn't have to go far. One girl whose perky ponytail swished as she skipped over said, "Hi. I'm Wendy." She didn't look like she wanted to shake hands. Still, she seemed friendly enough.

"Hi ,Wendy. I'm Bliss."

Claudia let go of Bliss's arm and said, "Wendy, I'd like you to show Bliss how we do things here. Just let her shadow you. She'll pick it up quickly, I'm sure. So when she says she's ready to go it alone, let her. She can always ask you if she has any questions, right?"

Bliss wondered why Claudia was giving the girl so many explicit directions. *Maybe she's got one of those brains with a dimmer switch, but her perkiness covers it.*

"Not a problem, Claudia. I'll just drop off this order and be right back."

"No hurry. I still need to introduce her to Robin."

"Oh. Okay. I'll see you later, Bliss."

As soon as Wendy skipped off, Bliss lowered her voice and asked, "Claudia? Is she always that perky?"

"Yup, if not perkier."

Bliss groaned.

Claudia led the way to the remaining waitress, who was wiping down a table.

"Robin, I'd like to introduce you to our newest employee. This is Bliss."

"Huh? Yeah, I guess. I mean it's always nice to have more staff, but bliss? That's a little strong, isn't it?"

Claudia chuckled. "Her *name* is Bliss."

"Oh!" Robin slapped her own forehead and giggled. "Oops. Sorry."

"No need to be," Bliss said. "You're not the first to make that mistake, and you won't be the last."

Robin giggled again, and Bliss got the distinct impression that she was even flakier than the other one. *Stop it. Don't be judgmental. You just met them.* Bliss hoped she was wrong, but her initial impressions usually proved to be fairly accurate.

She felt eyes on her and turned to see a gray-haired woman in a booth, shuffling tarot cards and staring directly at her.

Claudia led her over to the woman. "Bliss, this is Sadie. She's Anthony's aunt. Her tarot readings are a big draw here, and her customers have to meet a one-drink or two-soft-drink minimum. In other words, she's very good for business." Claudia spoke behind her hand: "Don't charge her or cut her off. Anthony lets her drink for free, and she's more psychic when she's had a few."

Bliss thought she saw one side of Sadie's mouth curl up in a sly smile. "If she's psychic, why are you whispering? Won't she know what you're talking about anyway?"

Claudia snorted. "Leave it to you to think of that."

At that moment, Wendy reappeared with a drink for Sadie. She set the cocktail in front of her and said, "There you go," in her sprightly voice. Then she whirled to face Claudia. "Is Bliss ready to be my shadow?"

"Ask her."

Bliss thought she saw Claudia smirk. *What's that about?*

"Okay," Wendy said, unfazed. "Are you ready, Bliss?"

Bliss pulled the order pad from her apron pocket. "As ready as I'll ever be."

A couple hours later, out of the corner of her eye, Bliss caught Claudia exiting her office with someone else. She led him right over to where Bliss was wiping down a table.

"Bliss, this is Anthony," Claudia said.

The tall, dark, and impossibly handsome man scrutinized her with such an intense stare, Bliss trembled inside.

Reverting to her old, flippant coping mechanism, she said, "Yo, Tony. How you doin'?"

His eyebrows shot up. Claudia gaped at her friend, and the activity near them ceased while people listened to the uncomfortable exchange.

"Um… Bliss," Claudia whispered, "no one calls him Tony."

"Oh." She wanted to slink off into a safe corner and give herself a time-out.

At last one side of *Anthony's* mouth turned up. "I'm 'doin'' well, thank you. And how you doin'?"

She didn't miss the mimicry and probably deserved it. Still, the fact that he went along with her Italian-American slang made her feel better somehow. If he was comfortable teasing his employees a little bit, maybe he wasn't the stick-in-the-mud Claudia had made him out to be.

After a deep breath, she said, "I'm quite well, thank you. And I want you to know how much I appreciate the job and apartment."

He nodded but made no comment. Focusing on Claudia, he said, "Can I see you in the office, please?"

Oh, shit. Claudia's probably in trouble with the owner for hiring me.

"Of course." Claudia followed Anthony to the small office where Bliss had changed into her uniform. She glanced over her shoulder and sent Bliss a wink.

Whew. She doesn't seem worried, so maybe she's right and he just appears *intimidating.* Bliss let out a deep breath. She couldn't afford to be shit-canned. At least not until she got her Hall-Snark cards back on line—but *not* online. There had to be a better way to protect her grand finale.

Wendy bounded over to her. "Did you just call him Tony?"

No sense denying it with half a dozen witnesses. "Yeah. And I'm afraid I said, 'Yo' too."

Wendy giggled. "That's funny."

"Why?"

She shrugged. "I don't know. It just is."

With that, she skipped off to the bar to give Angie her orders.

Bliss noticed Sadie smiling at her. Maybe she'd tell her if the owner was really the pussycat Claudia indicated he was, or if she'd completely blown her chance to make a good first impression.

Bliss made her way around the tables to Sadie's booth. The woman continued shuffling her tarot cards even as she smiled up at her.

"Um, Sadie. Did I do something terribly wrong by calling your nephew Tony? Does he hate that nickname or something?"

She chuckled. "No, dear. You're fine. I think you just surprised him. He isn't used to employees being comfortable around him. At least not right away. I think you made a good first impression."

"Seriously? I was already looking for another job in my head."

Sadie laughed melodiously. "Don't you go anywhere. You're a breath of fresh air around here." Then she held up her empty glass.

"Ah, I see you need a refill."

Sadie grinned. "I see I'm not the only psychic here."

Bliss smirked. *Psychic. Really?* "What are you drinking?"

"White Russians, dear. Always White Russians."

"Okay. In that case, I won't ask you in the future. But if you change your mind and decide you want something else…"

"I won't." Sadie stated it so matter-of-factly, Bliss couldn't help wonder what was so special about that drink. *Maybe she just knows what she likes*.

Bliss was about to go put in the order when Sadie said, "Oh, and dear…"

"Yes?"

"Be careful of Drake."

"Huh?" Drake hadn't even visited the bar while she'd been working. "How do you know about Drake and me?"

"I know a lot of things." Sadie spread the cards across the table. "Turn one over."

Bliss took a step back. "I—uh, I don't believe in letting tarot cards tell me what to do."

Sadie snorted. "The cards don't tell you what to do. They give you insight so you can use your free will accordingly."

Claudia said to keep her happy. "Okaaay." Bliss reached for the card closest to her and flipped it over.

It was a picture of two chalices and two people, or more accurately, a mermaid and a guy with a trident and a fishtail. Maybe Poseidon. It was kind of hard to see it at first, because Bliss was looking at it upside down.

Sadie smiled. "Well, it's better news than I thought."

Bliss waited quietly, not wanting to tell the old woman what she really thought of this hooey.

"It appears you've met your mate, but there may be some obstacle in the way. Don't worry. It's temporary."

"What do you mean? What's temporary?"

"Pull another card, dear."

Bliss did as she was asked. This time she reached for one in the middle of the deck that was sticking out a bit farther than the rest, almost begging her to take it.

The card read *Strength* in large letters, and it depicted a woman with a lion.

Sadie nodded. "As I thought... you will be facing some kind of formidable foe, and you may have to fight for what you want, but if you choose to do so, you will prevail."

Forgetting about playing nice with the overconfident so-called psychic, Bliss said, "You're not telling me anything specific. I can make that true about a few different things in my life right now. What does this have to do with Drake?"

"Earlier, when I looked at you, I had a vision of Drake standing beside you. I knew you two were connected in some way, but I'm guessing the relationship is very new."

A vision? The woman has visions?

Without waiting for confirmation, Sadie continued. "I'd say the cards are giving you the go-ahead, but I wouldn't expect it to be all smooth sailing."

Bliss smirked. "I've never heard of a relationship that was easy-breezy all of the time."

"Good. Then you won't presume it to be."

Bliss didn't know if she was any better informed now than she had been five minutes ago. What had she really learned? That the owner's aunt thinks she has visions. She somehow put Drake and Bliss together as a couple, and... and what? Their relationship would have the usual ups and downs of any other relationship? A big, fat "So what?" formed in her mind, but she kept her mouth shut.

"Well, um... thanks for the advice."

"You're welcome, but I didn't give you any advice."

She didn't? Bliss thought back to what she'd been told. The woman had simply shared what she saw, but she never did tell Bliss what to do about any of it.

"Hmmm… Well, it was interesting, nonetheless. I'd better get back to work. Even *I* can predict a thirsty customer or two will need my help soon."

Chapter 6

"MOTHER NATURE, WHY DIDN'T YOU STOP THE DRAGONS when you realized they were meeting?" Apollo asked.

"For the same reason we try not interfere in all human matters. It's important to give them a chance to figure things out for themselves. If Drake didn't realize Zina was bad news, I may have had to drum a few subtle hints into his thick skull. Fortunately he was smart enough to walk away on his own. Now, he's interested in someone else."

"But the female dragon knows he's here."

"Yes. And your point is?"

Apollo threw his hands in the air. "Aren't you afraid she'll hunt him down and convince him to have sex with her?"

Gaia chuckled. "Oh, she might try, but again we need to give the other dragon an opportunity to handle it."

"You must have a lot of faith in his ability to make good decisions."

"Not really. If it comes down to it, I'll huff and I'll puff and I'll blow their love nest right out of its tree, or something like that."

"But why sit around and allow them to possibly make mistakes?"

"Because that's how they learn. Why does Zeus let you make mistakes?"

"What mistakes? Gods don't make mistakes."

Gaia laughed. "Oh, you're precious."

———

Bliss looked up from the table she was wiping. Drake stood in front of her with a bouquet of flowers in his hand and a smile on his face.

"Hello, beautiful."

"Well, hello yourself. What brings you here with flowers?" *Are they for me?*

"It's a housewarming present. What time do you get off work?"

Yay, they are *for me!* She glanced at the clock. It was almost ten. "Not for another hour. Can you hang around that long?"

"Sure. I'll sit at the bar so I won't distract you from your work."

She set a hand on her hip. "Pretty sure of your shiny self, aren't you?"

His brows knit. "Uh, no. Did I sound like that?"

She felt like an idiot. Apparently he didn't get her poke at his male pride. "I was just teasing you. Sit anywhere you like. Maybe I should put the flowers in some water."

"Sure."

He handed them to her and she took a hearty whiff. They were really lovely and smelled like spring.

"Now to find a vase…"

Angie pulled a glass vase from somewhere beneath the bar and held it up for her to see. "Will this work?"

"Perfect."

Her new roomie half-filled the vase with tap water and set it on the bar. Bliss arranged the flowers in the vase and took another big whiff.

"Mmm... they smell heavenly."

Drake strolled up beside her and sniffed her hair. "You smell better."

She chuckled. "You like my herbal shampoo more than flowers?"

"What can I say? I'm a guy."

"That's for sure."

"Uh... miss!"

"Oops. I heard my name." Bliss located the female customer sitting near the door, holding up one finger. "Excuse me, Drake."

"Sure. Duty calls." He glanced at the customer and went stiff. His eyes rounded and he muttered, "Shit," under his breath.

What's that about? Sure, the woman looked a bit strange... kind of lethal, but so what? She was just sitting there. Hadn't he ever seen anyone wearing leather and dreadlocks before? And who was he to judge someone based on weird hair?

Bliss ignored his reaction and hurried over to the waiting customer with her order pad in hand. When she got closer, the woman sported a nasty smile.

"What can I get you?" Bliss asked politely.

The woman narrowed her eyes. "You can get out of my way."

"Excuse me?"

"You see that guy over there?"

Bliss glanced over at Drake. He quickly looked away.

"Yeah. What about him?"

"We went on a date recently and had a real good time, so I can't help wondering why my boyfriend is buying you flowers. Are you his sister or something?"

"Uh… no. We're not related." *And never will be, if he's trying to hide another relationship from me.*

"I see. So my question stands. Why did he bring you flowers?"

Bliss wasn't going to let this pushy broad get the best of her. She simply shrugged and said, "Ask him."

The woman rose. "I will."

Part of Bliss wanted to follow her and listen to what he had to say. The other part wanted to run for the hills. She opted for a compromise and asked the customers at her other tables if they needed anything.

Over her shoulder she noticed Drake leaving with the horrible woman. The cynical part of her that had been slowly fading away suddenly came back with a vengeance. *It figures. The minute I think I've found someone special, he disappoints me.*

Sadie waved her over. Bliss had almost forgotten about the tarot reading.

Crap. She strolled over to Sadie's booth. "Did you want another White Russian?" *Or did you want to say, "I told you so"?*

"Yes, dear. That would be nice, but I also wanted to give you a little more information."

Bliss was almost afraid to ask. "Another prediction?"

"No. Just a little psychic insight. When I told you to be careful of Drake, I think it had something to do with that woman. And it's not about protecting your heart. I think you need to protect yourself physically."

"Shi—I mean, shoot," Bliss stammered. "Wow. Do you really think she'd hurt me?"

"I was getting some very dark vibes from her. I'd say she's capable of it. Do you know martial arts?"

Bliss laughed, then she sobered quickly. "Do you think I need to take some classes?"

Sadie nodded. "It wouldn't hurt."

"It might. I don't have time for that right now."

"Why? What's so important that it comes before protecting yourself?"

"Only my whole future. Put it this way, if I survive because I learned self-defense, swell, but my quality of life won't be that great. If I don't survive but win the brass ring…" Bliss heard her own bizarre rationale and couldn't finish her thought. "I'm sorry, Sadie. Thank you for your concern. I guess I'll have to weigh the pros and cons."

Sadie smiled. "I understand. Exercising your free will is important."

Bliss had to put this new information on the back burner if she was going to do her job with any kind of competence. "Well, let me go get you your drink."

"Thank you, dear. Don't worry about that contest so much. I have a good feeling about your part in it."

"You know about the contest?"

Sadie shrugged. "Like I tell everyone, I know a lot of things."

Bliss thought about what else Sadie said she knew or had a feeling about, and her skin started to prickle.

—⁂—

Drake followed Zina onto the sidewalk. Charles Street was fairly quiet for a change.

"So, Drake, why are you two-timing me?"

"I just met you! And I met Bliss a couple weeks ago. I'm not committed to anyone yet."

"I thought we had a good thing going."

"We had one drink together, and to be honest, I wasn't planning to call you again."

"You *what*?" she shrieked. "Why the hell did you take my number if you weren't going to use it?"

Her eyes glowed and wings pushed at the fabric on her shoulders. He had thought she was wearing leather, but apparently it was something else. Something that stretched.

"I didn't want to insult you. Besides, I didn't take it. You practically forced it on me."

"Well, how do you think I feel now?"

He stared at what must have been her wings, pushing at the fabric again. "Probably lousy, but it would be worse to mislead you anymore than I already have."

"You bet I feel lousy. And you should know better than to piss off a dragon."

He focused on her rapidly reddening cheeks. This is what he was afraid of. If he'd refused her number, chances are he'd have seen the same reaction. Who knew what she'd do in a crowded restaurant. She could begin hurling chairs or get so "steamed" she'd shift.

"Look, I'm sorry I upset you, but—"

"But nothing." She aimed right for a male dragon's vulnerable spot. His throat. And with two fingers she jabbed him in his Adam's apple, hard.

Drake collapsed to the ground, choking. While he was down, she gave him a swift kick in the ribs with her steel-toed boot. He heard a crack, and pain shot through his chest. She stepped over him and sauntered off as if she didn't have a care in the world.

Unable to get enough air in his lungs, Drake felt the world spin and go black.

―⁂―

Bliss didn't think she'd see Drake again so soon, especially in the arms of a large, blond man who was carrying Drake's unconscious body into the bar.

"What happened?" Bliss wasn't the only one who shouted and hurried over to them.

The guy shoved one of the booths out of his way with his foot and laid Drake on the padded bench.

A moment later, Angie appeared beside Bliss and asked, "Nick, what happened?"

"Don't know. I just found him like this."

Drake groaned and started to writhe. The man Angie had called Nick held him in place and said, "Don't move, Drake. You're hurt."

Drake's eyes opened slowly. "Nick? Where am I?"

"You're in Boston Uncommon. Do you remember what happened?"

After a pause, Drake's expression grew dark. "Yeah, but I'm not telling you."

Nick straightened and crossed his arms. "Why not?"

"Because I got beat up by a girl."

Nick reared back and laughed.

Bliss kneeled by Drake's side. "Don't laugh. He's injured. Someone call a doctor."

"No. I'll be—" Drake tried to sit up but inhaled a sharp gasp and lay back down again. When his breathing steadied he said, "No, I guess I won't be all right. I think I broke a rib."

Bliss turned to her roommate. "Angie, call an ambulance."

"No." Drake put a hand on her arm. "Then my EMT buddies will show up and I'll never hear the end of it."

Angie jammed her hands on her hips. "Well, you can't just lie here for a few days."

"I don't need days. A few hours at most and—"

He glanced up at Nick. It was almost imperceptible, but Bliss saw Nick give him a quick head shake.

Sadie jumped in. "I have some emergency medical supplies in my bag. Someone can tape his ribs up tight. That's all they did for a friend of mine when he broke a rib."

Medical supplies? Did she know they'd be needed tonight, or is she always this prepared?

Sadie fished around in her oversized satchel and pulled out a roll of gauze bandage and adhesive tape. She handed them to Bliss.

"Look, I don't live far," Nick said. "I can carry him to my house and he can stay on my couch."

"Your couch?" Bliss didn't mean to raise her voice, but she was concerned about Drake, even if he *was* dating a first-class bitch who'd beaten him up. Bliss wondered what he'd said to cause that reaction. "You don't have anything better than a couch to offer?"

Nick sighed. "My wife and I just turned the guest room into a nursery."

Angie patted his arm. "It's okay. He'd probably be in too much pain if you carried him all the way up Mount Vernon Street. Carry him up to our place."

Bliss stared at her with raised eyebrows.

"Um… I mean, if it's okay with you, Bliss. We have that big sectional sofa, and if all he wants to do is lie down for a few hours…"

Now what? She'd look like a complete heel if she said no, especially in front of all these people. "But what about the hospital?"

"No hospital," Drake said, firmly.

"Well, then... Of course. Of course he can stay with us." Bliss hoped her pause wasn't too noticeable. "Wendy, will you be okay without me for a few minutes?"

"Yes, absolutely. Just take care of Drake," she said.

"I'll go get my keys." Bliss hurried to the office but remembered that Anthony was in there. She knocked and opened the door without waiting for permission to enter.

Anthony looked up from his desk. "Bliss? Is everything all right?"

Her expression must have given away the fact that all was not okay. "Drake's been hurt. I'm getting my keys to let him into our apartment upstairs, but I'll be right back down."

Anthony rose and buttoned his suit jacket. "Let me see him first."

Bliss followed Anthony out to the bar and pointed to the tight knot of people crowded around Drake. "He's over there. He was... mugged." *That sounds a lot better than "beaten up by a girl."* "He might have some broken ribs."

"Jesus," Anthony muttered and pushed his way through the crowd. When he got to Drake, he scratched his head. "A mugging? Where did this happen?"

"Right in front of the bar. I'm sorry, Anthony."

"Don't be sorry. Just be well." Anthony turned toward Nick and asked, "Can I help?"

"Sure. The two of us can carry him across our arms and he can lie flatter. I don't want those ribs to puncture a lung."

Bliss tossed her hands in the air. "Am I the only one who thinks taking him to a hospital might be a good idea?"

Several of the guys who were crowded around glanced at each other. Finally Drake spoke up. "I'm not going to a hospital. If you don't want me on your couch, I totally understand. I'll find somewhere else."

"Don't be ridiculous. I'm fine with your coming upstairs. I just think you should see a doctor so you don't heal wrong."

"He'll heal fine," Nick said. "I used to be a cop. Saw injuries like this all the time."

Bliss was outnumbered. "Okay. If you all think he'll be all right without medical attention, take him upstairs. But put him in my bedroom, and I'll sleep on the couch."

"Thanks, Bliss, but I think the sofa will be better for me. Your bed is kind of soft."

Sadie smirked and waggled her eyebrows at Bliss. *Oh, terrific. Now everyone knows he's been in my bed, even though we never got to the good part.*

Nick and Anthony grasped hands beneath Drake's back and thighs, forming a makeshift stretcher, and lifted him carefully. Bliss hurried to the door and held it open for them as they passed through it. Then she fumbled with the lock on her outside door until she managed to get the key to turn. *Damn sticky lock.*

She held the door open, and the trio slowly made their way up the narrow stairway to the landing in front of her apartment.

Bliss could tell Drake was in pain by his occasional wince, but he didn't moan or cry out, even when jostled. She felt bad for him but still wondered what had happened outside. Did she have a right to ask?

Hell, she was a Hall-Snark card designer. She could find a creative way to put anything unpleasant into words. So far she hadn't done nearly enough to resurrect her portfolio. She'd been waitressing every night for four nights in a row and sleeping late each day. But tomorrow was her scheduled day off. Perhaps she could get some work done as soon as Drake was feeling better. Right now he seemed to need her attention more than her cards did.

Anthony set Drake on the lounge part of the sectional sofa and straightened to his full height. "Stay with him, Bliss. If it gets busy, I'll have Angie and Wendy close early."

Bliss was grateful for an early night and doubted Anthony would dock her pay, but she could have used the tips. She figured he wouldn't have felt right letting his friend lie injured and alone in another person's apartment without someone who lived there present.

"I'll look after him," she said.

Nick and Anthony nodded to her, said good-bye to Drake, and left. When it was just the two of them, Drake reached out to her.

"Bliss, I want to explain..."

"You don't have to." She was about to walk away when he caught her arm and flinched. He sucked in air through his teeth, and she realized the effort must have caused him more pain.

"I want to. *I need to.* Please sit with me for a minute."

What harm could it do? Besides finding out the guy I like is a two-timing heartbreaker, that is.

She sat down on the sectional next to him and waited for him to speak.

"Before I found you again, I had tried everything I could think of. I called a bunch of greeting card companies in alphabetical order asking for Bliss, and I got hung up on, a lot."

She couldn't help chuckling.

He smiled and seemed encouraged. "I had no way of finding you. Because of the suspension, I was home going stir-crazy. Meeting you drove home what I'd been missing—a relationship—so I tried looking into those dating sites on the Internet. But then I got your card. It gave me hope that I might find you again, and I forgot about the dating site. Then a few days ago when I went to close my account, I discovered I had an answering email."

Bliss shrugged. "I get it. We didn't have an exclusive relationship. I mean, if I had known you were trying to meet anyone else, I'd have held back a little more. Just out of curiosity, how far into the alphabet did you get?"

"I got through the *A*'s, and was just about to start the *B*'s—"

"That's it? You gave up at the *A*'s?"

"My phone died. I made a mistake. I *wasn't* trying to meet anyone else. I was about to delete my account but then got sidetracked because duty called. By the time I got back from the run, I'd forgotten. When I went back to it, I saw her email. I shouldn't have even read her response, but I did and we seemed to have a lot in common. I felt I had an obligation to check it out."

Bliss raised her eyebrows. "You had a lot in common with *that… that…*"

"I know. She wasn't at all what I expected, but I shouldn't have even been curious. I really like you, Bliss. I hope I haven't messed things up with you completely."

She smirked. "You mean you'd rather be with me than Betty Bruiser? Then why didn't you call and break it off with her?"

He sighed. "I should have. I just put it off, knowing it was going to be unpleasant. I feel like a coward. A foolish, undeserving coward."

She couldn't let his self-loathing over one simple mistake continue, despite the temptation to get some payback. "I wouldn't say a guy who runs into burning buildings is a coward."

He sighed. "I know we didn't talk about exclusivity, but if you can forgive me, I'll swear to it now. I promise I'll be true blue, if you can find it in your heart to give me another chance, and I sincerely hope you can."

Bliss didn't want to give in too easily. Sure he was gorgeous and seemed like a great guy other than this "one mistake," as he called it. And having a committed relationship would be nice, but could she believe him? Did he really just forget to delete his profile? What was that little ditty she'd heard once? Cops beat, firefighters cheat? The fact that there *was* a little rhyme like that gave her pause.

She rose. "I need to think about it."

"I understand," he said softly.

Bliss strolled to the kitchen and put some water in the teakettle. For a split second she thought about her mother and how much she wanted Bliss to find a man, get married, have kids. Then she remembered that Drake, in the heat of the moment, had said he couldn't get her pregnant. *Stop it, Bliss. You're not living your mother's life. Decide what you want and go for it.*

As much as she hated to admit it, she wanted Drake…
at least the Drake she'd thought she was getting to know.
Was he really being honest with her? He hardly seemed
the type to avoid confrontation. Could he be covering
up a relationship he had going simultaneously while
romancing her? *Argh. It's all too confusing.*

Angie would be coming upstairs soon. Bliss wished
she and Drake could have it all sorted out by the time her
roommate got home, but life was rarely that neat. She
still didn't know Angie all that well and wondered what
she'd think of Bliss and Drake just picking up where
they'd left off after… *Knock it off, Bliss. You're doing it
again! Stop caring what others think.*

Bliss heard something from the living room and
poked her head around the support column. Drake was
trying to get up!

"Lie down," she squealed and rushed over to him.

"I—I shouldn't be here. It was nice of you to—" He
gasped and clutched his chest as if he had moved wrong
and reinjured himself.

"Stop." She jammed her hands on her hips. "Do I
have to push you back down on the lounger and sit on
you, or are you going to stay without a fight?"

He snorted. At last their eyes met and she saw
raw regret there. A corner of her chilly, suspicious
edge melted. She braced his back and helped him lie
down again. After he had sagged into the cushion, she
sat next to him. Her thigh molded against his shoulder. Heat seeped into her leg from his, as if he were
burning up.

"Wow, you're hot." She placed her hand on his cool
forehead. *That's weird. Maybe the blood is rushing to*

where he needs it more. "I don't think you have a fever, but you're really in no shape to go anywhere."

"I know, but if you want me to leave, I can call one of my buddies. The ribbing will stop eventually."

"I don't mind you being here. And I think Angie would be mad at me if I asked you to leave. She seemed as upset about the incident as anyone."

He smiled. "Yeah, Angie's a good kid."

"You think of her as a kid?"

"Sure. What is she? Twenty-two? Twenty-three?"

"Yeah, thereabouts. How old are you?"

"Five hundred and fifty."

Bliss laughed. "I didn't ask how old you *felt*. I asked how old you *were*."

"You know what they say... You're only as old as you feel."

She chuckled and focused on his face. His smile. His lips. She was just starting to lean in to taste his full mouth when the door opened and Angie appeared, carrying the beautiful bouquet that had started all the trouble.

"Hey, Drake. How're you doing, buddy?"

"I—I'll be right back," Bliss said, and hurried off to the bathroom. She'd remembered some pain pills left over from a badly sprained ankle. She checked her little medicine kit to see if they were still in it. *Yup.* The fact that she thought of offering him some pain relief meant she still cared about him. However, she had no intention of pretending she was okay with his desire to date her while looking elsewhere at the same time.

While she was in there doing her business, she got the idea for a new Hall-Snark card. This one was generic enough to use in her new line, but Drake was getting the first one.

You made a mistake, and that means you're human, but do it again and you'll see me fumin'.

She hurried to her bedroom to jot the words down before returning to check on Drake.

So many conflicting emotions whirled through Drake, he could barely handle just lying there, waiting for his regenerative powers to kick in.

What an idiot I am! Why did I bother meeting a dragon when I was still trying to find Bliss?

Because, Drake, ol' boy, you're a coward. You didn't want to go through the trouble and uncertainty of telling a human that you're an aberration.

I should have called Zina as soon as I found Bliss again. No, she probably wouldn't have taken the news well, but I should have told her. Now it looks like I was stringing both of them along.

Fuck… Bliss will never forgive me.

As he chastised himself, Bliss returned to the living room. He wouldn't have been surprised if she stayed away.

Strolling over to him, she held out a prescription bottle.

"I have these pain pills left over from a bad sprain. If you're not allergic to any medicines, you can have what's left."

She must really want to get rid of me… probably thinking, take a pill and get out of my apartment—out of my life.

Dragons were very hard to kill, so even an allergic reaction wouldn't hurt him. He doubted he had any allergies anyway. If he could limit the pain, he could probably walk down the stairs and get to his apartment.

"Sure. I'll take a couple, but not the whole bottle. I'm not *that* desperate to end it." He grinned, hoping she'd recognize his joke, but her eyes widened and her jaw dropped.

"You aren't… you know…"

"Of course not! I was just making a joke, or trying to. I'm not as good at that kind of thing as you are."

She let out a deep breath. "I'll get you some water."

While she was in the kitchen, he called out to her. "Bliss? I need to apologize more emphatically. I know you probably won't forgive me, but it's important that you know I'm so—"

The next thing he knew, she was bending over the back of the sofa, kissing him senseless, Spiderman-style. It didn't even matter that she was facing him upside down. Their lips fit perfectly. Her soft warmth eased the ache inside, not the physical one. The emotional battering he had been giving himself.

When she let up on the pressure, she gave him another tender peck and said, "You're forgiven, but I have something to tell you."

This was it. He had to be honest with her. Better she knew exactly who and what he was now, rather than test her trust again later.

"I have something to tell you too."

"Me first," she said.

She handed him the pills and glass of water, and as soon as he took them, she disappeared down the hall again. A door opened and didn't shut, so he figured she must be coming right back.

Waiting gave him a moment to compose his words, but what would they be? *By the way, remember during the fire when you thought you saw a reptilian form behind my face mask? Well, you were right... That was my alternate shape. I'm a shapeshifter. Had no choice in the matter. I was born that way. I hope you can accept my—um, uniqueness?*

It took a few minutes before she returned with a card in her hand. During that time, he'd composed his little speech a few times, but every version sounded ridiculous. She'd probably assume he was lying to her again.

He was almost relieved when he saw the card. Whatever she had to say in there, he could take it. Hell, he probably deserved it.

He grimaced. "It looks like I'm getting a card."

"Oh, yeah." She stood in front of the lounger and handed it to him.

Crap. It's the picture of the dragon again. Maybe she does know... Then he read the words.

"You made a mistake and that means you're human..." *Nope, she doesn't know.* He sighed and opened the card so he could read the rest. "But do it again, and you'll see me fumin'."

This time the dragon had smoke coming out of its nostrils. He couldn't help smiling, even if she was opening the door to his confession. The one he still didn't know how to tell her yet.

"Does this mean you forgive me?"

"With conditions," she said.

"Lay 'em on me, sweetheart."

Bliss crossed her arms and said, "If you want to see

other women, naturally you can, but if that's what you
decide, I'm out. And you'll tell me right away. Agreed?"

"I won't need—"

She lifted her palm as if to say, *I don't want to hear
it*, and repeated, "Agreed?"

"Absolutely."

She inhaled like she was taking a moment, thinking
something over. He waited to give her a chance to finish
her thoughts.

"Good."

"Is that it? You said conditions—plural."

"One more…" Bliss sighed. "Try to be honest with
me from now on. About everything. I'm a big girl and I
know how to take bad news without having a hissy fit.
I'd prefer an ugly truth to a pretty lie."

Drake gulped. *She said, try… How hard should I try?
Shit.* He knew what he had to do, but was she ready?
Were *they* ready?

"I have another card for you if this happens again."

"Uh-oh. What's that?" Drake asked.

"On the front I drew a beautiful old sailing vessel."

"Sounds nice. And on the inside?"

"Just two words… *Frig-it!*"

Chapter 7

AS THE MEDICATION KICKED IN, DRAKE'S PAIN WAS NOT the only thing growing duller. So was his mind. Did he dare discuss the truth with Bliss while he was less than sharp?

Fuck it. I have to.

"Blish, honey. There ish one thing I 'ave to tell you…" he slurred.

She chuckled. "Sounds like those pain pills are kicking in."

"Oh, mosht definitely."

She grinned. "Go ahead and tell me, if you can."

He took her hand in his and rubbed the pad of his thumb over her soft skin. "Blish, I'm a dragon."

"Yeah, I know. Medication will do that to you. It really makes you feel like it's dragging you down."

"No." He shook his head, and tried to enunciate. "I'm. A. Dragon." Then he remembered the card he was still holding. He pointed to the cute dragon on the front of it.

She laughed. "Sure you are…"

He needed to be clearer, but how? His brain was so muddled, he couldn't think of any other way but to insist she believe him.

"It's true. I *am* a dragon."

She frowned. "I know the medication is strong, but I didn't think it would give you delusions." Then she gasped. "Oh, my God. What if you're having an adverse side effect? I've got to call a doctor."

"No! No doctor! Promish me, Blish, you won' call a doctor."

She bit her lip. "I have to check the side effects on my computer."

She rose, but he grabbed her hand before she could walk off. "Promish!"

After a charged pause, she finally agreed.

The last thing he remembered was her gently placing a soft blanket over him and saying, "Close your eyes and rest. Just rest."

Then for the second time that day, he drifted off into unconsciousness.

Bliss brought her laptop to the living room so she could keep an eye on Drake. She was never so relieved as when the bathroom door clicked open and Angie reappeared from her bath in her pink terry-cloth robe.

"Oh, Angie. I'm in such a mess. Thank goodness you're here. I don't know what to do."

"Whoa, slow down. What's going on?"

"It's Drake. I gave him some pain medicine and he started talking crazy. He made me promise not to call a doctor, but I'm afraid he could be having an adverse side effect. What should I do?"

Angie reared back and stared at her. "Why did you promise not to call a doctor? It sounds like he needs one."

"I—I know, but he was so adamant… and we just had this big conversation about being honest and respectful of each other's needs and blah, blah, blah." Bliss opened her laptop and slipped on her glasses. "I looked up the medication I gave him on the Internet. Here's what it says: 'All medicines may cause side effects, but many people have no, or minor, side effects. Check with your doctor if any of these most common side effects persist or become bothersome.'" She waved away the useless information and continued. "That's not the part that upset me. Here's where it gets scary.

"'Seek medical attention right away if any of these severe side effects occur: Allergic reactions (rash; hives; itching; difficulty breathing; tightness in the chest; swelling of the mouth, face, lips, or tongue).' He seems to be okay there, so maybe he's not allergic, but listen to the rest of these: 'abnormal snoring or sighing; confusion; difficulty urinating; fainting; fast, slow, or irregular heartbeat; hallucinations; mental or mood changes; seizures; severe dizziness, drowsiness, or light-headedness; severe or persistent stomach pain, nausea, or constipation; shortness of breath; slow or shallow breathing; tremor; vision changes.'"

Just then, Drake started to snore.

"Oh, no! He's snoring. I'm afraid for him, Angie."

"Does the Internet say what you should do about it?"

"At the bottom here it says, 'If you have any questions about these side effects, contact your health-care provider.'"

Angie opened her purse and dug out her cell phone. "Well, *I* didn't promise not to call someone. I've heard of a hotline called Ask a Nurse. It may be a matter of semantics, but he didn't say anything about nurses, did he?"

"No, he didn't. Angie, you're brilliant."

She smiled. "I know."

She punched a few buttons and spoke with the information operator, who connected her to the hotline.

———— ∿∿∿ ————

Anthony let himself into the girls' apartment moments after they called him. As their landlord, he had a key and Bliss didn't mind him using it. She needed his help.

"How's Drake doing?" he asked.

"Terrible." Bliss wrung her hands. "We need you to help us take him to a hospital."

"Whoa, there. What makes you think he needs a hospital?"

She hung her head. "I gave him some pain pills and he had an adverse reaction."

Drake snored softly in the background.

Anthony cocked his head. "What kind of adverse reaction?"

Bliss didn't answer, so Angie chimed in. "I wasn't here when he was awake, but Bliss said he was hallucinating. He said he was a dragon."

Bliss cringed. "It's my fault. I gave him a card with a dragon on it, and the idea probably got mixed up in his head somehow." *Why the hell did I give him my medication?*

Anthony's lip twitched. Bliss thought she saw the start of a smile, but it quickly disappeared.

"Are you a doctor?" he asked.

Feeling about two inches tall, she answered softly, "Uh… no."

"I'll chew you out for prescribing medication without a license later. What did you give him?"

"Percocet."

"How much?"

"Just two."

"*Just* two? Those things are narcotics, not aspirin." He sighed and stuffed his hands in his pockets. "I don't think he needs a hospital. All he needs is to sleep it off."

Bliss was tempted to ask him if *he* was a doctor, but she knew enough not to get snarky with someone who they'd asked to help.

Angie took it from there. "But the Ask a Nurse hotline said to transport him to an emergency room right away."

Anthony stared at the ceiling and seemed to be thinking something over… hopefully how best to get Drake to Boston General.

"I know you don't know me well, Bliss, but Angie does. I'd never do anything to hurt my staff, friends, or customers. Isn't that right, Angie?"

Angie turned toward Bliss. "I've never felt safer since taking this job—and I grew up in the suburbs, so that's saying something. Anthony has gone out of his way to take care of all of us at one time or another. He'd never do anything to hurt Drake."

Bliss bit her lower lip. "You really think he'll be all right?"

Anthony placed a reassuring hand on her shoulder. He was surprisingly cool in more ways than one.

"I promise. When he wakes up, he'll be back to his old self. You'll see."

The following morning, Bliss awoke with the sensation that someone was touching her. When her eyes fluttered open, she looked up into Drake's smiling face. He smoothed her hair out of her eyes.

"Good morning, beautiful."

"Drake. You're up!" She levered herself to a sitting position on the sofa where she'd fallen asleep. She was still wearing her uniform, which was wrinkled beyond recognition.

"Angie said you took good care of me last night." He sat next to her.

"You look a lot better this morning. How do you feel?"

"I feel great. Perfectly fine." He glanced at his watch. "In fact, I should go into work soon. My shift is about to start."

"You don't have to. We called in sick for you last night."

He leaned back and scrutinized her. "You didn't say anything about my getting beaten up by a girl, did you?"

She laughed. "No, of course not. We said you were in an accident and left it at that."

He nodded. "Okay. Well, I should call anyway just to reassure them it was a minor accident, and I'm all right."

"Or you could go in a little late…" She finger-walked her way up his arm until he groaned and captured her hand in his.

He kissed her knuckles. "Did I thank you for all you did for me last night?"

"No, but I'll let you show me how grateful you are." Bliss raised her eyebrows, hoping he'd get the hint.

She wasn't horny as much as she was concerned about his pretending to be perfectly fine when he wasn't. Well, that wasn't entirely true. She was equal parts horny and concerned. If he turned down sex, he was either not a typical guy or still in too much pain to perform. Better to find out now than when he was riding around in a speeding fire truck or climbing a ladder.

He grinned, scooped her up in his arms, and strode toward her bedroom. Apparently her message was received, and he must have been all right to carry her like that.

"Is Angie around?" she asked quickly, before they reached her bedroom door.

"Nope. She went grocery shopping. Said she had a few errands to run too, and she'd be gone a couple hours."

"Handy." She reached down and twisted the doorknob.

"Very," he said, and carried her into the room, setting her down in the middle of the bed.

He began undressing, but Bliss still needed a bit of reassurance. "Just to be clear… you're not interested in the woman with the rat's nest hair who kicked the shit out of you, right?"

He reared back and laughed. "I couldn't be less interested in her…" Then he crawled on his hands and knees up the bed until he was looking directly into her eyes. "Or more interested in you. What you did for me, Bliss… I don't think many women would have been that forgiving. I wouldn't have blamed you if you'd added your own licks."

"Oh, I might still get in a few 'licks' but not the way you just meant it."

"How did I get so lucky? I thought you'd never forgive me. When Angie brought the flowers up, I fully expected to have them thrown in my face."

She caught sight of the lovely fresh flowers on her

dresser. They lightly scented the room and added a delicate beauty to it. "I think I knew what you were trying to say."

"You did?"

"Well, yeah. If I'm right, you felt bad for keeping your options open, even after you found the perfect woman... or you brought flowers to cushion the blow when you broke up with me and went off with Motorcycle Maddie."

He lay down next to her and gathered her into a warm hug. "Of course I wouldn't break up with you for—ugh—her, or anyone else for that matter. You're amazing. I want to keep you for as long as you'll let me."

Bliss was glad she'd asked for reassurance. Sometimes a little insecurity can bring out the nicest compliments. As long as they're not lines. She was fairly sure Drake was being sincere. Certainly he had been apologetic enough last night. He wouldn't humble himself like that if he didn't mean it, would he?

Her cynicism had resurfaced in a big way when she was confronted with the fact that he'd gone out with someone else while he was supposedly interested in her. Drake had admitted it was a mistake and promised her exclusivity in the future, but could any man be trusted if Heidi Klum came along? Then she almost snickered out loud. *How apt is that to happen? Not very.*

There were no guarantees, and Bliss had realized that long ago. That's why her Hall-Snark cards were so popular. People disappointed each other all the time, but that didn't stop them from trying again. If every relationship was effortless right from the start, she'd be out of a job.

While all this was going through her head, Drake was nibbling the column of her neck and popping open the buttons of her blouse.

Decision time, Bliss. Either you really do forgive him and take this relationship to the next level, or you hold a grudge and drive him away. What's it going to be?

She only needed a moment to realize what she wanted. She reached for his zipper and dragged it down. He lifted his pelvis so she could push his jeans over his hips. He divested her of her blouse, and then the rasp of a zipper over her ass meant he was getting rid of her skirt next.

She fumbled with the hem of his T-shirt until he stopped what he was doing and yanked it off. In another minute, she was wearing only her underwear, but she was determined that he be naked first. She took hold of his boxer's waistband and dragged it over the considerable bulge between his thighs. His cock sprang free, and what an amazing organ it was!

Drake watched her scoot down until she was at eye level with his cock, and then she grasped it tightly. He'd let her do whatever she wanted to him and couldn't wait to see what that would be.

She laved around the crimson head and ran her tongue down the sensitive underside. Tingles raced through him. Then she lowered her open mouth over his shaft as far as she could go, then sucked and pulled back at the same time. Incredible sensations shot through him, causing an involuntary moan to escape.

"Oh, God. You do that well. But you don't have to, you know."

She looked at him as if he'd lost his mind. "Of course I don't have to. I want to." She licked her lips. "Mmm... candy."

She returned to sucking his rod as if it really were a giant candy bar. He lay back and moaned his pleasure until he felt the inevitable tingle at the base of his spine.

"Bliss, stop. I can't take any more."

She lifted her head and smiled. "Are you sure?"

"Oh, yeah. Besides, it's your turn." He flipped her over onto her back and she squealed, apparently not expecting his quick reflexes. Then she giggled, letting him know she didn't mind a bit.

He yanked her red satin panties down and off, then reached for her matching bra's front closure. As soon as it opened, he dove for one of her gorgeous breasts. He suckled hard, then licked her nipples and blew on each of them, making her shiver and moan.

"*Please*, suck them again," she pleaded.

"I intend to." He took one nipple deep in his mouth and sucked thoroughly. She arched and moaned louder. As soon as he was sure he had pleasured that one enough, he moved to the other and gave it equal attention.

"Oh, God." She cupped his jaw and lifted his face until he was looking in her eyes. "I love that. Thank you."

Drake grinned. "My pleasure. Anytime."

"If I took you up on that, you'd miss a whole lot of work."

He chuckled. "Or I'd just have to find a way to work from home." *Damn, Drake. You've already got yourself moving in with her. Slow the hell down.*

"Um, are you up for the rest?" she asked.

Thankful that she'd let his comment slide, he murmured, "Oh, yeah. Where do you want me?"

"On a silver platter."

He chuckled and said, "The lady knows what she wants."

She winced. "Sorry. I can be bossy in the bedroom—well, not just the bedroom, basically everywhere—but right now I want to give you whatever you like."

"In that case, let's do it doggie style." *Perfect. That way if I begin to shift, she won't see.*

Bliss quickly rolled up onto her hand and knees, facing away from him. She looked over her shoulder. "Condom?"

Damn. How do I tell her I don't need them? "I—uh… I guess we should have had this talk before, but I still don't have any. The good news is I can't get you pregnant, and I don't have any diseases. The department insists on thorough checkups."

Bliss paused a moment, then said, "Works for me."

"How about you? Ever been tested?"

"I donate blood a lot. They'd tell me to stop if they found HIV or hepatitis C, and I don't have herpes or anything else."

She waved her tush in a provocative invitation. Drake groaned.

Positioning himself behind her, he tested her wetness. *Oh, yeah. No problem there.* "I'll go slow. Let me know if it hurts."

Bliss faced forward and nodded.

He positioned the head of his cock at her opening and rubbed some of her juices over it. He was large and *really* didn't want to hurt her. Fortunately, as he entered, she sighed.

He was only feeling now, inching into her until he was fully seated. With no sign of protest on her part,

Drake began a slow rhythm. He sucked in air and gave up breathing completely while heated sensations rose to a fevered pitch.

"Oh, that feels so good. You can go faster if you want to."

He wanted to, but he didn't want to give her a wham, bam, "Thank you, ma'am," either. He was already so turned on that his shaft was pulsing with need.

"Let me lead. I think you'll enjoy the experience."

"Oh yeah. I'm being bossy again." She snickered. "Sorry."

Drake leaned over her back and whispered endearments into her ear. He found her clit with his finger and rubbed it in a circular motion at the same slow speed as his thrusts.

She moaned but sounded a bit frustrated. *Good. It'll be that much sweeter when I finally make her come.*

Drake carried on like that until she whimpered.

He took pity on her, knowing she was as turned on as he was. "Are you ready for more?"

"Yes. Harder, faster, please."

He answered her by speeding up and increasing the pressure on her clit. He rubbed it so quickly that a vibrator couldn't have done better. She moaned and sped up her answering momentum.

Such pleasure. An animalistic instinct took over and drove him to take her without restraint. His heart pounded. He thrust faster and faster, pushing them toward the ultimate release.

He wanted her to come before him. He needed her to fathom all of what he was feeling and share every drop of joy.

Their bodies gleamed with sweat, and his breath puffed out, becoming a smoke curl against her neck. *Uh-oh*. He leaned over and licked her there, tasting her salty skin. He kept it up until she was so close, she was just a whisper away.

At last, she quivered and shattered, screaming her release. Drake felt like he was going to die if he held off much longer. His body temperature was rising, but he wanted her to ride out her orgasm to the very last aftershock.

He glanced at his arm and noticed the hardness that signaled his dragon scales were about to form. *Shit*. He had to let himself come and do it quickly before she noticed something strange.

Her quivering died down as did her screams, so he let his finger leave her clit. His climax exploded. He rode its waves of pleasure with his hands gripping her bottom—grateful they were still hands with fingernails instead of talons.

As the last aftershock rolled through him, he checked his arms and torso. *Whew*. He'd come soon enough to avoid shifting this time. He'd have to come up with a strategy to stop the heat buildup and possible loss of control over his shift. He smiled to himself as he realized the obvious answer was to have sex more often.

He withdrew and collapsed onto his side next to Bliss. She fell to her side, facing him. Despite her panting breaths, she appeared totally relaxed and sated. She didn't seem to have noticed anything strange. He gathered her into his arms and pulled her to his heaving chest.

That was a close one, moron.

Chapter 8

DRAKE CHECKED IN WITH HIS FIREHOUSE AND discovered that they were out on a run. His conscience kept pricking at him for taking a whole day off when he was no longer injured.

"Bliss, honey. I have to go to work."

"But I already called and told them you were in an accident. How would it look if you showed up feeling perfectly fine? And, while we're at it, how *can* you be in such good shape? I thought you broke some ribs."

Drake patted his rib cage. "They must have just been bruised, not broken. I'm still a little sore, but not like last night. Those pills you gave me... what were they?"

Bliss looked sheepish. "Percocet. I shouldn't have given you anything that strong without a doctor's prescription. They really knocked you for a loop."

Drake was aware of how he'd slurred his words when he told her he was a dragon. He was actually grateful for that. He hadn't thought through the best way to explain his alternate form and decide how the conversation should begin. "Hey, honey. I'm a dragon," didn't work out so well.

He really needed to plan it better. He'd have to let her see certain things he could do. He needed her to believe him next time, hopefully without transforming in front of her and scaring her to death. Since he'd given her zero preparation, it was a blessing she simply thought he was out of his mind.

But he *did* tell her. Later on, he could make that claim and she couldn't accuse him of being dishonest. Knowing Bliss, she'd think it, even if she didn't come right out and say it. *Who am I kidding? Of course she'll say it.*

She stroked his chest gently. "Are you sure you're all right now?"

He captured her waist and drew her against his hard length, letting his erection speak for him. She glanced down between them. "Ah, I see. You really are feeling better."

"And if I don't leave soon, I might feel *too* good to leave at all."

One side of Bliss's mouth turned up. "Oh, *well*, if that's the case, I'd better kick you out. I've got stuff to do today."

He laughed. *Typical Bliss.* "You should make a card for that."

"Oh, I have some. I call those the 'don't overstay your welcome' cards. You, however, are welcome whenever we have a few spare minutes."

She tipped up her face for a long, tender kiss. He cupped her head and let her silky dark hair glide over his fingers. As much as he wished he could stay there and fool around with this remarkable woman all morning, he really had to go.

"I'll call you later in the day. We can check our schedules and hopefully plan something fun to do together."

"That would be nice."

One more long kiss later, he managed to force himself out the door and downstairs.

———

Angie strolled around the corner humming. "Is he gone?"

"Yes, he just left. Nice of you to hum a warning."

She grinned. "I hope you'll do the same for me. Someday." Her smile suddenly diminished.

"Are you seeing anyone?"

Angie let out a long sigh. "Not really. Tory flirts with me, but… I don't know."

"Has he asked you out?"

"Not exactly. I mean, I think he would if I encouraged him, but…"

"Is it because he's black?"

Angie looked horrified. "No! Of course not." Then her shoulders slumped. "I mean, he's a great guy. Little things like that don't matter to me one way or the other, but you wouldn't believe how prejudiced my dad and grandparents are. They'd have heart attacks and die, and then I'd feel guilty because I'd know I killed them."

"Um, you're being a little dramatic, don't you think?"

"You don't know my family."

"True. Are you very close to them?"

"Hey, I spent twenty years with them, even my grandparents, under the same roof. You wouldn't believe how the multigenerational influence can mix you up. Sometimes you listen to passé values, and they almost make sense."

Bliss didn't want to be nosy, but she wished she could help. Angie seemed like such a nice girl. She deserved happiness without worrying about what others would think. *Ah ha! I see another card line needed.* Hmmm… *So what if he's black? He's got my back. Yeah, I'll work on that later.*

"…so you see," Angie was saying, "I'd be leading him on, and I try not to do that to guys."

"Huh? Oh, yeah. That's not right. You don't want to

be a tease." *Jeez, I'd better get into this conversation or start working on that new card line. I wasn't even listening to her for a moment there.*

Angie scrutinized her. "You did hear the part where my family wouldn't care about the color of his skin, right?"

"Huh? I thought you said they were prejudiced."

"They are. Or would be if they knew he's from New York. Bliss, he's a *Yankees fan!*"

Bliss's jaw dropped. "Is that what…" She gazed at the floor and shook her head. "Unbelievable."

"You seem distracted. Is everything all right?"

"Yeah." She straightened. "Everything's fine."

"Did Drake ever tell you who that woman was last night and why she hurt him?"

"I'd prefer not go into it." That was something Bliss would have to try *not* to think about. Repeating everything to her roommate would make it that much harder.

Angie shrugged. "I get it. Well, just know if you want to talk about it, or anything else for that matter, I'm here. I'm a very good listener, and I know how to keep my mouth shut too."

"That's probably what makes you such a good bartender."

"Yup. You'd be surprised how much gossip I hear."

"And you don't repeat any of it?"

A sly smile crossed Angie's face. "Only the really juicy stuff."

Drake found the firehouse deserted but waited around until the guys returned. They were covered with soot and sweat, which meant they'd had a hell of a job.

The chief eased out of the ladder truck first and strolled over to him. "I thought you were sick."

"Injured. But I'm okay now. Just some bruised ribs."

"Glad to hear you're okay. We could have used you back there. It was a two bagger in a three decker in Charlestown."

"Shit. Those things go up like kindling."

"No kidding. The second alarm was mostly to protect the neighborhood. The building itself was a total loss."

"Anything suspicious?"

"Talk to the other guys. I have to go fill out the paperwork." The chief strode off toward the stairs.

Benjamin shed his turnout gear and waved Drake over as he hung up his jacket. "Drake, what's up? We heard you'd be out a few days."

"Nah. I'm tougher than I look."

"I've always said so. What happened?"

"Stupid mugging. I thought I had a broken rib, but they taped me up, doped me up, and I was fine as soon as I sobered up."

Benjamin laughed. "Well, you're lucky you weren't in on this sumbitch. It got out of control real quick."

"Think it was a torch?" Drake knew better than to use the word "arsonist" out loud, so he went with the firefighter slang.

"Maybe. Or maybe a spark."

Drake hated to consider that. It meant one of their own had crossed over to the dark side. Even a firefighter wannabe could be bad news if the appeal was a fascination with fire.

"The neighbors said there was a guy all dressed in black leather wearing a biker helmet, poking around outside the back door. I saw someone like that hanging around when we got there. Then he took off. When the cops talked to the residents, no one was expecting any visitors and said they didn't know anyone matching the description."

Crap. It couldn't have been…nah. If Zina was taunting me, she'd wait until I was back to work. Although, if anyone knows the restorative powers of a dragon, it's another dragon. Damn it. She may have used her fire as a way of getting to me.

Bliss had spent her day not only redesigning many of her cards, but also thinking about how to prevent herself from ever losing them again. She hadn't liked Drake's idea of simply backing them up on one of the Internet storage sites. He didn't understand the cutthroat competition for this grand prize—and she wanted it as much as the other two finalists.

It was too much to simply trust his word that no one would be able to gain access to those sites. Hackers were able to do all kinds of things they shouldn't be able to do. No, she had to think of something else.

Suddenly it came to her. A safe deposit box! She could store her designs on a disk and put the soft copy in a safe hiding place. She slapped herself up the side of the head with a loud, "Duh!"

At that moment, the phone rang. She glanced at the caller ID and noticed it said District 3. *It must be Drake!*

She picked up the phone and said in a breathy voice, "Hello, big, strong, handsome fireman…"

She was met with silence for a moment. At last, a

voice she barely recognized answered, "Um, hello, dear lady. Is Drake there?"

Gulp. "Uh… may I ask who's calling?"

"Chief Tate. I told him to take the rest of the day off and come back for his shift tomorrow, but we're busier than expected and I could really use his help today."

"Oh," she squeaked. "I thought he went to work this morning."

"He did, but I sent him home, stupidly thinking he could use a little more time to heal. He said he might go to your place and left your number. That'll teach me to be a nice guy."

From what Bliss remembered of the chief, "nice guy" wasn't a description she would have used.

"Well, he's not here, but if I see him, I'll tell him to call."

"Never mind the call, just tell him to get his ass down here."

Yikes. "Okay."

"Oh, and honey? Thanks for the compliment," he added with a chuckle.

Bliss didn't know what to say to that, so she just mumbled, "Okay. Bye," and hung up.

She thumped her forehead on the table a few times and muttered, "Damn, damn, damn."

As Bliss headed for the bank with her disk, she thought she'd pop into the bar and say hello to Claudia.

She didn't expect to see Drake there having a beer with two of the regulars. He was at the back booth but spotted her immediately. He said something to his companions and rose. Tory and Kurt turned around and waved to her, then went back to their conversation. Meanwhile, Drake strolled over to her.

"Hey, Bliss. I thought this was your day off."

"It is. I was just on my way to the bank and thought I'd stop in and see Claudia. It's a good thing I ran into you, though. The chief called and wants you back at work."

Drake grimaced. "I don't know if that's a good idea. I've had two beers."

"You're not drunk, are you?"

He chuckled. "A couple beers just take the edge off. I'm not as bad as if I were under the influence of a couple Percocet."

She sighed. "I don't suppose I'll ever live that down, will I?"

"Sure you will, babe." He clasped her around the waist in a side squeeze and kissed her temple. "I'll never mention it again."

"Maybe you could call the chief and ask if he'd mind that you just had a little beer. It sounds like they really need you."

Concern crossed Drake's face. "Christ. What did he say?"

"Something about it being really busy. What does that mean? Is there a big fire somewhere? Or a lot of little ones?"

"It could be either. Even a bunch of false alarms take the guys away from the station. You're right. I'd better call and find out what's going on."

Drake reached for his belt where he kept his cell phone, but it wasn't there. "Crap. I forgot I lost the damn thing during the… incident on the sidewalk. I'll have to use the bar's phone."

"Here." Bliss fished her cell phone from her tote bag. "Use mine. I'll be in the office talking to Claudia."

"Thanks."

She threaded her way through customers and over to the closed office door to say hello to her friend and give Drake some privacy.

The door was ajar, so she knocked and peeked around it at the same time.

"Bliss," Claudia called out with a smile. "Come in. I was just making the schedule. Can you work this weekend?"

"Uh, sure. I guess so." *Crap, I owe her so much and I don't dare say no just because the show's producers are coming Tuesday.*

"It's going to be busy. The Boston Marathon is Monday, and a lot of extra visitors show up early."

"Great. More tips."

"Yeah, you'll make a mint. How's the greeting card biz, by the way?"

"I'm getting almost completely back on line… well, not exactly online. More on disk. I might be able to finish my presentation by the deadline after all." She reached in her pocket, and withdrew and waved the CD with all her latest designs on it.

"Careful," Drake said, as he came up behind her and plucked it out of her hand. "You don't want anyone to steal those."

"Hey! Give that back."

"Only if you kiss me good-bye before I go in to work."

She gave him a quick, closed-mouth kiss, then said, "Okay. *Now,* hand it over."

He chuckled and said, "Wow. Don't mess with the lady's work," then did as she asked.

"I'm on my way to the bank to open a safe deposit box. I think I found a way to keep from losing my whole portfolio if anything ever happens again."

"Still don't trust the Internet, eh?"

"No. I really don't."

He smiled. "Well, I'm glad you found a way to protect your interests, even if it's old school."

"Whatever works. So I guess your chief needs you badly enough to take you, beer-buzzed brain and all?"

"Yeah, I just can't drive the truck."

"That makes sense. How would it look if a firefighter wrapped the ladder truck around a tree, then flunked the Breathalyzer test?"

He gave her a look that said, "Really?"

She kissed him again but this time used her tongue. She tasted a little beer and detected some salt, probably from the pretzels, but he didn't reek. "You'll pass."

"Thanks." He handed her back her phone. "I'll call you when I can. It all depends on what's going on."

"The chief didn't tell you why they need you?"

"Looks like there've been a lot of small fires and some false alarms. I have a bad feeling it's only a matter of time before we see a big one."

A shudder rippled through Bliss. "Be careful."

He gave her a cocky grin. "Always."

It didn't help her shake the worry. How he did what he did amazed her. She still had panicky dreams of fire and choking on smoke.

Chapter 9

ZINA MUTTERED TO HERSELF AS SHE STUDIED A MAP OF Boston. "Stupid human. When I get rid of her, Drake and I can save the species." She glanced at the bed in her hotel room. "Hell, if it weren't for her, we'd be making baby dragons right now." *Ah, agony…*

The western dragons were given only a month-long mating window every five years, and it was already two weeks into the month. Maybe *others* had all the time in the world, but if Zina didn't get pregnant now, it would be a long wait for the next chance. *No wonder there are so few of us.*

The more she obsessed over how unfair it all was, the angrier she got. Scoping out the city had kept her busy for a little while, but now she was anxious to set her plan in motion. Over the past forty-eight hours, Zina had penciled in X's on the best targets in the area, then erased each and filled in the space with a red marker after she'd set a fire there.

Her goal was to stretch the fire department's resources so thin that they wouldn't be able to respond when she eventually went after her final target. The bar where the stupid human worked. She'd watched her for the last two days and determined the bitch lived in one of the apartments over the bar. *Perfect.* Zina had shouted with glee when she'd realized she'd be eliminating her competition's job and home at the same time. With any luck, she'd snuff out the human's interfering life.

Zina knew when the bar closed and planned to break in from the back at midnight. Then she'd open all the bottles of alcohol and pour them over anything and everything flammable. The fact that she breathed fire was the perfect cover for arson. She didn't leave any evidence behind—not so much as a matchstick for investigators to find.

"Drake will never know it was me who killed his girlfriend," she congratulated herself in the mirror. "And I know exactly what to do after the bitch is dead. I'll swoop in and comfort him in his hour of need. I'll show him I understand him the way only another dragon can. If that doesn't work, I'll use voodoo."

She whirled away from the mirror and ran her fingers down her long, bumpy dreadlocks. "Go ahead, girlie. Enjoy him while you can. It's just a matter of time before he understands and forgives my jealous outburst and comes back to me forever."

This plan had to be orchestrated very carefully. Nothing could be left to chance, so Zina went back to poring over her maps and choosing her timing precisely.

~~~

Drake dragged his tired body off to shower and prayed nothing else took him away from his bed for the rest of the night. His pillow beckoned him, and he wanted to lay down his head and kiss it. He hadn't called Bliss yet, but he was too tired to hold a phone, never mind try to listen and talk coherently. She'd understand.

How the hell had there been so many fires recently? Most were in the middle of the friggin' night. Some had happened almost simultaneously in the north or west end, and across the river in Charlestown. *All in my district. It can't be a coincidence.* But how did Zina know in which district he worked? He hadn't told her.

She must have followed me. That in itself was unsettling. *Or, crap... maybe she grabbed my cell phone while I was passed out on the sidewalk.*

So far, none of the fires had the usual earmarks of arson. No accelerant. Nothing to make a spark. And since that fire a couple days ago, no one had seen a suspicious person hanging around and watching. *It's as if she's deliberately trying to confuse me.*

If Drake hadn't been so tired, he would have spent more time going over the facts, trying to figure out if Zina had something to do with this anomaly and why. He suspected she did.

Maybe if I had found a way to let her down gently... He mentally shook himself. Guilt wouldn't solve anything. Besides, it was better to know what she was capable of sooner rather than later.

He knew what she wanted. His seed. But if he got her pregnant, it would be too late. A pregnant female had to be protected by her mate. To desert the one extending the species would be unconscionable.

Drake didn't know anything about the Caribbean dragons. Hell, he didn't even know there *were* any before meeting Zina, but her Jamaican accent and Rasta name pretty much proved her origins.

How could Zina be pulling this off, if she happened to be the culprit? She either had help, or she was risking being seen in flight. Both were uncomfortable thoughts.

If he hadn't been so tired, he would have obsessed longer. As it was, he had to get some sleep, so he made himself put thoughts of arson aside and think of something more pleasant. Perhaps if he thought of Bliss, he'd dream about her. A nice erotic dream where he'd feel her soft skin, taste her sweet mouth, and make love to her with the tenderness she deserved...

As those thoughts ran through his head, he realized *he* was the one who wanted to make love... not just have sex.

I love her.

The revelation should have made him uncomfortable. That meant he was giving up on his dream of having children, on his promise to his mother, on his species, but the thought didn't trouble him. Instead, he drifted off to sleep with a smile.

Mother Nature paced with her hands clasped behind her back, her mood in stark contrast to the beautiful spring day outside her glass bubble. As if the other gods and goddesses could sense her frame of mind, they gave her a wide berth.

Finally, she halted, threw her hands in the air, and yelled, "What the fuck is going on out there?"

Apollo, probably realizing he was one of the few gods she could almost stomach, approached her cautiously.

"Gaia. Would you like me to summon Mr. Balog for you?"

She snorted. "Balog. What good would he be?"

"Perhaps he's heard some rumblings among the paranormals in the Boston Uncommon bar? After all, he lives on the third floor of the building and keeps an eye on the patrons for you."

"You mean my little spy might come in handy?"

Apollo shrugged. "It's worth a try. After all, these fires are occurring in multiple locations, almost simultaneously. They seem beyond a human arsonist's capability. We know they generally work alone."

She blew out a deep breath. "I suppose so. I can't stand the thought of my beloved city being ravaged by these fires—and if I find out it's a *paranormal* doing it…" She shook her fist. "I'll… I'll—Gaaaah!" A cold wind rushed through the room, causing the gods to pull their togas tighter.

Apollo slapped his hands over his ears, expecting thunder. The other gods wisely decided to stay out of it and carried on with their poker game.

"Fine. Fetch Balog. Let's see if the little weasel knows anything."

"As you wish, Goddess."

"Wait! Bring me that dragon who frequents the bar too—in his human form."

"But I thought you took away his fire-breathing ability."

"I did. That doesn't mean he doesn't miss it. Perhaps he's working with someone else. Didn't we find out he was related to that asshole who started the Chicago fire over a century ago?"

"Yes. But—"

"But nothing… Bring him to me!"

"So, Bliss…" Angie began as she placed the washed and rinsed dishes in the drainer.

Bliss looked away from the pouring rain out the window and wiped dry one of the mugs they'd had their coffee in that morning. "Yes?"

"We know each other well enough now to ask personal questions, don't we?"

Bliss leaned away and eyed her roommate. "How personal are we talkin'?"

"Don't worry. I don't want to know what brand of tampons you use or anything…"

"Since you can just look in the bathroom vanity, that would be a waste of a personal question."

Angie chuckled. "Yeah. And believe me, I don't give a rat's ass about that. What I really want to ask you has more to do with work."

"Okay. Have at it."

"You seem to be a really good cocktail waitress. Since you get to live and work with wonderful me, why are you slaving so hard to get your other business off the ground? You seem to spend every free moment on the computer."

Bliss worried her lip and thought about how to word it for a moment. It wasn't as if she hated waitressing. In some instances it could be a lot of fun. But working in a bar for the rest of her life wasn't her idea of fulfillment. How could she say that to Angie without hurting her feelings?

"Well, it's like this… I used to work at a job I hated. The pay was okay, but my boss was mean and the work was boring. Yet, I continued to work there simply to make the rent. And I should let you know that rent is absolutely essential. If I lived with my parents for one more flippin' day, I'd have wound up in an asylum."

"Ah. So you're not making enough money at the bar?"

"Huh? No, that's not it. The money is fine. I need a place to live and enough money to pay the bills while I get my portfolio back on track. The waitressing is great for that, and even though my diplomatic skills are tested from time to time, it's not like being president of the United States."

"But why is the card business so important?"

"Other than the fact that I love doing it? Well, there's my sister."

"Your sister? I didn't know you had a sister."

"Yeah, she's in India. My big sister went and fell in love with a guy from West Bengal. Now she lives there." Bliss stifled a sigh. *How proud would she be at this moment, watching her little sister take her original idea and catapult it into the spotlight?*

Bliss didn't even know if India would see the show. It hadn't aired anywhere yet, of course. The whole thing was taped first and released soon afterward—and did the orphanage where her sister worked even have a television? Her village barely had electricity.

"So what does she have to do with the card business?"

"Oh! Yeah, I didn't quite connect the dots for you, did I? She started the business. When she decided to move to India permanently, she offered me the gig. It was her baby and I don't want to let her down."

Bliss finished drying and putting away the last of the clean dishes and folded the towel. "My sister may have started it, but it's turned out to be more than that for me. I found it's a great way to express my snarky sense of humor and stay independent. I love being my own boss. It was such a happy day when I could give my nasty old boss a big raspberry." She grinned, thinking about the day she quit her boring, frustrating, sometimes revolting tax job.

"Okay, I get that, but you seem so driven. How are you having any fun? I haven't seen you with Drake in days."

"Drake's been crazy busy at work. Haven't you noticed all the fire engines whizzing past and sirens blaring lately?"

"Yeah… Hey, if you need someone else to hang out with, we could do something together."

Crap, how can I make her understand?

"I have an important deadline. I've got this huge finale coming up. When my building burned, all my work went up in smoke. Actually, it melted, but that's beside the point. I still have a contract with the show, and if I don't make good on my promise of delivery, I'll screw up their ending, lose all credibility—and probably have to pay back the advance money they gave me to produce the designs."

Angie shrugged. "Okay, I guess I can see what you're up against. If I can help out in any way… take over some of the chores or anything…"

"Aw, that's sweet of you, but I'd never take advantage of a roommate that way. I need to pull my weight."

"Well, it seems like you're pulling a lot of weight everywhere. You'll burn out if you don't give yourself a break."

"Actually, there is something you can do."

"Really?" Angie perked up. "Name it. I'd love to help."

"The producers are coming to check up on me in a couple weeks. A little less than two weeks, actually. They like to meet the important people in the finalist's life. That's usually the people they're living with."

Angie gasped. "Are you saying I might be on television?"

"You'll have to sign a waiver, giving them permission to use the film with you in it."

Angie whooped and jumped into the air. She looked like she was headed for Bliss with a headlock of a hug.

At that moment, a knock sounded at the door. *Phew, saved by the fist.*

"I'll get it," Angie volunteered. She was still grinning from ear to ear. "Anything I can do to help out a TV star."

Bliss rolled her eyes.

When Angie opened the door, Drake was leaning against the door frame, looking soaked and haggard.

"Drake! We were just talking about you," Angie said. "Come in."

He raised his eyebrows. "You were?"

He entered slowly as if they might have been berating him.

"Yeah, I mentioned to Bliss I hadn't seen you around much, and she said you've been really busy."

He shrugged out of his raincoat. "Not my choice. It's been crazy lately. Believe it or not, this rainstorm is a welcome relief. A good soaking like this might keep fires from starting and give us a few minutes of peace."

Angie took his coat and hung it on the coatrack. "Thank God it's not snow, or we'd be buried!"

Bliss came over to give Drake a kiss and noticed Angie had pulled on her own raincoat. "Are you going somewhere, Ange?"

"Oh, yeah. I have stuff to do, and then I think I'll go in to work early. You two will have the place to yourselves." She winked.

"Just don't tell anyone what we were discussing, okay? I don't want it to turn into a circus."

Angie pulled an invisible zipper across her lips, then mumbled as if she couldn't talk if she wanted to.

Bliss smiled, and even though she was grateful, she didn't want her roommate going out into a driving rainstorm just to give them privacy. "Do you really have 'stuff to do' or are you making yourself scarce and giving us the apartment?"

Angie grabbed her backpack and slung it over one shoulder. "I really have 'stuff,' so you can have the place to yourselves for the evening. I'll just toss my work clothes in my backpack so I won't even have to come back to change."

It took her about two seconds to run to her room and back, still stuffing her black pants and white blouse into the zippered compartment.

She waved. "Have fun."

"Thanks, Angie." Drake grinned. "Just knock loudly if you decide to come back."

Bliss slapped his arm. "Drake, she lives here. She doesn't have to knock."

Angie laughed. "Don't worry. I will."

~~~

The minute the door closed, Drake pulled Bliss into his arms and kissed her ravenously. When he finally let her lips leave his, he breathed heavily. "God, I missed you." He bent his head so his forehead rested against hers.

She smiled and looked up at him through her long, dark lashes. "I missed you too. All those fires… Does anyone know what's going on?"

He hesitated, not knowing what to tell her. *Should I share my suspicions or wait until there's more evidence?*

She stepped away. "You must be frozen. Come in and sit on the couch. I'll get you some coffee. Or do you prefer tea?"

"Whatever's easiest for you."

She smiled softly and left for the kitchen while he found a comfortable spot on the sofa. Maybe, depending on how the evening progressed, he'd know if he should talk about Zina or not. The last thing he wanted to do was spend one precious minute discussing that cow when he could and *should* be making love to this wonderful, patient woman.

"How have you been?" he called out toward the kitchen.

"Not bad. Keeping busy."

"How's the greeting card competition going?"

She rounded the corner. "Snarky, but that's a good thing."

"Had lots of inspiration lately?"

She chuckled. "I haven't started a new line of 'why haven't you called' cards, if that's what you mean, but I did think it might be a good idea."

He hung his head. "I'm sorry about that. Last night I was so tired I was asleep *before* my head hit the pillow."

The microwave dinged, interrupting their conversation, and Bliss returned to the kitchen.

Drake sighed. *I guess I'm getting instant coffee. It's probably all I deserve.*

When Bliss returned, she set two mugs of hot chocolate on the coffee table. Just picking up and holding the warm mug, then smelling the soothing aroma, relaxed him.

He took a sip. "Ah... this is good. You're the best, Bliss."

She shrugged. "I know."

He chuckled and leaned over, giving her another quick kiss.

"I need to ask you something," Bliss began.

"Ask away."

"Well, the TV host and producer are visiting a week from Tuesday. They'll bring a camera crew and will want to talk about how it's been for me... you know, working on my designs for the finale."

Drake leaned back and scrutinized her. "And you needed to ask me something?"

"Yeah. They like to meet the people who have been important to the finalist during their time at home."

Drake felt the tingles at the back of his neck. Did she want him involved in the interview? He'd like to be supportive, but would he be able to with everything else going on? Hopefully, by then, he'd have found and contained Zina, but what if she was still running him ragged? He wished he knew at what point Zina was in her fertility cycle. If she missed her window, maybe she'd forget about him and leave, but somehow he doubted that.

"Would you be willing to sign their release form and let them film you along with me and Angie?"

"I—I will if I can. My schedule isn't something I can count on right now. I've worked a heck of a lot of overtime, and they've needed me for every shift."

"I understand. I just thought it would be cool if they could meet the firefighter who saved my life and *tried* to save my computer with all my work on it."

Drake laughed. "You'll have quite a story to tell them, with or without me."

She smiled. "Oh, you can bet they'll eat it up. It's just the kind of harrowing experience that brings drama to the show."

They were just getting into the rhythm of an easy conversation when someone knocked. Bliss strode to the door. "Angie must have forgotten something."

Or changed her mind about drowning outside…

The open door revealed a young man, no more than sixteen or seventeen.

"Hello," he said formally with a slight bow. "My name is Adolf Balog, and I live upstairs."

"Oh, it's nice to meet you." Bliss held out her hand, but he ignored it.

"I'm here to talk to him." He indicated Drake with a quick uptick of his chin. "S'up?"

"Me? Why?" *And why is he acting like we're buddies? I've never seen this kid in my life.*

"I need to speak to you privately." He shot a glare in Bliss's direction.

Something about this kid didn't sit right, but Drake's impending doom alarm wasn't going off. His curiosity quickly outweighed any reservations he had, plus it seemed like a good idea to put some distance between this stranger and Bliss until he knew more about him.

"I'll be back in a minute, sweetheart." Drake gave her a peck on the cheek and stepped outside the apartment, closing the door behind him.

Facing the kid head-on, Drake asked, "What's this about?"

The kid extracted some kind of powder from his pocket and tossed it up in the air. It shimmered gold as it covered both of them, and the next thing Drake knew, he and the stranger were… somewhere else. Bright sunshine streamed through a glass dome, telling him that much.

A woman with long, white hair came forward. She wore a long white dress belted with vines. Something about her was familiar. Others in plain white robes that he didn't recognize were scattered in small groups but paid little attention to them.

The woman crossed her arms and said, "I'll take it from here, Balog Junior."

The kid bowed and retreated. Drake glanced behind him and noticed a bank of elevators toward which the young man strode. Apparently that was the way out. Good to know, if he needed to escape.

"What is this place?"

The woman tipped her chin and studied him. "You don't remember me, do you?"

Drake didn't remember precisely where he'd met her, and he *really* wanted an answer to *his* question first, but he seemed to be at a disadvantage. He'd have to wait for an explanation.

"Not really. Who are you, and how did I get here?"

"I'm Gaia. Mother Nature. Goddess and creator of lesser gods, goddesses, and other living things. How you got here isn't important. *Why* you're here is."

"All right." He mimicked her crossed arms, trying not to let her intimidate him. "Why am I here?"

"You're a dragon. And to answer your original question, you're still in Boston. This is where much of the Supernatural Council is based now."

"But it's a sunny day. I must have lost some time getting here, because when I left it was a rainy night in Boston."

"That was to keep the city from burning to the friggin' ground! You didn't lose any time. Unless you're a nonbeliever. You must *know* Mother Nature can create any kind of damn weather anywhere she pleases, right?"

"I—I guess so."

"So, because Boston is important to the Council, I like to keep the place in balance and harmony. You know, four seasons and all that shit. Rain and snow are necessary. That doesn't mean I like to live in them."

Drake couldn't help wondering if he had fallen asleep on Bliss's couch and was having some kind of freaky dream. What had he had for lunch? Oh, yeah. Tacos. *Maybe they were a little too spicy.*

"I can tell by your vacant look that you're not convinced."

"I didn't say that. I'm just… reserving judgment."

She jammed her hands on her hips and leaned toward him. "I'm not here to be judged. *You are.*"

"Me? What did I do?"

Her expression and posture relaxed. "Maybe nothing," she said in a calmer voice. "But you can't deny that fires have been plaguing Boston and that dragons have an affinity for fire."

Drake was shocked speechless by the implication for a moment. "You think *I'm* setting the fires?"

She began to pace with her hands clasped behind her back. "You have to admit, it's more than coincidental that your uncle was the one who set the Chicago fire. *That's* when I took your family's fire away. You probably explained it as evolution." She laughed.

"That was you?"

"Of course, but let's not get off track. I happen to know Boston was your uncle's next target, and he wasn't about to be stopped by his lack of dragon fire. He actually captured a young fire mage to do the job for him."

He knew his uncle had been involved in some dirty dealings, but Drake had helped his detective friend Nick put the guy away, and then his uncle had a heart attack in prison. Drake didn't even attend his funeral. So why would this... goddess blame him?

She stopped pacing and tapped her lower lip as if reasoning something out. "Now, what could I take away to make sure he didn't succeed?"

He didn't answer right away.

"I won't wait for your poor little pea brain to figure it out. I'll tell you. I took away your family's immortality."

"Is that why my mother died after only a minor accident?"

"Yup. It turns out your family isn't bulletproof anymore."

"Are you saying I'm no longer *fireproof* either? I could burn up and die in any fire I try to put out?"

She shrugged one shoulder. "Dragon clans are connected, so what I'm saying is, be careful if you want to survive."

Holy shit. That explains how my family had lasted for hundreds of years but suddenly small things like heart attacks and accidents managed to kill them off. Prior to that, Drake's great-grandfather had been beheaded... and now the guy who did it was being called a saint, just because he knew how to kill an immortal.

"I see the wheels spinning in that head of yours. So, if you have anything to tell me, I suggest you do it now. I want to know who's responsible for setting my city on fire, damn it!"

Drake's knees quivered and felt weak. "Y—yes. I may have some information. May I sit down, please?"

She smiled smugly. "At last. A bit of respect." She pointed to a spot on the floor between them where a small bistro table with two chairs suddenly appeared.

Chapter 10

DRAKE TRIED TO HOLD HER STEELY GAZE AND FIGHT off the urge to hyperventilate. It wasn't every day a guy was dragged off to the Supernatural Council, accused of crimes he didn't commit, and then told he's suddenly mortal!

"First off, did you know I'm a firefighter?"

"I haven't really been paying attention to you... *until now.*"

He heard the veiled threat loud and clear. It was time to clear up some of these misunderstandings. "Goddess, I've dedicated my life to fighting fires. I've witnessed the destructive power dragons possess, and it hasn't filled me with a sense of superiority or imperviousness. If anything, it's given me a sense of responsibility. I've never used my fire for anything but light and heat in the safety of a rocky cave."

She leaned back in her chair and folded her arms. "Say I believe you... What's going on out there?" She pointed a long, tapered finger at the bottom of the glass dome.

"A female dragon is visiting Boston. I think she's from the islands."

Mother Nature's eyes narrowed. "Which islands? I made over a million of them."

"I don't know, specifically. Somewhere in the Caribbean. She has an accent... maybe Jamaican. Her hair is..."

Gaia held up one hand. "Don't tell me… black with a white streak in her widow's peak?"

"Yeah, how did you know?"

Mother Nature turned her face away and muttered, "Shit." She rose and began to pace again.

Drake wasn't sure he wanted to know, but he had to ask. "What? Who is she?"

Gaia sighed deeply. "The clan is small. That's the good news. Only one female and her brother are left."

"And the bad news is?"

"They're extremely dangerous."

She stared at Drake, sizing him up, as if she was deciding whether or not she could trust him. "Look, I'm not proud of this, but when I created dragons I didn't foresee the problems they would cause if they came up with their own agendas. I had a completely different purpose for them."

"Really? What's our purpose?"

"You mean, what *was* your purpose… It was a long time ago, long before humans invented the airplane."

He raised his eyebrows. "So we were supposed to be the first Cessnas?"

"Right. I tried flying horses, but they died out too easily. I thought I'd make a tougher animal that lived in caves. When I saw them shivering with cold I felt for them, so I gave them a way to light a fire for warmth— with their breath, so naturally they had to be fireproof. And then, because I'd gone to so much trouble, I made them almost impossible to kill. Boy, was that a mistake. Suddenly, they felt all powerful and thought nothing of swooping down and burning up some of my favorite creations. Forests. Villages. Innocent people."

"So, what did you do?"

"I marked the whole race for extinction. Your parents hid you well in Canada, or you wouldn't be here like the rest of the Eurotrash I took out. But you seem like a good guy." She rose and paced as she finished her story.

"Before I could wipe out the dragons of Central America, one momma dragon saw what was going on and sought out a voodoo priestess. She managed to put a spell on those kids to protect them, even from *me*."

Mother Nature let out a long sigh. "Because they grew up with no parental guidance, they're… well, I hate to label anyone, but does the word *sociopath* mean anything to you?"

"Uh, kind of. I'm not a shrink, but I could look it up and learn about it if you think it might help."

"Nothing will help, but you might as well know what you're up against."

Drake's dragon warning tingles vibrated wildly.

"Here's what I want you to do," Mother Nature said. "I want you to trick her into coming to me."

"Huh? How?"

"That's your problem."

"Look, with all due respect, I want nothing to do with her. She already attacked me, and now that I know I'm not immortal and she is… Besides, I don't even know where you're located and how to get back here."

Mother Nature threw her hands in the air. "Must I do everything?"

One of the robed gentlemen strolled over to them. He was not a handsome man. Some might even call him ugly. His face was wrought with deep lines. His eyes were too small and his nose was too large. "Gaia, may I be of service?"

She closed her eyes and mumbled something that sounded like "brownnoser," then turned to the god with a bright smile. "Thank you, Hephaestus. Actually, your help would be very much appreciated."

Drake's eyes widened. "Hephaestus? Greek god of fire?"

The gentleman straightened and puffed out his chest. "That's me. You may have heard my Roman name as well. Vulcan. You may call me either."

"Which do you prefer?" Drake asked.

"Actually, I like Vulcan. It reminds me of my workshop in my Italian volcano." His smile faded. "Although on earth these days, people seem to think I was named after a race on a TV show."

"Oh, that would be *Star Trek*," Drake said. "Great show."

"That's little comfort."

Mother Nature snickered. "Well, it looks like you two are hitting it off, so I'll let you get on with your business."

"Wait," Drake said. "My girlfriend."

Mother Nature frowned. "Sounds like a complication. I hate complications." She let out a defeatist sigh. "What about her?"

"I was just visiting her. I was only there a few minutes before that Adolf kid practically kidnapped me and dragged me here."

"Is she human?"

"Yes." *And in some ways, you remind me of her*.

Gaia's eyes widened. "She didn't see you disappear, did she?"

"No. We were out in the hall. I closed the door, but right before I did, I told Bliss I'd be right back."

Mother Nature laughed. "Yeah… never say that." Then she pointed straight at his chest. "And never—I mean *never* reveal your knowledge of this Council. As far as you're concerned from this moment forward, we don't exist. Got it?"

Drake glanced around. "Did somebody say something?"

Gaia patted him on the head. "Good boy."

Bliss paced across the living room, wondering what the heck was taking so long. "We finally get some time together, and some kid comes and takes him out in the hall," she muttered. *Well, too bad. I'm not going to stand for it.*

Prepared to do battle, Bliss marched over to the door and threw it open. *Odd. There's no one here.*

She heard a cough coming from the bottom of the stairs. Thinking Drake might have been beaten again, she hurried down the steps. At the landing where the stairs took a right turn, she stopped. It was Angie. She was sitting on the bottom step, reading a book.

Bliss rested a hand on her hip. "Is this the 'stuff' you had to do?"

Angie startled, then swiveled so she could look at her roommate. "Oh, I didn't see you there. I was engrossed in this book."

Bliss noted Angie's dry hair and coat. "Have you been there the whole time?"

Angie gave her a sheepish grin. "Kind of."

"What do you mean, 'kind of'?"

"Well, I was gonna go out and do some errands, but I decided to wait and see if the rain let up."

"Then you must have seen Drake leave. Did he say where he was going?"

"Drake? I thought he was upstairs with you."

"No. The kid who lives upstairs asked to see him privately, and I thought he just stepped into the hall. He said he'd be right back, but it's been about an hour."

"Adolf? Maybe they went upstairs to the Balogs' apartment. I can get engrossed in a book, but I'd have noticed if a couple of guys stepped over me to go outside."

"Yeah, that must be it."

Angie had been giving them their privacy, and Bliss just fell in love with her roommate a little bit.

Hmmm… to intrude or not to intrude? "So, do you know the people upstairs?"

"Not very well. They keep to themselves, and that's fine by me. They're kind of creepy."

"Creepy, huh? Now my curiosity is piqued. Want to go upstairs with me?"

Angie's jaw dropped. "You're going up to the Balogs' apartment?"

"Why not? I haven't met the creep I can't outrun."

Angie giggled. It may have been a nervous giggle, but a moment later she jumped up. "I'm in."

The girls tromped upstairs. Bliss heard music on the other side of the door. It sounded like an acoustic guitar and a violin harmonizing, and the melody had a Gipsy Kings quality.

When Bliss knocked, the music stopped. She and Angie waited for quite a while before she knocked again. Even after the second knock, no one came to the door.

That's weird. She frowned and knocked a third time. "Hellooo," she called out. "It's Bliss Russo, from downstairs." They waited. Still nothing.

She and Angie stared at each other. At last, Angie shrugged. "I guess no one's going to answer the door." She headed back down the stairs.

"That's kind of rude, isn't it?" Bliss whispered.

"I guess so, but it doesn't surprise me. They've always kept to themselves."

"Isn't that what the neighbors of serial killers always say?" Bliss felt a shiver pass through her.

Drake and Vulcan shared one of the small tables in the bar. Robin dropped off their beers and, without a word, proceeded on to Sadie, who had one finger raised. Even Drake knew what she wanted. *Another White Russian, please.*

He tried to focus his attention on Vulcan, even though getting back to Bliss occupied the back of his mind like a constant itch.

"Why Boston?" Drake asked.

Vulcan cocked his head. "What do you mean?"

"Why is the Supernatural Council located in Boston? I thought you guys hung out on Mount Olympus."

"Oh, we do… sometimes. But Mother Nature likes it here."

"Why? We have hot, humid summers and cold, snowy winters, rainy springs and well, I guess there's nothing wrong with fall."

Vulcan smiled. "Ah, yes. Autumn in New England is perfection, but remember who you're talking about.

Mother Nature likes to view her handiwork and the seasons are all here."

"But why Boston? Why not some mountaintop?"

"Boston is a modern city with an old soul. That's what attracts paranormals to it, and wherever they are, we need to be."

"I see. I moved here hoping to find others like myself. I had heard the city was highly populated with paranormal beings. Although I never found another dragon until Zina, and she came a long way, if I'm not mistaken."

"Yes. How did she find you, anyway?"

"The Internet. I posted a personals ad on a dating website. I worded it so no one but a dragon would answer."

"Really? What did it say?"

"I said I wanted a woman so hot she could breathe fire. Most women have such low self-esteem that a guy with high expectations like that would scare them off. Oh, and I said I was a fireproof five, so anyone on the fence wouldn't want to bother."

Vulcan laughed but sobered quickly. "Obviously Zina doesn't have a self-esteem problem. She was treated like a princess all of her life—because she is a princess. We need a plan. Obviously this dragon won't come willingly."

Drake scratched his head. "Assuming I'm able to trick Zina into going to the Council, how will I know where to take her? I still don't know where the Council is."

"That's where I come in. I'm afraid you can't get there without a member of GAIA."

"GAIA?"

"Yes, that's what Mother Nature named the Council. Gods and Immortals Association. She said she liked the 'ring' of it. We all know she just wanted to name it after herself." He rolled his eyes.

Drake suppressed a smile. "Okay. So, where will I find you when I need you?"

"Don't worry. I'll find you."

Drake still didn't see how this could possibly work. "How will you know when I'm ready?"

"Hmmm... good question. I don't think you'd appreciate my spying on you constantly."

"You got that right."

"Let's come up with a code word or phrase. Something you could yell, and when I hear that above the constant drone of earthbound creatures, I'll come right away."

"You can do that?"

Vulcan smirked. "I'm not a god for nuthin'."

"Okay. Let me think of a code. How about, 'Ow, ow, she's killing me'?"

Vulcan raised his eyebrows. "Let's hope it doesn't come to that. I was thinking more along the lines of, 'What a beautiful day!' Something like that."

A couple at the next table, still soaked from the rain, shot twin glares in their direction.

Drake lowered his voice. "Yeah, right. And what if Mother Nature makes it rain or snow that day?"

"Fine. Think about it while I finish these fine hops."

"I've got it. I'll yell, 'Taxi!' She'll think I'm calling a cab to take us wherever the hell I told her I'd take her."

Vulcan smiled. "I'll recognize your voice and I will be your taxi. You're quite clever, Drake Cameron."

"Gee, thanks. *Now* can I get back to my girlfriend?"

"Aren't you going to finish your drink?"

"No, getting back to Bliss is more important to me right now. She's not the most patient woman who ever lived."

"As you wish. I know something about impatient women."

"I'll bet you do." Drake rose and pulled out his wallet. As he left the money to cover the tab and tip, he thought again about how Bliss and Mother Nature seemed to share certain personality traits. Maybe all women did. Maybe Gaia liked creating more than names in her honor.

The intercom buzzed and Bliss, now in sweatpants and her comfy oversized T-shirt, padded over to it. She pressed the "talk" button and asked, "Who the hell is it, and what do you want in the middle of the friggin' night?"

When she pressed the "listen" button, Drake's voice answered.

"Bliss, honey, I—"

"Save it." She pushed the button to unlock the outside door and waited to hear his footfalls on the stairs.

Before he knocked, she threw open the door and crossed her arms. Trying to look frowny, she wasn't quite ready to welcome him back. She knew she would eventually, but for now she wanted to pout.

"Where were you? Angie said you never passed her on the stairs, and she was sitting there the whole time. After about an hour, we went up to the Balogs' apartment because we thought you might have been abducted by the creepy neighbors."

"Uh—what did they say?"

"Nothing. They didn't answer the door." She thought she noticed a flash of relief before his expression returned to one of concern.

"May I come in? I promise I'll make it up to you?"

Damn it. He probably means with sex, and I've been horny all night. She decided it was time to forgive him and probably jump his bones.

She stepped away from the door, allowing him entrance. As soon as he'd crossed the threshold, she locked the door behind him and launched herself into his arms for a desperate hug.

"You had me worried sick."

He caressed her back and murmured more apologies. Eventually she leaned away to look at his face, and he ran the backs of his fingers over her cheek.

"I'm afraid I can't tell you what was happening... not right now, anyway. I will when I can." He gently held her chin between his thumb and forefinger. "Soon."

Bliss narrowed her eyes. Maybe if she squinted he wouldn't look so mouthwateringly gorgeous. *No such luck.*

He leaned in for a tender kiss. She met his lips, tentatively, but the inevitable magnetic pull demanded that she open to him and caress his tongue with hers. She was heating up fast. *Damn, he gets me hotter than any guy I've ever known.*

The next thing she knew, he had scooped her up and was carrying her to the bedroom. They fell onto the bed together. He whispered the sweetest words in her ear as he pushed up her T-shirt and found her bare breasts.

Bliss arched into his hand and moaned with the

gratifying sensations his touch provided. "This is what I've wanted since the first time I kissed you outside my burning building," she murmured. She pulled his shirt up, freeing the hem from his belted waist.

He paused just long enough to pull his shirt over his head and toss it on the floor. Bliss followed suit, losing her T-shirt. He bent down to suckle her breasts while, at the same time, pulling the drawstring on her sweatpants. She raised her bottom, allowing him to work her pants down her legs until they were bunched at her ankles.

Her free hand moved up his side over his bare, heated skin. He shivered as she trailed her fingers down his ribs, continuing toward her goal—the large bulge he was thrusting against her thigh. When she gripped what she could through his pants, he lifted his head and groaned.

As he unbuckled his belt, he said, "Finally, after all the daydreaming, you're right here in my arms."

She sighed. "You daydreamed about me, too?"

"Every waking hour. The real woman is so much better. Hot, wicked, and sexy."

Say something not stupid, Bliss. But she couldn't think of a thing. Her mind was turning to mush and all she could do was feel. *Ah, hell... thinking is overrated.*

She grasped his zipper and heard the quick rasp as she yanked it down. She plunged her hand under the waistband of his underwear and tried to envelop his girth. He was too thick for her to close her fingers.

When he opened his eyes, they held a golden glow. She had seen that before, but was now the time to mention it? Hey, when had she ever held anything back? "Your eyes—"

Suddenly he flipped her onto her stomach. Then next

thing she knew, her sweatpants were torn off and his pants soon followed them onto the floor. He lay on top of her and whispered, "Do you mind doing it this way again?"

She almost laughed. "Mind? Please do. Or should I say, 'Do me, please'?"

"Relax," he whispered in her ear. "Let me give you a massage first."

"A massage? You mean, on my back?"

"I said I'd make it up to you."

"Wow." *How many horny guys stop to give a girl a massage?* "And after that?"

He chuckled. "Then I'll lift you up and massage your front."

"In that case… yes, please."

Drake applied just the right pressure as he massaged her tense muscles all the way down her back on either side of her spine. Bliss turned her head to the side and relaxed in the warmth of his take-charge hands and fingers. When he reached the bottom of her spine, he kept going.

"Ah… that feels fantastic, even if you're using it as an excuse to manhandle my butt."

"It's a big muscle. The gluteus maximus."

"Hey, it's not *that* big."

He bent over and whispered in her ear. "Relax. It's perfect." Then he gave her right butt cheek a little smack and returned to working his way up from base to shoulders.

Despite the tiny sting, Bliss could have melted into the mattress.

After the thorough massage, good to his word, he lifted her onto her hands and knees and positioned himself behind her. He dipped his fingers into her core to test her wetness, but she could have told him she was plenty ready.

Without a word, he thrust into her and she welcomed him by pushing back and meeting him halfway. Being filled with him felt so good. So right.

He began his rhythm and added the promised massage to her clit. Pleasure spiked through her like an electric current.

"Ohhh." She couldn't think of anything else to say, but talking didn't seem necessary at this point anyway. Instead, she rocked a little harder against him.

He leaned down and placed little kisses all over her shoulder. "You have the right name. You're absolute Bliss."

It seemed as if all she could do was drown in the sensations and moan her appreciation. A spiral of delicious pleasure was building within her. "I'm close."

"So am I."

They tumbled over the edge together. She screamed as she climaxed, and the orgasm lasted longer than usual.

"Oh, God," she said when they collapsed. "Oh, God; oh God; oh God."

"Yeah," he agreed breathlessly.

Drake withdrew and turned her over. He gathered her into his arms and held her close while their panting breaths returned to normal.

She couldn't have been more relaxed if she'd had a Valium. As Bliss was about to drop off to sleep, Drake said, "Bliss, honey. There's something I need to tell you."

"Now?"

"Yes. Before I lose my nerve."

Chapter 11

BLISS ROLLED UP ONTO HER ELBOW AND RESTED HER cheek in her palm. "You have to go back to work tonight, don't you?"

"No. I've worked all the overtime I'm allowed to for a while."

Facing him and frowning as if waiting for a firing squad to be called in, she said, "Okay. Tell me."

Drake propped himself up against the pillow so their eyes were even. "Actually, there's quite a lot I have to confess to you, but if at any point it becomes too much, tell me to stop."

"Confessions?" She flopped back onto her pillow. "Uh-oh. This doesn't sound good at all."

"There's both good and bad."

"Give me the good stuff first."

He sighed. There wasn't really anything good that didn't start with something bad... oh, except possibly one thing.

He stroked her cheek. "I love you."

The wrinkle in her forehead disappeared and her lips twitched into a smile. "I think I love you too—but I reserve the right to take it back, depending on what else you have to say."

Oh, great. Someone who admits to conditional love.

He inhaled a deep breath. "Okay. Here it is... I told you before that I was a dragon. You laughed it off because, as far as you know, nothing like that exists, right?"

She smirked. "Well, of course dragons don't exist. Oh, wait. Maybe they do. Let me go ask my unicorn."

Drake rolled his eyes. "Okay, not unicorns. We know they died out when Noah couldn't get them to come onto the ark, but why not dragons? Don't you think they could exist?"

She stared at him for a few moments. "Are you saying *you* believe they do?" She reached out and felt his forehead. "You don't seem to have a fever."

He smiled. "I'm fine, honey. There are all manner of beings that have been talked about in legends, but how do you think those legends got started?"

"Um… in the old days people had big imaginations to answer their questions, instead of science."

"Believe me, people back then were no more imaginative than they are now. And as for science, a lot of folks think that if they haven't seen something with their own eyes, it doesn't exist, but science has proven the existence of all kinds of things you can't see. Tiny molecules, germs, plus planets so far away you'd never be able to see them with the naked eye."

"Yeah, but… dragons? They'd be kind of hard to miss."

"Not if they don't want to be seen. And after all the talk of St. George destroying the last dragon, why would any unknown survivors come forward? Are they going to say, 'Oh, hey, Georgie… Look, you missed one!'"

Drake thought about how his mother had kept him hidden for years, because they were safer with humans believing the extinction rumor. His great-grandfather *had been* that "last" dragon—or so the humans of the time thought. Most of his other relatives had been slaughtered long before that. Knights just loved to sneak up on and kill dragons. Then they'd brag about it upon their return to their respective castles.

Bliss faced away from him, as if talking to her furniture. "Damn. And he seemed so normal... even smart."

He laid his hand over hers. "I can prove it."

"You can prove dragons exist?" She chuckled. "How?"

"I can show you my alternate form."

She began to pull her hand away, but he grasped it tighter. "Do you remember seeing my eyes shimmer?"

That stopped her momentarily. "Uh... yeah. I wondered about that. They're green most of the time, like now, but I thought I saw them turn gold a couple times."

"It's what happens when I begin to shift."

"Shift?" She shook her head slowly. "What are you saying?"

"I'm saying I can change my form. Several centuries ago, as a way to survive, some dragons found a wizard and convinced him to use his magic to help them blend in. I'm descended from those dragons. I understand the Asian dragons found a way to do the same thing, but I'm not sure how. We look human most of the time, but if necessary, we can return to dragon form."

"Any time now, you can give up and tell me you're joking. I won't hold it against you if you admit it—soon."

Damn, she still doesn't believe me. But at least she didn't appear ready to run off, so he blundered on.

"I have a few advantages in my alternate form. As a dragon, I'm fireproof. It comes in handy when fighting fires—I just wish I could let my chief in on that little fact. And my vision improves tremendously. Think about the first time you saw my eyes glow gold."

"It was during the fire. I couldn't see you well under

all the protective equipment you were wearing, but I did notice your eyes."

"I had to shift when I was inside the building. The fire was so hot, and flames were everywhere. If I hadn't taken on my alternate form, I might not have survived, and I certainly couldn't have seen through the flames and smoke to find my way out."

She reached out and touched his cheek. Her expression was deadly serious. Maybe he was reaching her, at last.

"You don't have to go through this alone, Drake. We'll find you a good doctor. I've heard with medication they can treat all kinds of delusions."

Oh, crap. We're back to square one.

"Bliss, honey. I'm not delusional. I can show you my dragon transformation, but I don't want to scare you. If you see me as a dragon you might be afraid, but I can assure you, I'd never hurt you."

"I believe that. If you didn't hit back when that awful biker chick was kicking you in the ribs, I don't think you'll hurt me for giving you a little ribbing. Although, you might rib me back. I'm pretty sure that's what you're doing now."

He dropped his head and let out a deep breath in a whoosh. *I'm still not getting through.*

After a long silence, she lifted her chin. "Okay. Prove it."

"Really? You'll let me show you my transformation?"

"Sure, why not?"

"Think about it. If you see something you really don't believe in, it'll change your perspective forever."

Bliss flopped onto her back and threw her hands in the air. "Do you want to show me or don't you?"

"You won't be scared?"

She rolled back onto her elbow, propped herself up, and looked him right in the eye. "I won't be scared."

"Promise? Because it would be perfectly normal to be a little bit nervous."

"I'm not perfect, nor am I normal."

"You're joking again."

"That's how I cope." After a long pause, she worried her lip. "Okay. I guess I'm a little afraid *for* you, but I'm not afraid *of* you."

That was good enough. *This is it. Now or never.*

Drake got up off the bed and backed away a few feet. He closed his eyes and concentrated on his dragon form. His back vibrated, letting him know his wings and tail were ready to emerge. When he opened his eyes, he saw Bliss still on the bed and not running for the hills. The shimmer he knew could be seen in his eyes colored his vision for a matter of seconds. He transformed briefly but didn't flap his wings or tail. He truly didn't want to scare her.

Her eyes had rounded and grown huge throughout the process. Perhaps she wasn't moving because she was frozen in fear. He'd made his point and didn't need or want to impress her. All he wanted was her trust—and for her not to doubt him anymore. He quickly closed his eyes and concentrated on his human form. The tingling stopped and the glow faded.

As soon as he could speak with his human mouth he asked, "Are you okay?"

As if she couldn't quite make words come out, her mouth moved a little before she said, "I… I guess." She shrugged a shoulder, but he thought he saw it tremble.

He wanted to gather her close and hold her, but he didn't know if she'd welcome him. He had never let a human see his transition before. Hell, he wasn't supposed to let anyone see it now.

Maybe if I just tell her that... "I've never shown this side of me to anyone else."

"G—good. I imagine it would scare the pants off most people." She backed away for the first time since they'd begun talking.

"Are you *sure* you're all right?"

"Oh, yeah. I'm good." She grabbed her clothes with shaking fingers.

"Bliss, there's more I have to tell you."

She groaned but didn't stop pulling up her sweatpants or fastening the drawstring. "Uh—can we do it later?"

"Not really. The whole reason I had to tell you about dragons was to warn you."

"Warn me?" She finished tying her drawstring, then dragged her T-shirt over her head. "I thought you said you'd never hurt me."

"I won't. *I promise* you have nothing to fear from me."

"Then why do you have to warn me?"

"Because I'm not the dragon who means you harm."

She froze. "Are you saying there are more who do?"

"Just one. Possibly."

She jammed her hands on her hips. "How possible is this possibility?"

"It's a pretty good possibility. Remember the biker chick who kicked my ass?"

"Fuckin' A!"

"I know..." He started to stroll toward her until she held up one palm to stop him.

"I need a minute, Drake. Maybe a whole lot of minutes. This is a crazy amount of information to process."

"I understand. Please don't be afraid. Let me help."

"Help? What can you do to help? If you're fireproof, I expect she is too. And you can't possibly stand guard over me day and night."

"I know. That's why I need to come up with another way to protect you."

"Can you… you know, breathe fire like in the legends?"

"No. My family lost that ability centuries ago, but I don't know about other clans."

"There are clans? Is that because you're Scottish, or… Oh, fuck it. I don't even know what questions to ask."

"I'll answer any questions you have, later. Right now it's important to come up with a plan to keep you safe. I *can't* lose you, Bliss."

"Especially not to someone like her. I imagine that's why she wants to get rid of me—so she can drag you off to Hanalei or wherever it is that dragons live happily ever after."

"I can't lose you to *anyone*, Bliss. Not for any reason. I wouldn't have told you any of this—and you can't imagine how many rules I've broken—but it was important that you truly understand the danger. I'd never forgive myself if I could have warned you but didn't because of my own cowardice."

She stroked his cheek. "A coward is one thing you're *not*, Drake Cameron."

It had taken Drake another hour to calm Bliss down to the point where she could sleep. The one thing he

wanted most was for her to be safe. When he suggested
she move back with her parents, even temporarily, she
about lost her mind.

He couldn't tell her what to do. He could only make
suggestions and hope she'd see the wisdom in listening
to him.

She moved in his arms and mumbled something un-
intelligible, as if having a restless dream. Drake stroked
her hair until she calmed down and her breathing returned to the long, slow breaths of deep sleep.

He couldn't tell her that he was under orders from
the Supernatural Council. They had expressly forbidden him from sharing any knowledge of their existence.
He had also been told not to reveal his own paranormal
identity, but he had promised Bliss he'd be honest with
her, need-to-know basis or not. And yes... she needed
to know.

However, one promise kept and one broken with each
competing part of his life had seemed half as bad before.
Now he wasn't sure he hadn't blown it with both.

Warning Bliss had been the right thing to do. How
could he have explained the danger to her without re-
vealing the existence of dragons? She had to know that
Zina could probably breathe fire from twenty feet away.
His family lost their fire-breathing abilities when his
uncle tried to burn down the City of Chicago. But he
didn't know if Zina's clan was affected too. He didn't
get the impression that Mother Nature punished all
dragons equally.

Bliss also had to know that dragons could fly and that
Zina could spot her from the air.

Drake would never forgive himself if anything

happened to the woman he loved... especially if he hadn't told her what she was up against. Knowing Bliss, if Zina confronted her again, Bliss might say something she'd regret. If Zina let her live long enough to regret it.

Just because he hadn't seen Zina didn't mean she hadn't seen him. His skin had tingled several times when he was out on a job, battling blazes large and small. The sensation could have been a reminder that he was mortal now, but it seemed like more than that. Why hadn't his warning sense kicked in when he was rescuing Bliss's computer?

Maybe he was still fireproof but could be killed in other ways. Maybe Gaia was lying to him... but why? His uncle and mother had died within weeks of each other. It had made no sense at the time, but now it did. His mother had done nothing wrong, but the link between clans would explain why she became mortal as soon as her brother did. He died of a heart attack, and she had been in a car accident.

Just in case, he'd have to remember to listen to his chief from now on. The other guys relied on the chief to keep them safe, and now he should too. The last thing anyone needed was a firefighter's funeral to attend. He had to find Zina and stop her. With Vulcan's help, he might be able to pull it off.

Drake needed to get some sleep, but he couldn't stop imagining all the possible scenarios. Unfortunately, he couldn't come up with any in which Bliss would be safe and that the Council would approve. Her survival was completely up to him... and her.

He had to get her to understand. Perhaps in the morning she'd be thinking more clearly and would agree to go somewhere safe. But where? She'd refused to move back in with her parents and nixed the idea of living with one of her brothers' families—and Claudia wasn't open to guests. That left his place. But he'd had tingles when he returned to his studio apartment to change his clothes and pick up a fresh uniform, so he had to assume Zina knew where he lived. She had probably been watching him, so his place was out too.

There had to be someone. A maiden aunt who'd enjoy the company, perhaps? He'd explore that idea and others in the morning. If he could make her concentrate on her real business and forget about working at the bar, that might help. She had completed her designs and placed them in a safe-deposit box, hadn't she?

Wait a minute…

What if he could get her to stay with Sadie? The woman was a psychic. She might be able to warn Bliss ahead of time if someone was coming after her.

Drake felt better. Just having an idea that *might* work helped.

He curled his arms around Bliss until she was snug, being careful not to wake her. She cuddled into him and sighed. At last his eyelids became heavy and his mind, well, lighter than it had been.

———

Drake sat across from Sadie, hoping the psychic would hear him out. He had ordered a White Russian and set the one-drink minimum on the table in front of her. If all else failed, he could simply ask her for a reading. Maybe the cards would provide some insight.

"I'm hoping you can do me a favor, Sadie."

"You came bearing gifts, so I'll see what I can do." She lifted the White Russian in a mock toast and took a sip.

"Bliss is in danger."

"I know."

Wow. Either she really is psychic or Bliss had said something to her. He was fairly sure Bliss wouldn't talk about dragons and such—especially when she had sworn not to. However, she still claimed to be questioning her own sanity.

"How much do you know?"

Sadie set down her drink and began shuffling her tarot cards. "I knew getting mixed up with you was going to bring her stress. I told her as much, but her heart chose you anyway."

"Her heart?"

"Of course. Don't tell me you think she'd go through all this for just anyone—or simply to be nice."

He smiled. No. Bliss wouldn't put up with anyone's crap "just to be nice." She would, on the other hand, tell another guy who'd put her through this to open his Hall-Snark card.

"I appreciate knowing that, but now I need to know how to keep her safe. I was thinking that maybe she could stay with you for a while. Perhaps you could use your psychic ability to give her a heads-up and keep her out of harm's way."

Sadie puffed out a breath.

"What's wrong?" Drake asked.

"I live in a room the size of a closet."

"Oh." *Damn it. On to plan B*. "Maybe the tarot cards can give us another idea."

She nodded. "I'm glad I don't have to convince you of their value… or my abilities. That much is refreshing."

"I've heard your accuracy is pretty amazing."

She squared up the cards and laid the deck in front of him. "Cut it."

He picked up about half the pile and set it to the side, then piled the other half on top. The whole time he was thinking of Bliss, so he figured he must be imparting some kind of positive energy into the cards.

Sadie shuffled them again and then fanned the cards out in front of him. "Pick three, but don't turn them over."

He did as he was asked, taking cards from different areas.

Sadie flipped them over and muttered something under her breath.

"What?" He didn't tingle, but he could tell from her expression there was some kind of bad news in the cards.

"They're all reversed."

Glancing at the cards, he saw every one of the pictures had landed upside down. "I guess that's bad?"

"Not always." She gathered up the remainder of the cards and shuffled the deck again. Sadie set the pile in front of him and he cut it again.

She shuffled and fanned out the rest of the cards. "Pick three more."

He did the same thing as before. Sadie flipped them over and sighed.

"What? Is someone going to die or something?"

"Not that I see here, but there are a lot of sinister events revolving around you. Bliss is better off where she is."

"You're not just saying that because she serves you drinks, are you?"

Sadie reared back, her eyes wide. "How could you even think that?"

"I'm sorry." He raked his fingers through his hair. "I didn't mean to offend you. I've had very little sleep and I'm not myself."

She relaxed, but the frown remained.

"Can you tell me what the cards indicated? What made you think she was safer here?"

She lowered her voice. "I know more about the paranormal than you might think."

She knows? "I see. But I don't understand what that has to do with Bliss."

"Don't you realize how much protection she has here that she wouldn't have anywhere else?"

Drake glanced over at the bar. Two shapeshifters and a wizard were chatting casually while keeping up with a basketball game on the overhead TV.

"Shit. You're right."

"Of course I'm right. What better protection could she have from a misguided paranormal being? Here she's surrounded by a number of super-strong, super-protective supernatural friends. Each one of them believes in the value of their shared safe place. That means no one messes with their status quo."

Drake felt like an idiot. Why hadn't he thought of that before?

"You're too close," she said, as if she'd heard his internal question. "You feel like *you* need to be the one to protect her. The thing is, every one of them would be happy to help. All you need to do is ask. Let the others know the scope of the problem, and they'll give you all the support you need."

"Is that it? Is that all the cards can tell me?"

"What else do you want to know?"

"Are you telling me to avoid her for her own good?"

"No. Not at all. Just don't spirit her away from the safest building in the city."

"But what about at night? I can't always sleep here."

Sadie lowered her eyes and smiled, as if she were in on some kind of secret. "Even at night there are protectors here."

"What kind of protectors? You can't be talking about the family from the third floor."

"No, not the Balogs. But there are… others."

"Others? What others? Does Anthony live in the building?" He had always wondered where the vampire owner lived, but he didn't think there was an apartment on the fourth floor. He'd only seen two buzzers. One for the second floor and one for the third.

"It isn't important that you know who they are. They don't want to be bothered, and if you go poking around, you might not like the consequences."

"Huh?"

"Leave it alone, Drake. You have enough to worry about." She began to gather up the cards but stopped when he laid his hand over hers.

"Wait. These sinister events… Is there more than just the increased number of fires? Are there others involved in setting those?"

Sadie replaced and leaned over the cards, studying them for a few moments. "I don't see a whole lot of different events, and all of them seem to be perpetrated by one individual." She pointed to the Knight of Swords. "One very dangerous, determined individual." She gathered up the cards, marking an unmistakable end to the discussion. "Watch your back, Drake."

He honestly didn't care about anything other than Bliss at the moment. As long as she was safe, he'd cope with whatever else happened. *If only she were a dragon too, I'd know that Bliss could defend herself.* Unfortunately, the odds of a mortal surviving a dragon attack were slim.

He suddenly thought about his mother. He was sure she'd had good intentions when she asked him to save their species, but even she wouldn't have wished Zina on him.

"Thank you, Sadie. You helped tremendously."

She nodded. "Thanks for the drink. Next time, buy one for yourself. You need it more than I do."

Bliss had never felt so isolated in her life. Drake had asked her not to leave the building until he was able to deal with Zina. That meant she had two options. Sit in her apartment and try to work on another card, or sit in the bar and socialize. She had tried watching TV, but there was nothing on she wanted to watch. Angie didn't have a way to record shows, and Bliss hadn't planned to live there long enough to care.

She didn't dare get hooked on a soap opera. Her schedule wouldn't allow for it, although she'd heard viewers could miss several episodes and still pick up where they'd left off. Sounded like some kind of ripple in the time-space continuum.

She really didn't feel like socializing. Something as bizarre as learning there were dragons in the world made

"Look at this adorable necklace I got at a flea market" seem inane. She didn't think she could concentrate on designing her cards, and there might not be any books that would hold her attention when her mind inevitably wandered to dragons... *Hey, wait. Maybe I can find an ebook on dragons!*

It was a long shot. She was fairly sure anything she read would be legend, but as Drake had said, "Legends come from somewhere." Maybe she could do some digging and find out more than what she knew now... which was next to nothing.

She grinned. *Wouldn't it blow Drake's mind if I could spout a few dragon facts he hadn't told me yet?*

But what if she blew her own mind? And how would she know fact from legend? She dropped down onto her bed. "Argh! All this stuff is mucking up my mind."

Damn it. I'm going to talk to the one person who has never deserted me. The smartest, most loyal friend I have... me.

She rifled through her purse and grabbed the little notebook she carried just in case ideas struck while she was on a subway or shopping or anywhere away from her computer. It came with a little pencil she liked because she could erase the stupid words and leave only the good ones when she eventually made it home.

She wrote, *Dear damn diary...*

"Heh-heh. Good start. Give yourself hell, Bliss. If anyone can take it, you can."

What was I thinking? Maybe my mother was right. "No, no. Scratch that."

She flipped the pencil over and scrubbed the ridiculous words off the paper.

A dragon? Seriously? A dragon. I think I've finally met a guy who might be worth a shot, and he turns out to be some kind of circus freak.

I'd never have believed him if I hadn't seen it with my own eyes. Transform? Yeah, right…Then he did it! Ack!

I keep waiting to wake up and find out this is just a crazy nightmare. Nope. I've pinched myself and then slapped myself for pinching myself. Still not popping out of any coma.

I've even wondered if I was drugged. Drake never slipped me any pills. He didn't even bring me a beer. Nope. Nothing went into my mouth except, well… him. Heh-heh.

Hey, I wonder if dragon penis can cause hallucinations? Naw. That doesn't make sense. Because if it does, that means he's a dragon and I didn't hallucinate anything but the truth.

"Oh my God." Bliss slapped the side of her head and stared at the words she had just written. She sighed and mumbled her own reassurance. "It's okay… no one is going to read this. Just go ahead and let out all the crazy."

And while we're at it, no wonder he said he can't get me pregnant. We're not even the same species! Oh, man. If we ever got married, my mother would be in seventh heaven until she learned that little fun fact. Then she'd descend to the seventh circle of hell and never be seen again.

Why do I care what my mother thinks? Haven't I always known she means well, but…

Yeah, there are no words following that "but." Never have been. Never will be. Some things are better left alone.

So, back to Drake. What am I supposed to do with this information? He seemed relieved after he told me, but now I'm the one who's all jiggy. I don't know how I'll feel next time I look at him... if there is a next time. Didn't he say that biker chick was probably setting the fires and he had to stop her?

I may not have known him long, but one thing I'm certain of—he won't hit a girl. I doubt he'd even fight back unless his life depended on it, and it well might. She must be some kind of psycho to beat him up and then set fires all over the place. All because he brought me flowers? I swear, if he lives through this, I'll ask him never to bring me flowers again.

Bliss set down the paper and pencil. She rose and paced as the gravity of the situation sank in. She'd always coped with unsavory situations using her signature flippancy and irreverence. She wasn't feeling very flippant at the moment.

Chapter 12

DRAKE HAD GREETED THE OTHER PARANORMALS AT THE bar and gathered them together in the back booth. Kurt, the wizard; Tory, the shapeshifting coyote; and Nick, the werewolf. As they were waiting for Anthony, the vampire bar owner, to join them, Drake asked, "So, are there others we should invite to this meeting?"

Kurt, Tory, and Nick all exchanged glances.

At last Nick said, "No, why? Have you heard about more?"

"Yeah. Sadie said something about the building being protected even after everyone leaves for the night."

Nick chuckled. "I guess she's talking about the house brownies. I don't know how much protection they'd provide. They're about a foot tall."

All three of the other men stared at Nick. "House brownies?" they repeated in unison.

"Yeah. They were the first paranormals Brandee had ever seen. I'm glad my wife was introduced to the supernatural world though them. They don't present much of a threat. They're only goal is to clean the bar, and they're happy to do so as long as there are plenty of peanuts and pretzels to eat. If someone insults them, they might play some kind of harmless prank but that's about it."

Drake's irritation rose. "Then why did Sadie think they'd provide plenty of protection for Bliss after dark?"

"Maybe because they're down here in the bar after hours and could signal an early warning," Nick said. "From what I understand, they eat a few snacks, then they clean the place until dawn as a thank-you."

"Actually…" a deep voice said.

Drake whipped around to see Anthony standing behind him.

"They're quite protective of the place. As long as they feel valued, they will continue to keep everything in perfect condition. I can't tell you how many times Ruxandra has had a fit and trashed the bar. The brownies always put it back together before morning."

Anthony dragged a chair over and sat at the end of the booth.

"Where is Ruxandra these days?" Tory asked.

Anthony chuckled. "She thinks she's punishing me by depriving me of her presence."

"Wow." Nick leaned back, looking impressed. "Well done. What did you do to make her think that? Did you say, 'I can't miss you if you won't go away?'"

The others laughed, but Anthony shook his head.

"No. She's vain enough to have come up with that all on her own. In fact, she's probably on another recruiting mission, finding just the right guy to make me jealous."

Tory grinned. "Hey, maybe she'll find someone she likes better and finally dump your ass."

"I'd never get that lucky." Anthony sighed. "I made her, so she'll always feel… obligated to me. Never mind her. What did you call us together for, Drake? I assume it's not to talk about my vampire ex-girlfriend."

"No. I want to talk about my very human, *very special* girlfriend. I need your help to make sure she's safe."

Nick immediately went into his private investigator mode. "Why? What's going on?"

"The female who kicked the crap out of me last week... she's a dragon and I think she's kind of like Anthony's Ruxandra. She's hard to get rid of and jealous of any woman she perceives as getting in her way."

All four guys groaned.

Drake continued while he had the floor. "She hasn't left the area. I think she's been setting all the fires, but I have no proof. No one can find any signs of arson, but that just makes it even more likely that it's her. Unlike myself, she can still breathe fire, so she could easily touch off a wooden building or a pile of brush and leave no evidence behind. Also, I think she's targeting me since most of the fires have been set all over my district. And she may be using her wings. That puts us all at risk for discovery."

"Wait," Anthony said. "You work in *this* district, don't you?"

"Yeah. So far she's stayed away from this particular street, but I have a terrible feeling she's saving it for last."

"Crap," Nick said. "Do you know where she's staying? Maybe we can set up a sting."

"No. I haven't seen her, but I'm sure she's around. I have this sixth sense that tingles whenever danger is near. It's been driving me crazy—especially when we're out on a job. If she's watching, she's very good at staying out of sight."

"So, how can we help Bliss?" Tory asked.

"Look, I know this is going to sound like I broke the most important paranormal rule of all, but I had to..."

The others waited for him to say whatever he had to

say. *Shit*. *I did break the most important paranormal law of all*.

Drake leaned in and lowered his voice as he confessed, "I told Bliss about dragons. I even had to show her my transformation before she'd believe me."

Kurt gasped. In a whisper he asked, "What made you do that?"

Nick held up one hand. "I understand. I had to do the same thing with Brandee. My brother had to tell his human wife, Roz. As long as you and she never tell anyone else, and I assume you swore her to secrecy, I think you'll be okay."

"I did. And she promised not to tell a soul. She knows no one would believe her anyway. Hell, she almost had *me* committed."

Nick cleared his throat. "It's a little early though, Drake. I thought I jumped the gun with my wife. But Brandee and I knew each other as friends for a long time before we ever dated. Are you sure you can trust Bliss?"

"She had to know about Zina. If something happened to Bliss because I kept her—well, blissfully ignorant, I'd never forgive myself. I got her to agree to stay out of sight. If the dragon bitch sees her as a threat to a relationship she wants to have with me…"

"Then she's toast… literally," Kurt said.

Tory scratched his head. "What makes you think Zina still wants you even after you rejected her?"

"Because I'm the only one left to breed with—other than her brother, that is, and I don't think she's desperate enough to consider that idea. Can you imagine inbred dragons?"

"God, no," Anthony said. He rubbed the stubble on

his chin and appeared thoughtful. "It looks like you're right. Bliss needs our constant protection. I'll escort her home and keep an eye on her until she's safely locked in. Someone else will have to escort her *to* work because of my daylight limitations."

"I'll be glad to do it," Nick said.

Anthony thanked him with a nod. "If this Zina is anything like Ruxandra, your girl will probably be in danger the minute she's alone."

Nick folded his arms. "Remember when Ruxandra tried to harpoon Brandee?"

Drake's jaw dropped. "She threw a harpoon at your wife?"

"Yeah. That was back when she thought there was something going on between her and Anthony."

"There wasn't," Anthony said with finality. "I never even smile at my staff, if I can help it. I know how jealous Ruxandra is."

Nick sighed. "We pretty much had to prove to her that Brandee was with me, not Anthony. Even after that, Anthony had to be careful not to even look at her. A human stands no chance against most paranormals. Add to that female jealousy…"

Drake groaned and dropped his head into his cupped hands. "But if Ruxandra comes back, Anthony won't be able to help."

Kurt, who was sitting next to him, patted his back. "Don't worry, buddy. We're all capable of protecting her and willing to step in. Anthony can handle Ruxandra if necessary."

"But won't that put your staff at risk?"

Anthony lifted his chin and frowned. "I'll have you

know I've always protected my staff. I don't care if they're being threatened by another vampire or an ordinary bully. I'd put my undead life on the line for any one of them, and Ruxandra can go to hell if she doesn't like it. I think she understands that now."

"Let's hope so," Nick said. "Because here she is."

As predicted, Ruxandra waltzed into the bar arm in arm with a handsome stranger.

Crap, Drake thought. *I don't think I can take much more drama.*

The next day as Bliss opened the office door to drop off her purse before work, she spotted Claudia bent over an open drawer. Unable to stifle an irresistible tease, she wolf-whistled.

Claudia snapped to attention and swiveled to see Bliss grinning at her.

"Oh, it's you. Thank goodness. I thought I was going to have to kick one of the customers out of the inner sanctum."

"Nope. It's just little ol' me." She hung her purse on a hook in the closet provided for the employees.

"Didn't you wear a coat? It's still raining, isn't it?"

"No, sweetie. It's just a light mist and it takes two seconds to walk from my home to work. Gotta love the commute." She didn't mention having a big ex-cop escort her the few steps between her apartment and the bar.

"Glad to hear it. So, how's it going otherwise?"

"Otherwise? You mean like job-wise? Relationship-wise? Health-wise?"

"Sure. Why not? How's every little thing?"

Bliss shrugged. *How do I tell her everything's fine except, oh yeah, I found out I'm dating a dragon?* "You know... the usual."

"Good. Sometimes the 'same old, same old' is a welcome relief."

Bliss would have argued that point a few days ago. Now it seemed like sage wisdom.

"You know something? Lately I've been wondering if my mother isn't kind of right. I mean, wouldn't it be nice to live in the suburbs in a nice home with a nice, normal man and maybe raise a couple of sweet kids?"

Claudia almost dropped the folder she'd been holding. "Who are you, and what have you done with my friend?"

"Sorry. I didn't mean to give you a heart attack. It's just that... you know. Things have been a little crazy in the city lately. First all those fires, now all this rain..."

Claudia raised her eyebrows. "You don't think they have fire and rain in the suburbs?"

"Oh sure... rain maybe, but the fires? At least in the burbs you don't have to worry about one home wiping out a whole block."

"Are you worried about Drake?"

Bingo, but not because he's a firefighter. "Maybe a little."

"He's a professional, Bliss. He knows what he's doing, and from what I hear, he loves it. You shouldn't ask him to quit if you really care about him."

"Yeah, he's really... into it."

"So, is he *into* you?" Claudia sported a playful grin.

"Uh... you could say that." She couldn't help the soft smile. "He told me he loves me."

"Awesome. You two make a cute couple. Are you thinking of moving to the burbs and raising kids?"

"Probably not."

Bliss remembered what Drake had said when they first hooked up. *I can't get you pregnant.* She was in such a lust-induced haze that she hadn't paid much attention at the time. Now it made perfect sense. *I'm not a dragon. How could we possibly have children together?* Another thing made sense, too. Zina's claim on him.

Claudia must have noticed a change in Bliss's mood. She scrutinized her friend. "You look… sad. Is everything okay? Really?"

Bliss pasted a bright smile on her face. "Of course. I'm fine. Everything's great. I'm just worried about the contest."

Claudia didn't look like she quite believed her. "Okay. You know if you ever need to talk, I'm right here."

"Thanks. I know." She strolled toward the door. "I'd better get out there and serve those thirsty customers."

For once she was grateful for a busy bar. She wouldn't have time to ruminate, obsess, and otherwise drive herself crazy over the heady new situation that had slapped her upside the head.

About midway through her shift, Bliss heard sirens blaring… and they were getting louder. That meant they were close and getting closer. *Shit. Not again.*

Drake was working an overnight shift. He was probably in one of the trucks, if this was a fire. She hoped she was hearing police sirens instead. *How sick is hoping for a robbery or attempted murder instead of another fire?*

She grabbed a rag and strode to the table nearest the window, hoping to get a peek as either fire or police vehicles roared by.

Flashing lights lit up the night. *Please be blue, please be blue.* When the sirens deafened her, both red and blue light bars whizzed by. That meant both police and fire were responding. *Crap. Well, maybe they needed the EMTs, not the firefighters.* Somehow she knew that wasn't the case.

As the sirens slowed down and stopped altogether, she realized the incident couldn't be far away.

Suddenly the front door burst open and an excited man she recognized as a semi-regular shouted to the whole bar: "Hey! The bank on the corner is on fire."

Some of the customers took it in stride, not moving from their bar stools. Many got up—joking about cold, hard cash turning hot and crispy—and followed Phil out the door.

The bank on the corner? Horror struck Bliss like a punch in the chest. "My designs!"

She threw the rag on the floor and charged out of the bar. Running at top speed, she made it to the corner before the firefighters had completely unfurled their hoses.

She spotted Drake. Part of her wanted to rush over and beg him to rescue her safe-deposit box. The other part of her knew she should stay out of the way. He didn't need to get suspended twice in one month. Besides, how could he get into her safe deposit box without her key and the bank personnel? That's why they called it a *safe* deposit box. She cupped the sides of her face and gazed in horror.

She watched him work. He strapped on his protective gear and rushed up the steps.

"Give me the hydro ram," he shouted. One of the guys who followed handed him a sophisticated-looking tool. He had to try a few times but finally forced the door open. Smoke billowed out as Drake led the other firefighters into the building.

Her heart beat a little faster. Knowing he was fireproof certainly helped relieve some of her fear. Knowing he was such a heroic figure—and that he was hers—well, that got her heart pounding in another way. *No wonder so many women go nuts for firefighters.*

Someone sidled up to Bliss, and a female voice murmured, "Pretty cool, huh?"

Cool? A burning building? She turned toward the voice, ready to give the woman a piece of her mind, when she recognized her. *That's the woman who beat up Drake.*

"What are *you* doing here?" Bliss made sure the woman understood that she knew exactly who was standing next to her and was none too pleased to see her.

"I'm watching the excitement, just like everyone else is."

"Do you think you could do it from somewhere else?"

"Only if you come with me."

Bliss felt something hard touch her back. She whirled around and saw a gun pointed at her midsection. *Holy shit.*

Reason dictated she should stay quiet and wait for the woman to tell her what she wanted. But when had Bliss ever been reasonable?

"Gun!" she yelled and grabbed the woman's arm. She tried to press it over their heads and hold it that way until the nearest cop could reach them. She didn't expect the woman to be so strong.

"Bitch," the woman screamed. "You can't have him."

The weapon jabbed Bliss's temple. The next thing she knew, she was being dragged across the street, away from the crowd.

"Halt!" Two cops already had their weapons drawn and trained on both of them.

"You don't want to shoot," the woman cried out over the noise and confusion. "You might hit an innocent woman." Then she lowered her voice and growled in Bliss's ear, "And by that I mean a not-so-innocent, boyfriend-stealing bitch." Even though the woman had an accent, Bliss understood every word.

She still thinks she's entitled to Drake. Bliss didn't know what made psychotics tick, but right about now she wished she did. *Maybe if I play along I'll live long enough to get out of this.* Not only didn't she know if that was the right thing to do, but she couldn't bring herself to do it.

She saw one of the cops speaking into his radio. Hopefully he was calling for backup, but would they arrive in time? The nasty Rasta dragon had managed to spirit her around the corner and out of sight. A moment later, Bliss was able to answer her own question with a resounding "No."

Something strange was happening. She felt as if claws were digging into her shoulders. Suddenly her feet left the pavement and she was soaring up into the night sky. For some damn reason, she pictured Dorothy being kidnapped by flying monkeys.

Do something, Bliss! The only thing that came to mind was to follow Dorothy's example and let out a bloodcurdling scream—so she did.

An animalistic sound that might have been a laugh was the only response.

—∿—

Drake and his buddies wrestled the fire under control in about half an hour. The bank suffered irreparable damage, not only by ravaging flames, but smoke and water destruction too. The overhead sprinklers helped save some areas, but not all.

His dragon warning tingles had begun during the fire, but he'd chalked them up to the possibility of his being in mortal danger—now that he was mortal. However, they hadn't subsided.

Drake had been focused on the job, and it wasn't until they pulled into the station that he wondered whether or not that was the bank in which Bliss had stored her CD. He'd call her as soon as he could. If nothing else, he'd be able to reassure her that the vault and safe deposit area weren't affected.

She might experience a slight delay getting to her valuables, but she had until Monday to produce the designs she had been working so hard on. He was proud of himself for recalling a detail that was important to her but not so much to him. Too often he'd known men who only half listened to their wives or girlfriends and paid the price later.

He hung up his gear and trudged upstairs, looking forward to a shower. Bliss would still be at work, so he could wait to tell her about his day.

A little voice in his head argued, No. You need to call her now.

Not one to ignore so many portents, he grabbed his

new cell phone and punched in the number for Bliss. When her voice mail offered to take a message and get back to him, he hung up and called the bar.

"Boston Uncommon, Angie speaking."

"Hi, Angie. It's Drake. Is Bliss there?"

"No. I was about to call you. She took off like a bat out of hell when the fire trucks drove by earlier and hasn't come back yet. It's busy and we need her."

"She left you in the lurch? That doesn't sound like the Bliss I know."

"You don't think something has happened to her, do you?"

Drake didn't know what to say. Should he reassure Angie when he was almost positive something *was* drastically wrong? *Hell*.

"I'm going out to look for her. When I find her, I'll call you and let you know what's up."

"Call Anthony. He's worried about her too. Really worried."

"Can you put Anthony on the phone?"

"Sure. Give me a minute."

Drake paced as he listened to the sounds of a noisy bar. A few anxious moments passed before he heard Anthony's voice.

"Drake. What's going on?"

"Apparently Bliss is missing. Angie said she ran out during the fire, and I can't get in touch with her."

"That much I know. You didn't see her at the scene, did you?"

"No, but she could have been there. I was focused on the job and didn't pay much attention to the crowd."

Anthony hesitated but eventually said, "I followed her

scent as far as I could. The smoke may have thrown me off, but on Branch Street her scent just—disappeared. Do you think Zina may have something to do with it?"

Drake swore. "I didn't want to even entertain the idea, but yeah. It's quite possible. If she's the one who set the fire, she may have been nearby."

Anthony sighed. "I'm sorry, Drake. I said I'd be responsible for her and I feel terrible. I was in my office and didn't know she was missing for quite a while. I think the staff was covering for her."

"Don't blame yourself. Neither of us would have expected she'd run off in the middle of her shift."

"That's not much comfort, is it?"

Drake dropped onto his cot. "No. It isn't." After a short silence, he said, "I've gotta go."

"Let me know if there's anything I can do."

"I will, if I think of something. I don't even know if there's anything *I* can do."

Suddenly Drake had an idea. It might backfire, but it was all he had.

"Talk to you later, Anthony." He hung up and tucked his cell phone into his pocket. Then he ran downstairs to the street and yelled, "Taxi!"

Chapter 13

BLISS WAS TIED UP AND GAGGED. IF SHE WEREN'T SO scared, she'd be amused that the woman seemed more intent on gagging her than tying her to a chair. Bliss's mouth had always been her best weapon, and yet she hadn't even taunted the bitch. *I could have… Oh, I could have.*

Thank goodness she'd thought better of it. All she'd done was try to reason with the woman. Apparently reason didn't appeal to psychos. Now that Bliss was forced to sit and think, she should have been planning a way to get out of this. Instead she was furious and chiding herself for getting into this predicament at all.

Why did she care if the bank burned? She had her designs on her computer and could have simply created another CD. But for some damn reason, worrying about an arsonist—and knowing all her designs could be lost *again* if anything happened to her laptop—had her seeing things a little cockeyed.

If I get out of this alive, I swear I'll make dozens of CDs and mail one to each person I know before Monday's presentation.

The she-dragon had flown them all around the city before landing in a deserted park. That's where she found a dirty, disgusting sock and shoved it into Bliss's mouth. A nasty sweater lay nearby, and the dragon had used that to tie Bliss's hands *and* blindfold her. Probably a couple of kids were canoodling in the park and something scared them off before they could grab all of their clothes. Maybe they saw a dragon swooping down on them.

And if they were drinking, they'll probably never touch alcohol again.

Bliss glanced around the room, trying to figure out where she was. It looked like some kind of warehouse. *How clichéd.* A forklift and numerous boxes were clearly visible from her vantage point. High windows wouldn't aid her escape.

She twisted her torso, trying to see what was behind her, but boxes obscured her view of the door. The woman with the long dreadlocks walked out from behind a pile of boxes, zipping up her leather pants.

She halted and stared at Bliss. "What? You didn't think dragons had to go potty once in a while?"

Bliss tried to mumble something around the sock, but it was useless. The she-dragon sported a mean-looking grin and strolled over to her.

"What's that? Speak up. I can't hear you."

I really don't want to play this game. Bliss let out a defeated sigh and let her shoulders slump.

The woman ripped the sock out of her mouth. "Go ahead. Scream. No one will hear you."

Bliss lifted her chin. "I wasn't trying to scream. I just thought the idea of a bathroom sounded good right about now."

The woman got down into her face. "Oh, yeah? Do you need to pee?"

Bliss *so* wanted to answer her with sarcasm. She could hardly resist the urge. *Oh, what the hell. I'm probably going to die anyway.*

Dragon Lady grabbed hold of Bliss's hair and yanked her head back. "I asked if you need to pee."

"No. I want to put on my makeup."

To her surprise, the woman let go of her and laughed. "In another life I might have liked you. Unfortunately, we're in this one, and *you* are in my way."

"What's your name?" Bliss asked.

"Why do you want to know?"

She shrugged. "I just want to know what to call you besides, 'Hey you.' That seems rude, and I really do have to go to the bathroom."

"Well, since you want to be polite, you can call me Zina, like the warrior princess."

It was all Bliss could do not to burst out laughing. She pasted on the blandest expression she could muster. "Seriously?"

"Yeah. What's wrong with that? I'm descended from dragon kings in the Amazon and my name is Zina, with a *Z-I*—not an *X-E* like the chick in the old TV show."

"Gotcha. Okay, Princess Zina, may I use the bathroom, please?"

Zina blew out an exasperated breath. "I just asked if you needed to pee." Then, as if she'd thought of something funny, she chuckled and threw her hands in the air. "You should have gone before we left the house."

"I almost went in midair."

Chuckling manically, Zina untied her. "Fine. Go, but be quick about it."

As soon as she was free, Bliss prayed the bathroom would offer some way to escape. Although if Zina the warrior bitch was letting her go, she'd bet there wasn't one.

Striding around the boxes, Bliss spotted a small door near the windows. She prayed there would be a stack of boxes, like stairs, leading up to an open bathroom window. *Yeah, and with my luck, flying monkeys would be waiting on the other side.*

Deciding she had seen too many movies, Bliss opened the bathroom door and took in the small windowless room. *Damn.*

"Disappointed, are you?" Zina called out.

"Why should I be?" Bliss yelled back.

"There are no windows to climb out of."

"Gee. I never thought of that. All I wanted was a toilet, and it seems to have one. Maybe I'm not spoiled like you."

The woman was silent.

Frig. Maybe I went too far. Bliss had to remind herself not to taunt the psycho. Kind of like not taunting tigers in the zoo. Hopefully, if she could just stay alive long enough, some kind of opportunity to escape would come up.

While she did her business, Bliss pondered possible scenarios, concentrating on the ones in which she'd get away in one piece. Zina would have to leave at some point. Bliss remembered reading an article on how to present your hands to be tied if you're ever taken hostage. There was a way to look cooperative while giving yourself enough room to slip out when you changed hand positions later. *Yeah, that's what I'll—*

Suddenly, she wasn't alone in the tiny room. A man was standing right in front of her! She blinked to be sure she hadn't imagined him. *Nope. He's still there.*

The well-dressed older gentleman was not an

attractive man. His eyes were small and too close together. His face looked like a worn-out leather jacket, but if he was real, maybe he could help her!

He put his finger to his lips as if to say, "Shhh," although he didn't make a sound. Thank goodness he seemed to be aware of the danger on the other side of the door.

Bliss leaned forward, not only so she could be heard but also to protect her modesty—slightly. There's nothing quite so embarrassing as being caught on the potty. "Who are you?" she whispered.

He smiled and whispered, "I'm your rescuer. Now get dressed." He turned his back to give her a bit of privacy, so she quickly yanked up her panties and straightened her skirt.

"What's going on in there?" Zina yelled.

Bliss started to panic when she heard heavy boots tromping in her direction. The man whirled around, grabbed her arms, and seconds later, she was blinking against a blinding light.

"What the…" She tried to shield her eyes with her hand but still couldn't see past the gentleman who called himself her rescuer. He let go of her arms.

A female voice called out, "Who the hell is this? And why did you bring her here, Hephaestus?"

"I'm sorry. I just needed a moment to scan the area I'm returning her to, so we won't be seen appearing out of thin air."

"Well, that's a moment too long. Get her out of here, now!"

The guy sighed and grasped Bliss's arms again. Suddenly they were standing in a dark place. It took a moment for her eyes to adjust, as if she'd just had a flashbulb go off in her face.

"Wh—where are we?"

"In the alley behind the bar where you work. You've been gone for quite some time. You'll need a reasonably believable story to explain your absence."

Bliss focused on the man as soon as she could see again and set a hand on her hip. "You mean they won't believe a dragon snatched me off the ground, flew me all over the city, and held me in a warehouse until some guy with magical powers got me out of there and took me to someplace brighter than the sun?"

"I think it would be a good idea to tweak the truth a bit, don't you?"

"Well, yeah, of course, but damn... what do I say to my boss?"

"You could start by apologizing for running off and worrying everybody."

Well, that's a no-brainer. "I probably won't need to explain where I was. I'll just get my stuff and start looking for another job and place to live."

"I don't think you'll lose your job."

Something about the way he smiled made her realize he wasn't as ugly as she'd originally thought. There was a goodness inside the man, and she felt ashamed for not realizing it before.

"I never thanked you. You probably saved my life."

"Oh, there's no 'probably' about it. I don't usually like to interfere with mortals, but this was a special case. Now, I'm off to wrestle with a certain nasty dra—I mean, person."

Mortals? "I have so many ques—" She stopped when

she blinked and realized she was standing there alone, talking to herself. *What the… How does he do that?*

———

Bliss stepped through the back door and headed toward Anthony's office, fully prepared to pick up her stuff and get out. *If only Claudia was back there, but she's home in bed by now.*

Before she reached the door, she was spotted. Someone called out, "Bliss!" It may have been Tory. He was standing at the bar talking to Angie. Angie whipped her head around and gasped when she saw Bliss.

Drake burst into the bar through the front door.

Before Bliss could take another step, Angie lifted the bar top and rushed through it, almost tackling her.

"Bliss! Oh, God! Where have you been?"

"I don't know, but you may have just guessed who I was with."

Angie took a step back. "God? You were with God?" Her hands flew to cover her second gasp. "You saw God? Did you have a near-death experience?"

Hey, that's as good an explanation as any… "Yeah, I think so. In all the confusion, I was—um… I got knocked down and I think I hit my head."

"On the street? But didn't anyone stop to help you?"

Drake battled his way through the crowd.

"Uh… no. You know how big cities are."

Angie glanced around at the people that were watching as if to say, "Do you believe this shit?"

Drake reached her and pulled her into a giant hug. "Bliss, honey. We were all worried about you, but I think I speak for everyone when I say we're just glad to have you back." Raising his voice he announced, "Bliss needs time to rest and regroup. Let's give her some breathing room."

Everyone murmured their assent and stepped back. Most folks returned to their tables. Kurt and Tory stayed nearby, probably to make sure she was all right.

"Thanks, Drake. I need to tell Anthony I'm okay and get yelled at, or more likely fired."

Drake smiled. "He's not going to fire you."

"Wanna bet?"

"How much?" He placed his hand on the small of her back, guiding her toward the office.

Tory laughed. "You're seriously betting on whether or not she gets fired?"

Drake grinned at him. "Why not? I know I'm going to win. Maybe I can get something I want from her in the bargain." He winked at Bliss.

His calm demeanor and good humor relaxed her somewhat, but she wondered how he could be so sure of himself.

As soon as they reached the office door, he opened it.

"Drake! We always knock first."

Anthony strode right over to them and opened the door wider. "Come in, Bliss."

"Can I join you?" Drake asked.

Anthony gave a slight bow and backed away enough to let both of them into his office.

"Anthony, I'm so sorry…" Bliss began.

He held up one hand. "I'm sure you had your reasons. There's no need to go into them right now. Are you all right?"

"Yes. But I'm so sorry…"

"Are you able to finish your shift?"

Her mouth opened in surprise. She had been ready to defend her poppycock story, but it didn't appear as if she had to. Not only that, but she wasn't losing her job or even being warned about repeat behavior.

"Uh... yeah. I can get out there right after I wash my hands, if you want."

"Then please go ahead. I'd like to talk to Drake for a moment."

"Sure." She fished in her pocket. Somewhere during all the sky travel and rough landings, she'd lost her order pad. "I, ah... I just need a new pad and pen."

Anthony opened a side drawer of his desk and found the needed items. "Here you go," he said with a smile.

This was all too weird. He didn't even appear upset. But not wanting to look a gift boss in the mouth, she grabbed the pen and order pad and scurried out the door.

Drake strolled to the couch on the far wall of Anthony's office and made himself comfortable. Anthony took the adjacent chair.

"You must be relieved."

Drake blew out a deep breath and dropped back onto the cushions. "You can say that again. If it hadn't been for Vulcan, we might never have found her."

Anthony shook his head. "I don't know if I like having the Supernatural Council here in Boston or not. Nick met them and seemed to feel uncomfortable about it. Of course, Mother Nature *did* threaten to drop him into an active volcano."

"That would give anyone cause for alarm."

"Yes. Well, I assume it's only a matter of time before they call me in. The Balogs tried to discourage me from opening the bar, and I assumed it was simply because they didn't want that element near their home. Now I understand from both you and Nick that the Balogs seem to be in the Council's employ."

"I think you're all right as long as humans don't discover the bar's real purpose as a safe place for paranormals to meet and get to know each other as fellow, well, creatures."

"It's more than that. They don't want humans knowing about our existence at all. I can understand their concern since I employ humans. I've tried to find paranormals to work here, but most aren't interested in such mundane duties and lousy pay."

Drake laughed. "Can you blame them?"

"No. If I didn't firmly believe in my theory that hostilities between the factions would cease if everyone just got to know one another's daily struggles and challenges, I wouldn't be doing this, either."

"It's a positive message and I, for one, hope it's working."

Anthony nodded. "For the most part. I've had to mesmerize a couple of employees who'd seen too much, but it was absolutely essential. They had to forget about our... uniqueness."

"I understand. But Bliss knows about me, and now that Vulcan has intervened, she may know a lot more."

"She's a smart woman, and I trust her not to blab. You must too if you're sitting here and talking to me casually. I thought you might ask me to mesmerize her."

"As you said, she's smart. I think she knows no one

would believe her, and I trust her not to jeopardize my safety. Just now, she made up a crazy story about being knocked out and having a near-death experience."

Anthony's brows shot up. "That's a little much, isn't it? Why not temporary amnesia?"

"I don't know. I'll ask her about it later. Right now I want to wait until her shift is over and see if I can talk her into going to my place for the night."

"You don't believe she's safe here anymore?"

"It isn't that. She's probably safe anywhere. Vulcan said he was going after Zina and Bliss was back at the bar. You have no idea what a relief that was. The Council must have Zina in their custody by now.

"I can't imagine that Bliss would have been able to escape without their help. That's probably why she made up that bullshit story about seeing God. I can hardly wait to hear what really happened."

"Ah, I think I understand now."

"If I'm right, we should have nothing to fear from Zina from now on. Thanks for your help while she was being a menace."

Anthony chuckled. "I may ask you to return the favor someday. Wait until you see Ruxandra on a rampage."

～～～

Mother Nature screamed a string of obscenities. "Are you kidding me? You had that dragon bitch in your grasp and you lost her?"

Vulcan's gaze dropped to where his white robe met his bare feet. "I'm sorry, Gaia. She was about to open the bathroom door and I panicked. I grabbed the mortal and returned her to safety instead of grabbing the immortal and going back for the other one later. You're absolutely right. I should have done it the other way around. I don't know what I was thinking."

"You were thinking it would be easier to deal with a helpless mortal than battle a nasty fire-breathing dragon."

It chafed, but she was probably right. That's why Vulcan didn't visit earth very often. He was much more comfortable in his solitary workshop or among his own kind. Mortals were so frail and easily broken, they made him nervous.

"Not only that, but you actually brought the mortal here." Mother Nature tossed her hands in the air. It was never a good sign when she began talking with her hands. "*Here!* No mortal has ever—or *should* ever—be aware of our location. They need to think we're everywhere. Otherwise there will be chaos wherever we're not."

"Yes, Goddess."

"Fortunately I was able to blind her with über-bright direct sunlight. If I hadn't, she could have seen everything. How would you have explained it to her then?"

"I don't know. I am very, very sorry."

"Well, get your sorry ass back down there and find that friggin' dragon. You know how I hate dragons! I've almost wiped them out completely, but if this one manages to get pregnant... Gaaaah!" Thunder rumbled in the distance.

Vulcan had never seen Mother Nature this angry. Well, no, that wasn't quite true. She'd caused some impressive earthquakes and tsunamis when she was *really* on a tear. Vulcan wondered what kind of destruction was taking place on earth during this tirade, but he wasn't nearly as concerned about that as he was with his own hide at the moment.

"I'll find her, Goddess."

"Damn right you will, because you won't be allowed back here until you do."

Why did I ever volunteer to help in the first place?

Chapter 14

"I THOUGHT YOU DIDN'T WANT ME TO LEAVE MY building. Don't get me wrong. I'm glad to be out and about again. I was beginning to feel like I was on house arrest."

"I'm pretty sure you're safe now, or I wouldn't have suggested coming here."

Drake unlocked his front door and led her down the hall of the old brick house. Near the end of the corridor, he unlocked another door and let her go inside first.

"I know it's small. Someday when I have more money saved, I'll look for a bigger place. Basically, it was affordable and convenient to walk to work."

"Your place is… cute." Bliss took in the entire apartment from her vantage point. The room couldn't have been more than twenty by twenty-five feet, but he had managed to make every square inch useful. There was one door in the middle, which had to be the bathroom. On the left side stood a very efficient kitchen.

A set of bookshelves ran the length of the opposite wall, but built into the middle was a dresser and, on top of that, a TV. The wall unit looked as if it had been custom made. Perhaps it was. She remembered his telling her about making his own Murphy bed and desk combination. She spotted them on the other side of the bathroom door and walked over. "Am I in your bedroom now?"

"Oh, yeah," he said in a sexy, low voice. "And you look mighty good there."

She chuckled. "Where do you sit and talk? You *do* still want to talk, right?"

"We should. Let me fold down the bed. It's my sofa too."

She backed up out of the way, and he made short work of flipping up his desk, fastening it in place, and dropping down a queen-size bed.

"You made that look easy."

"I'm used to it." Then he gestured to his bed, inviting her to sit on it.

She couldn't help but wonder if other women had been to his place. It really wasn't an entertainer's paradise. She had a hard time reconciling her social guy with a place like this. Bliss took a seat on the end of the bed and tried to cross her legs at the ankle and tuck them beneath her. She was a little too close to the ground for a ladylike position.

Drake sat down next to her and pulled her close for a long, warm kiss. Afterward, he rested his forehead against hers and spoke so softly, she almost didn't hear him.

"I've never been so worried about anyone in my life."

"I'm sorry. I shouldn't have put you through that."

He brushed a stray lock of hair behind her ear. "It's not exactly your fault. It wouldn't have happened if you weren't involved with me in the first place."

"Yeah, well, I'm glad I am. I just don't understand why Zina wants you so badly."

He looked surprised and she realized how that must have sounded. Her face heated and a nervous giggle escaped. "I mean... you're a great guy and everything, but the only thing she said to me was that I was 'in the way.' She seemed to have some kind of plan for you."

Drake hung his head. "She wanted to mate with me. Dragons are only fertile once every five years and the cycle only lasts for a month."

"Oh." Bliss didn't know quite what to say to that. She hadn't known him a month yet? It seemed at times like they'd known each other for years. And what if they were still together in five years? Did that mean she'd have to worry about Zina coming back?

"Look. You were never 'in the way' because I was never going to be with her. If I had just been honest from the beginning and told her I wasn't interested…"

"I don't think it would have mattered. She seemed to think you were her property. If she really is a princess as she claimed, maybe she's used to just telling people what to do and being obeyed."

"She certainly acted like a spoiled princess," Drake agreed.

"So, now what happens? Is the month over? Will she just give up and go away when it's too late?"

Drake shook his head. "I don't think we'll have to worry about her anymore." He ran the back of his fingers over Bliss's face, tenderly. "I know you were probably told not to tell anyone how you got away, and I won't say anything, but I figure we should talk about it… just between us."

"Oh, um, that." She looked at her lap, not even sure if *she* knew what happened. "I—I don't mind telling you, but please don't laugh."

"Laugh? Believe me, I won't laugh." His voice sounded sure and sincere.

She gazed up into his eyes and took a deep breath. "God helped me. I know it sounds nuts, but I was sitting on the toilet in a disgusting tiny bathroom in a warehouse. No way out. Zina standing guard. I thought I was done for. Suddenly this... guy appeared. He turned around just long enough for me to pull up my panties and then zing... we were somewhere else. It was so bright, I think it was heaven... but maybe not. I heard a woman's voice, and she sounded angry. Then, zing... we were standing outside in the alley behind the bar."

"Zing?"

Bliss waved away the word in frustration. "I don't know what to call it. There wasn't a noise involved. I was just somewhere and then I wasn't there anymore. Then I was suddenly somewhere else."

"And you think God took you to heaven and brought you back?"

"Either that, or he was some kind of angel and the angry woman was God... or a goddess... Oh, I don't know." She rose and paced toward the windows. "I knew you'd think I'm crazy."

He followed her and grabbed her by the arms almost as the mystery man had. "You're not crazy." He turned her in his arms and kissed her. "You're perfectly sane. I don't know *why* you're not losing it after what you've been through, but I'm glad you're not."

She blinked. "You don't think I'm crazy?"

"Put it this way, crazy things happen. Maybe denying that is crazy."

She threw her arms around his neck. "Thank goodness you understand."

—⁓—

Back in her hotel room, Zina paced and muttered to herself, "So that human thinks I'm spoiled? Nothing could be further from the truth. I had a very critical father. Nothing I ever did was good enough for the king of the Amazon. There was no pleasing him. He said he was toughening me up for the world. You know what? Now I just want to punch the world in the face."

She punched her own palm, then shook it to release the sting.

"Come on, Zina, think. You have three more days to get this Drake guy to sleep with you." She snorted and a curl of smoke left her nostrils. "Yeah, willingly or not. At first, I thought I only had to show him my charming side, but nooo... that wasn't good enough.

"Now I not only have to come up with a plan to get him alone, I also have to think of some way to threaten him into cooperating. I thought for sure, holding his woman hostage would get him to do anything. Now I find out she has some kind of magical power that lets her escape through walls. Damn it! I can't catch a break."

As she paced, she became angrier and angrier. "Why the hell would he allow the whole dragon species to die out? Am I that repugnant? He knows how few and far between we are. He said so himself. And I know that Bliss bitch isn't a dragon. I mean, we're good, but even a dragon can't escape though a solid wall without leaving a big, gaping hole. What the fuck?"

She halted in her tracks as a kernel of an idea came to her. "Maybe I can just threaten to burn the city to the ground. He knows I can do it, and I don't think he'd let that happen." The more she thought about it, the better she liked the idea.

~~~

Drake tucked a loose strand of Bliss's hair behind her ear. "A couple days ago you said you thought you loved me but reserved the right to take it back. Now that we're safe from Zina and all her crazy distractions, do you have a definite opinion on that?"

Bliss smiled and lay back on his bed. "I do. Come here and let me show you."

Nice. It was all he could do not to tear her clothes off and make love to her. Now it looked as if they'd get there after all. But he didn't want to assume and be wrong, so he lay next to her and waited to see what she'd do next.

She reached for the buttons on his shirt and undid them slowly. The heat in her eyes spoke of good things to come, and she didn't look away. Perhaps she was waiting to see if his eyes turned gold. Regardless, making love face to face was something he'd wanted to do from the start, and now that she knew his secret, he could.

As soon as she'd removed his belt, he reached out and unbuttoned her blouse with the same care she'd shown his uniform. It took a lot of restraint, but he managed to get her clothes off without tearing anything.

She rolled him onto his back and kissed him. Their tongues found each other instinctively.

Drake hadn't expected this slow seduction to appeal to him, but it did on many levels. The heat inside him built more slowly, and he finally felt like he had total control over his shift. That didn't mean he was reacting any less. His balls were tight and his blood was pounding. When she took his cock in her hand, he had to force himself to breathe.

"I see we have a situation here," Bliss said.

"A situation?"

"A situation that might need my attention."

"Oh, yeah. I think you're right."

Bliss slid down the bed until she was at eye level with his cock, stroking it the entire time.

He thought he might explode right there. "I should point out that this 'situation' is entirely your fault. If you weren't so damn sexy—" He gasped when she took him into her mouth.

Her hair dark fell forward, obscuring his view, so he swept it back over her shoulder. Watching and feeling was almost too much stimulation for a man or dragon to bear. He had to close his eyes for a moment. He was rigid, hot and ready. Too ready.

"Bliss, honey. I can't take much more."

She eased her mouth off his throbbing cock and kissed the swollen tip. Then she tongued his hole and he almost short-circuited. He grasped under her arms and hauled her up, then flipped her so she lay looking up at him.

"That mouth of yours is sheer magic. Let's see if I can do the same for you."

He bent over her breast and circled the hard nipple with his tongue. When he covered the entire areola with his mouth and sucked, she arched and moaned. His hand found her other breast and cupped its fullness, then he stroked her nipple with his thumb.

After thoroughly suckling one breast, he switched to

the other. She breathed out his name as he moved. If possible, she moaned even louder when he latched on to her nipple and gave equal attention to that side while adding a rub to her clit.

"Oh, God," she rasped. "I need you—inside me. *Now*."

He let her breast pop out of his mouth and grinned. "I believe in giving a lady what she wants."

"In that case, I want to be on top."

Drake had no objections to her taking control. If their situations were reversed, he'd want to watch her face as they made love too. She might want to watch his eyes for a change in color, or perhaps she just wanted to gaze into them, but either way he was ready to let her.

She positioned herself over his hard erection. She sank her slick channel over his length, and there was no question about her readiness to accept him. Incredible sensations took his breath away for a moment. Then he grasped her waist and let her ride him how ever she wanted. They made eye contact and didn't let go. A wicked little smile teased the corners of her mouth, but her eyes burned with passion.

As the pressure built, she changed her tactic and moved in a circle, grinding down on his pelvis. A sudden spike in pleasure brought on the inevitable tingles at the base of his spine, signaling a sweet release was imminent.

"I can't hold on much longer, Bliss."

"Then don't. Just let go."

"You're coming with me." He rubbed her clit and she bucked like a wild horse. At last, she doubled over and howled just as he spilled his seed. The pleasure that ripped through him was more powerful than anything he'd ever felt before. "Good God!"

Bliss tumbled off to one side, breathed out, "That was amazing," then panted like she'd run a marathon.

He wrapped her in his arms and kissed her damp forehead. "Indeed it was."

They lay happily sated for several moments, allowing the air to cool their overheated bodies. When Bliss cuddled closer, he grabbed the sheet and dragged it over them.

"Your eyes didn't glow this time," she said.

"Not to worry. All of me is glowing inside right now."

They held each other in silence, basking in the lovely serenity for a few minutes. Bliss eventually stirred.

"I guess we can't lie here all day, as much as I'd like to."

Drake chuckled. "I know what you mean. I'm a little hungry. Can I take you out for a late dinner?"

"That sounds perfect. I'd like to go home and change, though."

"Really? You don't want to wear your uniform out to dinner?"

"I would if it were cute and didn't smell like beer."

"Gotcha. I'll walk you home. And because tomorrow's your day off and I don't have to report for duty until five p.m., why don't you pack an overnight bag?"

The following morning, Bliss awoke to bright sunshine. She and Drake had made love so many times during the night, they'd slept in to recover. Trying not to disturb her still-sleeping boyfriend—or dragon friend—or whatever, she rolled over and was about to get up when she noticed a male figure sitting on the end of the bed. She shrieked and pulled the sheet up to her neck.

Drake sat bolt upright. "What's the matt—Oh, it's you," he said to the man-angel who'd rescued her from Zina's clutches. "Bliss, this is Vulcan, a friend of mine. There's no need to be afraid."

"Vulcan? I—I'm not afraid. I'm stark naked under here. Jeez, guy. First you pop in on me while I'm sitting on the potty, and now I wake up to you sitting on the end of my boyfriend's bed. What is it with you? Don't you ever knock?"

Vulcan gave her an indulgent smile. "I'm sorry, but it was necessary."

"How do you get through locked doors? Is that something Vulcans can do? Can you do that mind-meld thing too?"

Vulcan cleared his throat. "I'm not *that* kind of Vulcan—but let's not focus on me. You have bigger problems."

"Why? What's wrong?" Drake grabbed his underwear off the floor and tugged it on while exposing his tight butt.

Bliss had no hope of reaching her clothes, which were on his side, so she pulled the sheet loose and wrapped it around herself.

"It's Zina. I'm afraid she got away," Vulcan said. "I searched all night, but wherever she is, she's managed to conceal herself quite well."

"Shit," Drake said. Then he looked at Bliss. "I'm sorry. Please excuse the language."

"If you hadn't said it first, I would have." She focused on their unexpected guest as she rose. "So, now what?"

"Now you can take precautions. I imagine she'll show herself again. Perhaps more directly. I have the feeling she's becoming more desperate. I'll stay with you, Bliss. Drake, you should be safe as long as you're surrounded by people. I doubt she'd reveal her supernatural identity in public."

"Why not?" Bliss asked. "If she's getting desperate, why wouldn't she use all the powers at her disposal?"

Drake picked up the rest of his clothes and tossed them in a hamper she hadn't noticed. It was neatly concealed in his nightstand drawer. "Because paranormals know better than to do that. There would be far-reaching repercussions."

"But what if she just loses it? She seems easily unhinged and doesn't care about anyone but herself."

"If she was caught, can you imagine what would happen to her?" Drake exchanged a look with Vulcan, making her think there was more to it than just government experiments. Drake crossed to his dresser, grabbed a pair of jeans from the bottom drawer, and hopped into them.

"No, I can't. Why don't you tell me? We promised to be honest with each other, didn't we?"

Vulcan groaned and looked away.

"What?" *Now I know there's definitely more to it.* But would she be able to drag it out of one of them? She sighed, then thought about how her mother always advised that she'd catch more bees with honey than vinegar. Maybe she could try that approach.

"Drake, my darling, my love, what is it you're not telling me?"

He bit his lip and looked to Vulcan as if distressed.

Vulcan raised his hands, palms up. "Don't look at me. You're the one who made that stupid promise."

"Stupid?" Bliss was indignant that this *whatever he was* would call total honesty in a relationship "stupid." It made him seem less like an angel. Maybe he was some kind of demon, but why would Drake call him a friend?

"No one is saying honesty is stupid, honey. It's just that some things require the right timing or circumstances."

"And some things are on a need-to-know basis," Vulcan added.

Obviously, she didn't need to know whatever they were trying so hard not to say. Bliss bit out the word, "Fine," between clenched teeth, then grabbed her overnight bag and stomped off to the bathroom.

Chapter 15

WHEN BLISS SHUT THE DOOR A LITTLE FIRMLY, Vulcan looked at Drake and shrugged. "I'll never understand women."

"What's so hard to understand? She knows we're hiding something and deliberately keeping her in the dark. Considering it may have to do with a crazy she-dragon who wants to kill her, I think she has a valid point."

"But you *cannot* tell her about the Council. Mother Nature's adamant about that."

"I know. I wasn't planning to do that anytime soon."

"Is that how you keep your promise to Mother Nature and also manage total honesty with Bliss? I'll tell her... but some other time? Like on her deathbed?"

Thinking about Bliss dying brought him up short. Yes, some day he would lose her. The Council, on the other hand...

Drake sank to the floor with his face in his hands. "What can I do to end this? If you can't find Zina, I doubt I can."

"I think she'll find you. I just need to keep Bliss out of the way."

He sighed. "Yes, I know. It's for her own safety, but I'd like to tell her what I'm planning to do if I find Zina."

Vulcan raised an eyebrow. "And what would that be?"

"Just that I'd turn her over to you. I don't have any

idea what you'll do with her after that, and if you don't tell me, I won't have to lie about it."

Vulcan paused and tapped his lip. "I think that might work." Then he started to laugh.

"What's funny?"

"Man, you really screwed yourself with that total honesty promise. There are so many things you should *not* tell a woman like her."

"What do you mean… like her?"

"A woman with a temper."

The bathroom door flew open and Bliss stood there, looking fabulous. She had changed into some tight jeans and a super-soft-looking light blue sweater. Her hair was still a mess, but with a hairbrush in her hand, she looked as if she was planning to remedy that—or beat him with it.

"You look gorgeous." Drake got up and strolled over to her. *No raised hairbrush. That's a good sign.*

She started to smile, then quickly pasted on a frown. "Is it safe to come out now? Are you two finished planning your super-secret strategy?"

"There's not much in the way of strategy, hon. If I see Zina, I'll call Vulcan and he'll take it from there."

She stuck a hand on her hip. "That's it?"

"Well, yeah. Keeping it simple seems best."

"You aren't planning to lure her somewhere?"

Drake shrugged. "Like where? And how would we do that? We don't even know where she is."

Bliss turned to Vulcan. "Have you checked the warehouse?"

"Several times," Vulcan said. "She doesn't seem to be staying there."

Bliss blew out a deep breath. "So that's it, then? You just have to wait until she finds Drake?"

"Pretty much." Drake rubbed her back and hoped she'd let the subject drop. But this was Bliss, and she wasn't about to let anything drop.

"How will you keep in touch with each other?"

"We have a code. If I yell a particular word, Vulcan will hear it and find me."

"What word?"

"Taxi."

"That's weird. Vulcans can find people from miles away? I never saw Spock do that."

Vulcan sighed. "I'm not *that kind* of Vulcan." He rose and wandered toward the front door. "But, yes, I can find people most of the time. The way I found you in that warehouse bathroom." He tapped the side of his nose.

Whatever that meant… Did he smell her? She wrinkled her nose but finally stopped questioning Vulcan. Instead, she put her arms around Drake and said, "Well, I guess I'm going out for breakfast with Vulcan and planning my day from there. Will you call just to let us know you're okay at some point?"

"Absolutely."

"Good." She let out a deep breath and lowered her voice to a whisper. "I love you. Don't get killed."

———

"So, are you ever going to tell me who you really are and how you did what you did?" Bliss swirled the dregs of her coffee and set the cup down.

Vulcan glanced around the fifties-style room. "Cute

little diner. If you didn't know where it was tucked away, you'd never find it. And the food…"

"Don't try to change the subject." Bliss leaned back against the padded booth and crossed her arms. "I mean it. I want to know."

Vulcan leaned in and lowered his voice. "There are certain things I'm not at liberty to tell you and, fortunately, I never promised you total transparency."

Bliss snorted. "Are you really upset with Drake for promising to be honest with me? That seems like an important part of a successful relationship."

He smirked. "Sure, honey. Tell yourself that. You'll learn."

"What?" Outraged, she was about to toss her napkin onto the table and storm out, but she'd promised Drake to let the maddening Vulcan watch over her, so she was stuck with him. *Well, Drake didn't say I had to be pleasant company, did he?* She was tempted to toss a snark bomb at Vulcan, but again her mother's warning chimed in the back of her head. *Honey, not vinegar, Bliss.*

"Fine. We can agree to disagree on that, but I really want to know what you *can* tell me."

He cleared his throat. "You already know too much."

"Why? Are you in the Mafia? Do I have to worry about getting whacked?"

Everyone in the North End diner immediately fell silent and turned to stare at them. Bliss wanted to slink down until she disappeared under the table.

Vulcan did what anyone in that situation would do. He laughed out loud. Pounding the table might have been overplaying it a bit, but at least the rest of the patrons relaxed and went back to their own conversations.

Bliss tried to think of another tactic to get the

information she wanted. Realizing it might be fruitless, the only thing she could come up with was hammering at him until she wore him down.

"Seriously, there must be something you can tell me—just a morsel of information."

He sighed. "Well, you already know about Drake. That must tell you something…"

"Like what? That there are certain legends that might be true after all?"

"Now you're getting it."

"Ah. So you're something of a legend yourself."

He smiled. "Something like that."

Bliss racked her brain for what legendary creature could materialize through solid walls and transport a person from one place to another in seconds. All she could come up with were her memories of *Star Trek* and the Vulcans with pointy ears using their transport pad—or whatever they called that thing that turned them into a column of bubbles. *But does a TV show qualify as legend? Maybe if it's in reruns…*

"Why don't we finish up here, and I'll walk you back to your apartment," he said.

"Why walk? Why don't you just transport us there instantly?"

He raised one eyebrow. Suddenly, he looked just like the Vulcan on TV who used to do that. Pointy ears, severe haircut, the works.

"Oh, come on. Now you're just messing with me."

He chuckled and returned to his former countenance. "Sorry. I couldn't resist."

"Believe me, I understand not being able to resist a good joke… but it *was* a joke, right?"

"Yes."

She balled up her napkin and gave her fingers a final wipe. "Weren't you afraid others in the diner would see you change your appearance like that?"

"Like what?" He tipped his head as if he had no idea what she was talking about.

"Like Dr. Spock."

"I think you mean Mr. Spock. Dr. Spock was a pediatrician and authority on parenting."

"Hmmm… I imagine you'd have to have a doctorate in *something* to run a spaceship."

Vulcan looked like he was about to burst out laughing. He covered his mouth as if to hold it in, but his eyes danced with mischief.

When he seemed more composed, he said, "I understand why Drake likes you. You're very… entertaining."

She didn't know if that was a compliment or not. At any rate, she was ready to get out of there. She waved the waitress over. "Check, please."

The bubble-gum-popping waitress said, "Sure thing, honey," and produced an order pad from her apron pocket, much like the one Bliss used herself.

"Are you getting the check or am I?" Vulcan asked.

Bliss thought he might not have any money, so she was prepared to pay with her credit card, but the idea of his treating her to breakfast held a certain appeal. It might make up for the frustrating company.

She leaned back. "You can pay, if you want to."

"Okay." He retrieved a wallet from his back pocket. "What do you use for currency here?" Opening his wallet revealed money in all sizes and colors.

"Uh… forget it. I'll pay with plastic."

"I was just kidding. I know how the dollar works."
He plunked down enough American cash to cover the
tab and a generous tip. "Let's get you home."

"Please. At least there I can hide in my room while
you watch TV or something."

"Awww... am I not good company?"

*Bite your tongue, Bliss... If he can transport you
through walls, he could probably drop you off in the
middle of a bridge abutment.*

Bliss talked Vulcan into dropping her off at home and
then going on his merry way. She said she'd use Drake's
code word and yell, "Taxi," if she needed him.

Wondering where Angie was, she strolled to her
bedroom. Maybe she could find a good book and spend
her day wrapped up in someone else's problems for a
change. Her door was partially open. *That's weird. I
usually close it.*

Upon walking in, she spotted Angie reading her journal.
"What the hell?"

Angie dropped the pad of paper and her face flushed.
"I—um... I'm sorry. I just came in to see if you had any
laundry I might put in with mine."

"And you just happened to find my diary and decided
to read it?"

"I thought it might be a grocery list. I'm going shopping afterward."

Bliss couldn't tell if Angie was being sincere or not.
How long had she been reading? If she'd followed her
nutty thoughts about Drake being a dragon... *Oh, shit.
How do I explain that?*

"I'm really sorry, but who has a diary with no cover? It's just a pad of paper."

"That's because it's not a regular diary. It's just a bunch of crazy thoughts that go through my head. Sometimes I get ideas for cards and I need to jot them down."

Angie worried her lip. "Those were thoughts for a card?"

Think fast, Bliss. Try to remember what you wrote. Oh shit. I started with "dear damn diary." "Or not. Sometimes I write down weird dreams first thing in the morning so I don't forget them. We all have weird dreams, right?"

"I guess..." Angie pointed to the floor where the damning evidence lay. "But this is so detailed. That must have one helluva dream."

"It was."

"I thought dreams only lasted a few seconds."

Damn it, Angie. Can't you just drop it? "I have a very creative mind."

Angie stared at the pad of paper. "I'll say..."

Bliss moved toward her roommate, intent on guiding her out of the room. "Look, why don't you—" As she reached for Angie, the frightened girl's eyes widened. She flinched and took a step back.

"What's the matter? I was just going to say that if you'll wait in the living room, I'll get whatever laundry I have together."

"Oh. Sure." Angie scooted around her and practically fled from Bliss's room.

Crap, crap, crap. She picked up her "damn diary" and scanned the contents.

A dragon? Seriously? A dragon. I think I've finally

met a guy who might be worth a shot and he turns out to be some kind of circus freak.

I'd never have believed him if I hadn't seen it with my own eyes. Transform? Yeah, right... Then he did it! Ack!

Okay. That could have been a dream... and then she read on.

I keep waiting to wake up and find out this is just a crazy nightmare. Nope. I've pinched myself and then slapped myself for pinching myself. Still not popping out of any coma.

I've even wondered if I was drugged. Drake never slipped me any pills. He didn't even bring me a beer. Nope. Nothing went into my mouth except, well... him. Heh-heh.

Hey, I wonder if dragon penis can cause hallucinations? Naw. That doesn't make sense. Because if it does, that means he's a dragon and I didn't hallucinate anything but the truth.

She dropped the pad on the bed. "I am so fucked."

Now what? *Should I yell "taxi" and traumatize my roommate further if an ugly old dude appears out of nowhere?* Bliss dismissed that idea quickly. What could he do anyway? She needed a time machine to help her go back to the moment she set her diary on her nightstand. Better yet, to the time before she'd written down all the stuff she'd promised not to tell anyone—ever.

She racked her brain for a solution as she pulled a few things out of her hamper. She heard the front door slam shut and realized Angie must have taken off. "Damn!"

Darting out of her room and around the corner, she noticed Angie's jacket was missing. So was her backpack. "Crap!" *I can't let her tell anyone else what she's read.*

At a complete loss as to what to do, Bliss stood in the middle of the room, looked at the ceiling, and called out, "Taxi." When no one appeared, she waited a few moments, raised her voice, and shouted, "Taxi!" Still nothing.

Frustrated, she stomped her foot and yelled, "Taxi, taxi, taxi!"

The front door opened and Drake rushed in with Angie on his heels.

Drake pulled her into his arms and held her close.

Angie stared at her with a worried expression. "D—don't worry, Bliss. Drake and I will find you a nice taxi."

Bliss closed her eyes and muttered, "Oh, for Christ's sake…"

Chapter 16

"I'LL TAKE IT FROM HERE, ANGIE." DRAKE STOOD next to Bliss and draped an arm over her shoulder.

Angie looked unsure about leaving and backed toward the door slowly. "Should I… call anyone?"

Bliss slipped her arm around Drake's waist and seemed to relax. "I'm perfectly all right, Angie. Really."

"Oookay. If you say so."

"We both do," Drake said.

Angie bit her bottom lip and didn't look convinced, but she finally reached the door and turned the handle. "I'll just go and do… something."

"Laundry?" Bliss asked cheerfully.

"Yeah. Laundry. That's where I was headed. I'll see you later."

"Hold on," Drake said. After a brief hesitation he added, "I might need you."

"Oh? Oh, yeah. I guess you might."

"Could you wait in your room for a few minutes?"

"With the door closed," Bliss said.

"Sure." Angie gave her a funny look as she scooted around her.

For God's sake, even if I was off my rocker, that wouldn't be contagious.

As soon as Angie's door closed, Drake and Bliss stared at each other.

"Poor Angie," Bliss whispered, then sat on the couch. "What did she tell you?"

"Not much. Just that she thought you were losing your mind."

"Is that all?"

Drake settled next to her and leaned in for a kiss. Bliss met him halfway. When their lips parted, they weren't alone anymore.

"Vulcan," she blustered in a loud whisper. "Will you ever learn to knock?"

"Sorry." He disappeared.

A moment later, a knock seemed to come from the air in front of them.

Bliss rolled her eyes. "Oh, for the love of—"

"Vulcan, buddy," Drake said, "come in."

The god appeared in front of them again. Drake couldn't help being amused by how easily Bliss ordered the god around and how he obeyed. She probably still didn't know he was a god. To her, he was part of a TV-show race, and that's how he and Vulcan wanted it to stay.

Bliss folded her arms. "What are you doing here?"

"You called me, remember?"

"Oh. That was so long ago, I'd forgotten. Where were you?"

Vulcan strolled around the living room, looking at the pictures on the walls and the books in the bookshelves. "I was engaged in a conversation with someone I couldn't simply run out on."

Ah, Drake thought. Mother Nature, most likely.

"Did you locate Zina?" Bliss asked.

"No." Vulcan addressed Drake. "Did she locate you?"

"No. I made myself plenty visible too. Hung out right in front of the bar."

Bliss rubbed his arm. "So that's how Angie found you so fast."

"Yeah. Why did she think you had lost your marbles?"

Bliss blew her bangs out of her eyes and hesitated. At last, she admitted. "She read my diary."

"You keep a diary?" Drake asked.

"Not really. It's just a little notepad I use when I get ideas for cards. This was the first time I actually used it as a diary."

Vulcan raised an eyebrow. "And what did she read?"

Bliss grimaced. "Look, I needed to talk about all the craziness of late, but I couldn't. I swore I'd never tell anyone, um… other things existed, and certainly not that I had one of them for a boyfriend. But after Drake's little confession the other night, I was a bit unsettled."

Drake rubbed her back. "That's putting it mildly."

Vulcan paced with his hands clasped behind his back. "I understand, but how did your roommate discover it?"

"She went into my room to see if I had any laundry she could do for me. She's always trying to be the perfect roommate—unfortunately. I think she misses the close friendship she had with her old roomie and wants us to become just as tight."

"She seems to be quite considerate," Drake said. "I don't see that as unfortunate. Well, except in this case."

"True. I tried to tell her it was all a dream and I'd jotted it down before I forgot the details. I figured she'd think I was going to tell you later so we could laugh about it."

Drake took her hand. "That was smart. Why didn't she believe you?"

"Because in the diary, I said I *wished* it was a dream, but it wasn't. So, now she thinks I'm crazy."

"Hmmm…" Vulcan seemed deep in thought. Hopefully he had an idea that could undo the damage. "Drake. You should tell Anthony about this."

Bliss shot to her feet. "Anthony? Why should he tell my boss? Do you want to get me fired?"

"Not at all. I think he might be able to help."

Drake rose and held Bliss's shoulders. "He knows how to hypnotize people. He could make Angie forget the whole thing."

Bliss raised her eyebrows. "Really?"

"Yeah. Just one problem… He never arrives before seven and Angie's shift will start a couple hours before that. Do you think she could keep quiet about it until he gets there?"

Bliss sighed. "Probably not. I sure wouldn't."

"Who would you tell?" Drake asked.

"Claudia. But she's my friend. That's how I got the job. Maybe Angie could be convinced to avoid worrying her and go straight to Anthony."

Drake thought it over and realized it was risky, but it might work. "If I could convince her to talk to the big boss privately in his office, she'd be right there so he can… do his thing. I can call him first and explain."

"How? Won't he wonder why I was writing crazy stuff in my journal?"

Damn. How do I tell her Anthony knows about me? I sure can't tell her that Anthony is a vamp and knows about everyone who frequents his paranormal bar. He decided to go with partial honesty. He'd stop short of blowing the identities of the other patrons. It wasn't his right to reveal that information anyway.

"Bliss, honey, Anthony is aware of my secret."

"He is? And he's okay with you hanging out in his bar?"

"Yes. He's… um… very understanding."

Bliss was silent for a few moments and appeared to be mulling it over. "I guess it could work. I still don't understand why you told Anthony. I thought other than Zina and Vulcan, I was the only one who knew."

Drake gave her a charming smile. "You're one of a very select few."

"Huh. Well, whatever. How do we proceed?"

"I suggest you and Vulcan leave so I can talk to Angie alone."

"Where will you say I went? To the booby hatch?"

He chuckled. "No, but it wouldn't hurt to say you made a doctor's appointment, just to get checked out."

"Great. She'll think I went to see a shrink about a dragon."

"Or that you decided to get a blood test to make sure there wasn't some kind of physical cause."

She jammed her hands on her hips. "I'm not admitting there's something wrong with me when there isn't."

Frustrated, he said, "Fine. I'll say you had a dentist appointment."

Bliss dropped her hands by her sides. "I guess that'll do." She faced Vulcan and said, "Okay. Shall we go get root canals?"

"Not me, thanks. My teeth are just fine."

"Then let's go get some ice cream with sticky caramel sauce and make some cavities."

Bliss stayed out of the way until it was time for her work shift. By the time she'd run upstairs to change into her uniform, Angie was already gone. *Perfect. I didn't want to answer any more of her questions anyway.*

When she arrived at the bar, she gave Angie a jaunty wave, but her roommate just ducked behind the bar and grabbed a rag. Then she proceeded to polish the bar with unnecessary force.

Uh-oh. That doesn't look good. Rather than worry about what Angie was thinking, Bliss simply glanced around at the customers to see who might be thirsty.

She went about her usual duties until Anthony arrived and entered the office. A few moments later, Claudia exited wearing her spring coat and carrying her purse. Bliss wanted to talk to her friend, but she left the bar so quickly, she must have had an errand to run.

Sadie caught Bliss's eye and waved her over.

"Hi, Sadie. Let me guess, you want a White Russian?"

"Later, dear. Right now I want to warn you about something I just saw in a vision."

Bliss wanted to plant her hand on her hip and say, "Really?" in a blasé tone, but she knew making fun of the psychic's "gift" would be frowned upon. Instead, she asked, "What did you uh… see?"

"Someone with malicious intent is coming."

Bliss glanced behind her. "Who? Where?"

"I wish I knew more. All I can say is the energy is disturbed. Someone with a great deal of rage is nearby."

Bliss sighed. "Nifty."

Sadie lowered her voice. "I don't think there's anything

you can do to intervene. I just wanted you girls to be aware of it, so you can take cover if things start to fly."

The hair on the back of Bliss's neck stood up. "Fly? What's going to fly?"

"Again, I'm sorry. I wish I could be more specific."

"You said 'girls.' Did you talk to Angie?" Bliss glanced over her shoulder and caught Angie staring at them, then she quickly returned to wiping down the bar. Malcolm, the other bartender, entered through the back door and Angie looked relieved.

"Yes. Both you and Angie were in my vision. Not Robin or Wendy. Just you two."

"Again... nifty. So *something* is going to happen. We can't stop it. All we can do is duck for cover. Is that it?"

"That's about it."

Bliss glanced over at the bar again and noticed Angie heading to Anthony's office. Malcolm was behind the bar, so it looked as if she'd been waiting for him to relieve her.

"Did you ask Angie to tell Anthony about this danger?"

"No. She might have decided to do it on her own, though. Angie's been here a long time. She might feel a little more protective of the bar than you do."

Bliss didn't like the implication that she didn't care about the bar. It provided her with a much-needed part-time job and a place to live. She was about to say so when Sadie glanced at the front door as it was opening, and a horrified expression flitted across her face. It was only there for the briefest of seconds, then she schooled her features and began shuffling her cards.

Bliss cast a glance over her shoulder to see what had upset her. A pretty blond in a red dress waltzed in, smiled, and waved to a few of the regulars. She looked harmless enough.

"Who's that?" Bliss asked.

Sadie didn't look up. She mumbled, "Ruxandra. Anthony's old girlfriend."

"Sheesh. You looked like you'd seen the devil himself walk in."

"I'm not sure you're wrong. She's trouble."

Bliss snorted. If that was the "vision" Sadie had talked about, there was nothing to worry about. Bliss hadn't met a blond she couldn't best in a battle of wits.

A customer in the next booth held up one finger.

"Well, I'd better get to work, Sadie. Thanks for the heads-up."

She nodded but didn't take her eyes off the cards.

Bliss happily waited on the other customers and headed to the bar to give Malcolm her order. She noticed the blond was missing. Perhaps she had come to see Anthony and was in his office. She was fairly sure Angie was still in there too.

Suddenly she heard shouting coming from inside the office. Even though the words were muffled, she could make out a shrill female voice. Angie raced out of there like her heels were on fire. She ducked down the back hall as if headed to the ladies' room, but instead Bliss heard the back door burst open.

Tory and Kurt were on their feet and moving toward Anthony's office. One of them clicked the door closed and leaned against it.

What the hell is happening?

At that moment, a fist smashed through the office door. Bliss saw a series of rings on the delicate fingers and deduced it must belong to the infamous Ruxandra. But how did she shatter a solid oak door? She must have hit it with adrenaline force.

The fist withdrew, but now with a hole in the door, everyone could hear what was being said. Well, everyone except Phil, who was hard of hearing. Regardless, he was riveted to the scene like everyone else.

"Calm down, Ruxandra," Anthony demanded.

"Why? Because I frightened your little chit?"

"It's not what you thought."

"Are you kidding? I'd have to be blind to miss the two of you gazing into each other's eyes. I should have known it was Angie all along."

"There's nothing going on between me and Angie."

"Liar!"

At the sound of items smashing, Tory opened the door and rushed in with Kurt right behind him. Phil moseyed over and stood just outside the office.

Bliss looked to Sadie for direction. If this was what she foresaw, maybe she knew where things were headed. The woman was spreading her cards out in front of her and flipping a few of them over.

Now? She's doing a reading now? Bliss was on her own. She stood on a chair and announced, "Patrons, I think it might be a good idea to leave and come back later."

A few tourists got up and moved toward the front door, but one guy she'd seen a few times swiveled his stool toward her and said, "No way. We haven't seen a good bar fight in months."

"Months?" She walked up to Sadie and planted her hand on the table right over her cards. "Did he say this happens every few months?"

Sadie sighed. "Any time Ruxandra perceives a threat to her relationship with Anthony."

"What relationship? I thought you said she was an old girlfriend... as in *ex*?"

Sadie rolled her eyes. "I'm afraid she and Anthony have different opinions on where they stand."

Bliss covered her eyes with her order pad. "Oh, for the love of..."

The door burst open with Tory and Kurt holding the kicking, screaming blond by each of her arms and carrying her toward the back door. Bliss wanted to shout, *Not that way! That's where Angie went,* but thought better of it.

If the woman thought she could catch up with Angie, she'd probably hunt her down and... *Oh crap*. The blond was making threats that involved Angie's exsanguination. Bliss shuddered for her roommate.

Phil led the procession to the back door, and Bliss moved carefully so she could see what was happening but still duck behind the bar if she needed to. As soon as Phil opened the door, he stepped into the alley and looked both ways. "She's safe," he said, and walked back into the bar.

The two men holding Ruxandra swung her back and forth, chanting, "And a one, and a two, and a threee..." On three they launched her into the air and slammed the door behind her.

"Oh. My. God." Bliss jogged to the bar. "Malcolm, aren't you going to call the cops?"

Anthony rushed out of his office. "Do *not* call the police."

Malcolm held up one hand. "I know the drill. You'll handle it."

The sound of pounding on the back door ensued, accompanied by more of Ruxandra's high-pitched shouting. The guys held the emergency exit bar shut against a number of heavy pulls. At one point, Bliss heard a loud crack and was afraid the door had come off its hinges.

Anthony groaned and stared at the door. The two guys gave him sympathetic smiles, nodded to each other, then opened the door and rushed out. More of Ruxandra's threats could be heard, but they were aimed at the guys. Thankfully, a few moments later the volume began to fade. It sounded as if the three of them were moving farther away.

Anthony returned to his office and slammed the door shut. Bliss could see him through the hole, pacing.

"Bliss, dear?" Sadie waved her over.

She approached the psychic half expecting a "See? I told you so," but instead the older woman just smiled at her and said, "I think I'll have that White Russian now."

The fire station was experiencing a welcomed lull. The guys seemed relaxed. Kelly and Benjamin were watching TV. Bruno was on the computer. Drake pretended to read. He couldn't concentrate on anything except what Zina might be up to next.

He had to call Bliss to make sure she was all right. Her shift was almost over, and he'd vowed to wait until it was. He checked his phone for the umpteenth time and *finally* it showed the time as eleven o'clock. He hit the speed-dial number for Bliss. Number three. He refused to make her number two, and the station had to be number one.

Several rings later, she picked up and he breathed a sigh of relief.

"Did I interrupt your cleanup duties?"

"Not really. We don't actually do a lot after closing. I understand there's a cleaning crew that comes in around midnight."

Ah, yes… the "cleaning crew" consisting of two house brownies. "Nice gig. So, where are you now?"

"Just on my way out the door."

"Is anyone with you?" He may have asked too quickly, but he had to know she was taking his appeal for an escort seriously.

After a brief hesitation she said, "Yeah. Anthony's right here. Do you want to talk to him?"

He let out a deep breath and said, "No. I'm just glad you have a bodyguard."

She was quiet again for a few moments.

"Bliss?"

"I'm here. Drake, are we going to have to do this much longer?"

"It depends on Zina."

"Any sightings?"

"No, and that makes me nervous."

He heard her thanking Anthony and assumed she must be inside her apartment. A moment after he heard the door click, Bliss began whispering frantically.

"Oh my God, you wouldn't believe the insane night I've had."

"Why? What happened?" *Shit, and here I thought I might be able to relax for five minutes.*

"Anthony's old girlfriend showed up."

"Ruxandra?"

"Yeah. That's what Sadie called her—although she didn't actually talk to her. Well, Angie was in the office with Anthony, and this blond bombshell went off like a, well, a bomb!"

Drake dropped his head in his hand. "Oh, crap. I've heard about her legendary jealous fits, although I've never seen one. Please tell me Angie's all right."

"She took off but never came back. Hang on... let me check her room."

Drake waited an anxious moment.

"Nope. She's not here."

Crap. "Did Ruxandra go after her?"

"If so, Angie got a good head start."

That didn't help ease Drake's worry for the young bartender. Ruxandra was a vampire. She could smell her and outrun her.

"Wait. I just got a text."

"Is it from her?" Drake mentally crossed his fingers.

"Yeah. She says she's staying with a friend tonight. Not to worry. She's safe."

"Whew. I'm glad to hear that."

Bliss put on her sexy voice and said, "That means I'm all alone tonight. Care to come over and get my cat out of a tree?"

He lowered his voice. "I'd love to, but I don't dare leave the guys, just in case."

"Well, maybe I'll use my newfound privacy to take a long bubble bath or something."

"Mmm... I'll picture that as I'm falling asleep. Maybe I can join you in an erotic dream or two."

She sighed. "I guess that will have to do."

Zina couldn't believe her lucky break. The back door to the bar was almost off its hinges. One good tug and she'd be inside.

She grabbed the metal handle and yanked. Surprised, she stumbled back a few inches when the whole door came off in her hand. Stifling a maniacal laugh, she glanced around the alley to make sure no one had heard the noise—no need to add more suspicion if she laughed out loud.

Fortunately, no one appeared out of the shadows, and no lights came on upstairs. *Almost too easy.* She set the door aside and strolled into the bar. *No need to rush. Why not savor the moment?*

She flipped up the hinged section of the bar top and perused the various bottles of liquor. There was a nice selection of top-shelf spirits, as one would expect in a bar on classy Beacon Hill.

One scotch on the rocks, please. On second thought, hold the ice. I'm going to need a nice hot mouth soon. She grinned and poured herself a tumbler of scotch, then poured the rest of the bottle over the bar. *What fun!*

She took a swig of her scotch, letting the liquid burn her throat—in a good way. She shook her head hard and chuckled her approval. *Nice stuff, but that empty bottle looks lonely.*

Zina set bottle after bottle on the bar, opening each one. She threw the caps and corks on the floor. No need to be neat when the whole place was going to be ash in a few minutes. When she'd finished her scotch, she was giddy. She staggered out to the main floor and grabbed two bottles at a time—one in each hand.

Wobbling from one table to another, she drank and poured, drank and poured. Soon the entire contents of the now-empty top shelf coated every surface. And just for good measure, she splashed quite a bit on the walls, too.

"Time for my grand exit," she muttered.

Standing in the corridor that led to the back door, she removed her shoes and stayed on the only dry spot. Zina quickly stripped off her clothing and shifted into her dragon form. Gripping her clothes in her talons, not wanting to leave a single clue behind, she took a giant step backward toward the door—or more accurately, the hole in the building that used to be the door.

She inhaled deeply and leaned forward as she blew out a column of fire about twenty feet long. The room erupted in flames. She waited just long enough to be sure the sprinklers in the ceiling were as woefully inadequate as she'd expected.

With a giggle of glee, she took off into the night and waited atop one of the buildings high on the hill so she could watch the place go up in flames. She'd have to use her imagination to picture Drake as he tried in vain to save her nemesis, but the mental image was worth a thousand laughs.

Chapter 17

BLISS AWOKE TO THE SMOKE ALARM BLARING AND IMmediately kicked into high gear. She couldn't believe this was happening again! She didn't bother getting dressed—just grabbed her precious laptop and a robe, then fled to the apartment door.

"Wait. The CD," she said out loud. She had just received the backup design disk from the bank and it was in her room. "Screw it."

As she was about to open the door, she felt heat on the other side and ran to the window where the fire escape was. *Was* being the operative word. The damn thing was leaning away from the building on bolts that looked rusted through. *Crap! When did that happen?* Now there was no other way out. *Damn old buildings.*

She heard pounding on her door. Maybe Drake was here to save her again. She rushed over and threw it open. To her surprise, Adolf Balog stood there.

"Where's the other one?" he asked.

"Angie's at a friend's house." *Lucky Angie.*

"Hurry. Upstairs," he said.

One glance and she understood why. Fire was licking up the wooden steps from below. "Won't we get trapped up there?"

"No. There's a secret passageway to the next building under the roof."

"Let's go," she shouted and hurried up the staircase behind him.

Mr. and Mrs. Balog were already prying open the door to the attic. Why they didn't have a key she had no idea, but at least they knew a way out existed.

"Pop the hinges, Father," Adolf said.

"I've almost got it." Mr. Balog grunted, and with one more herculean effort, the lock broke, allowing everyone entrance to the attic. The men stood back and allowed Mrs. Balog to climb the narrow wooden staircase first. Then with a grand, sweeping gesture Adolf indicated Bliss was next. *What a time to be chivalrous!* But it was heart-warming to realize heroes came in all shapes and sizes.

What she had to climb wasn't a ladder, but Bliss had to turn her size nine feet sideways to avoid falling off the tiny steps. *People must have had much smaller feet back in the seventeen-hundreds.*

At last all four of them were under the rafters on their hands and knees. Mrs. Balog said something in a language Bliss didn't understand, but she figured it meant something like, "Follow me" or "This way."

Bliss cradled her precious laptop against her chest, which gave her only one hand to hop across the dusty floor.

"Leave the computer," Adolf said from behind her.

"Not on your life," Bliss said, and then she realized how appalling that sounded under the circumstances. "Um… I mean, I can't."

"Fine. Hurry."

Why hadn't the fire department arrived yet? Bliss wondered. Yes, it was the middle of the friggin' night, but didn't they have their clothes and boots next to their beds all ready to jump into?

Bliss noticed what looked like a couple of doll beds and some doll clothes. *Did kids really play up here?* Because of the momentary distraction, she almost rammed Mrs. Balog in the ass. Finally they had arrived at the end of the loft.

The older woman found the door to the next building, turned a wooden latch and gave it a shove. Surprisingly, that was the only security to keep the next-door neighbors from crawling over the Balogs' heads. *I guess back in the day people trusted each other.* Then Bliss remembered the locked attic door. *Or not.*

"We should go two or three buildings over," Bliss said, even though her wrist was beginning to hurt from hopping on one hand. "My boyfriend is a firefighter and said sometimes if they can't get to the fire fast enough, the next building will go up too."

Mr. Balog rattled off some words in another language and Mrs. Balog nodded. A moment later, they were crawling again.

Why me, Lord? Do you really want me to drop out of this competition or something? At last Bliss heard the faint wail of sirens. *Thank God. Drake, what took you so long?*

Their little parade paused at the next door just long enough to turn the latch and crawl through. Mrs. Balog located the stairs and led the four of them down to someone else's attic. Then she pounded on the door with both fists.

Shit. It hadn't occurred to Bliss that they could be trapped in a wall if no one let them out. The Balogs weren't calling out to anyone, so it was up to her.

"Hey! People! Let us out before we become crispy critters!"

A lump lodged in Drake's throat when he heard the address of the job they were responding to. It was midnight, and the place was fully engulfed by the time they got there. He suspected a certain dragon lady had been planning this all along. If he could get his hands around her throat, he might forget she was a female.

The windows had burst from the intense inferno inside, and rather than wait for his fellow firefighters to bash down the front door, he grabbed a hose and leaped through the opening. He was glad he was the first one in there; otherwise the humans would have met with a shocking surprise.

Two little men, no more than a foot tall, stood on the bar spraying soda water at whatever they could reach. Their droopy felt hats and suits would have caught fire except that they seemed to have sprayed themselves first. The miniature firefighters glanced up at Drake, dropped the soda sprayer, and looked as if they were prepared to run away—right into the blaze.

"Wait," Drake shouted. "Let me help you."

He reached them in a couple of long strides and opened his jacket. "In here." He grabbed his suspenders and stretched them out enough to make a pocket in his pants to accommodate the little guys. They glanced at each other with their alien-like, totally black, almond-shaped eyes, then leaped off the bar and into the safety Drake was offering them.

"You're not afraid of us?" one of them asked in a Munchkin-like voice.

"Afraid of a couple of house brownies? Nope. Are you afraid of dragons?"

"Yes," both of them answered simultaneously.

It figured. *I hope I don't shift*. "Just stay out of sight." Drake zipped up his jacket, hiding the little fellows who were clinging to his suspenders. His fellow firefighters had finally managed to break down the front door. When Benjamin rushed inside, Drake handed him the hose and said, "I have to find Bliss."

Benjamin had to shout to be heard over the crackling blaze and the powerful spray of the hose. "Is she here? Now?"

"She lives upstairs," he yelled.

"Always in heat for your hottie, aren't you?"

Drake ignored the obvious dig and quickly disappeared into the back.

If she made it out, she must have used the fire escape. He hadn't seen any residents standing on the street out front. He prayed that he'd see her far down the alley, safely out of the way.

Drake was surprised that the back door was missing. That must have been how Zina got in. He rushed out into the night and frantically cast a glance all around, hoping to see Bliss somewhere. The fire escape hadn't been lowered. In fact, it looked like it was about to fall off the brick facade. Meanwhile, the roof of the bar caved in.

Crap. He unzipped his jacket and said, "Out you go, boys. You're safe now."

The brownies hopped out of his pants and landed on the pavement. They paused just long enough to thank him and waved as they ran away.

He heard one of them mutter, "Boys. Hmmph."

True, they had white hair and beards, and goodness

knows how old they could have been. They might even be immortal like he was… rather, like he used to be.

Drake backed away, hoping only smoke had reached the upper floors. Smoke was deadly too, but he had on lifesaving equipment. If the floors could support him… Horrified, he watched as fire roared and smoke billowed out of every window.

He was needed back inside, but there was no way he could survive without shifting into his dragon form. Fucking Zina. She wanted this to happen. He threw his jacket on the ground and was about to drop his pants in order to shift so he could fly up to Bliss's apartment on his dragon wings.

A window in the building next door opened and a couple of frightened men stepped out onto the fire escape. It's a good thing Drake was there. They had no idea how to use it and simply froze. Drake directed them down and stayed to help the other five people from the third and fourth floors. Damn it.

Hoping Bliss had gone somewhere safer, Drake pointed at the charred shell behind him and asked, "Did anyone from this building come over to yours?"

The residents glanced at each other and shook their heads. One of the men who came down first said, "We opened the front windows to see what was happening, and the fire chief said to go out the back, using the fire escape. They were about to hose down our building too."

"Do you think our building will burn?" one of the women asked, trembling.

"Probably not. They do that as precaution." Although with the heat of this particular blaze, Drake figured anything wooden and dry might catch. That's why the chief had sent them to the fire escape, not the stairs.

But where was Bliss? And what about the Balogs? He knew Angie was out for the night, but that left at least one family who may or may not have been paranormals and his very mortal girlfriend.

The nearest side street was only two buildings down, so he directed the residents to get to the chief out front and report that they were all accounted for.

"Go."

When they didn't move faster than a stroll, his frustration got the better of him and he yelled, "Run!"

A couple people glanced over their shoulders briefly, then they all took off at a flat run.

Finally, I can get up there and look for Bliss. Drake made sure all the people he had helped were safely out of sight before he shed his clothes. Then he shifted until he could spread his dragon wings and flew up to the second-floor windows.

At last Bliss heard voices on the other side of the attic door. A key rattled; the door opened; and four dusty, exhausted people tumbled into the room of a very surprised couple.

"What the heck…" the man began to say.

His wife or girlfriend asked, "Did you escape the fire through the attic?"

"Yeah," Bliss said. "Thanks for letting us out." She set her computer on the bedside table and rubbed her sore wrist.

Mr. Balog bowed formally. "We apologize for

entering your home like this. I am afraid it couldn't be avoided."

Gee, ya think? Bliss almost laughed out loud. It sounded as if the Balogs had been invited to tea, not escaping a harrowing death.

Suddenly Bliss realized that perhaps this wasn't the first time the Balogs had escaped something nasty. She could picture them hiding and running from communists or something. The strange language sounded Slavic. *Honestly, the stupid things that run through my mind sometimes. I should be thanking them for saving my life.*

Bliss embraced Mrs. Balog. The woman stiffened, but when Bliss murmured, "Thank you," she relaxed and patted Bliss's back.

In English she answered, "You are welcome."

Drake soared through the window that led to Bliss's bedroom and hovered over the parts of the floor that were still intact. She was nowhere to be seen. He could see his buddies below still battling the blaze. He had to go up in case Bliss and the Balogs were waiting for rescue on the third floor.

He sought a place out of sight of the firefighters if they were to look up. In the back bedroom, which would have been Angie's, he scanned the area for some place to break through to the next floor. Grasping a heavy lamp in his talons, he smashed it against a spot in the ceiling that looked weak. Plaster rained down on him, which he didn't care about. However, additional pieces fell below and his firefighter buddies jumped out of the way.

Shit. Seconds later, he heard the window above burst.

A way in! He flew out the second-floor window and up to the third floor. Fire blasted out that window, so he sucked in a deep lungful of air and flew through it.

His eyes watered, but he could still see. He flew from room to room and found no one. *Thank God.* Maybe they'd made it out safely after all. He took one last look and spotted the attic door open. *Oh, crap. Could they be hiding up there?*

He flew up to the rafters and looked left, then right. No one was there. Suddenly another awful possibility occurred to him. *What if Zina took her?*

Dejected, Drake scanned the area for onlookers and found it was safe to descend to the ground and shift. As soon as he was dressed again, he took off for the side street at a flat run. He couldn't lose hope yet. Maybe she was standing out front.

As he rounded the corner, he saw residents all along the block leaning out of their windows, trying to see what was going on.

"Drake!" someone yelled.

He slowed down, scanned the building up to the top floor, and saw Bliss leaning out the fourth-floor window. She appeared a little ragged but unharmed. To him she had never looked more beautiful.

"Are you all right?"

"Yes," she called down. "Thanks to the Balogs."

"Are they there with you?"

Adolf appeared in the window. "We are all here. All safe."

"Thank God."

Bliss held up something rectangular. "I even managed to save my computer this time!"

He would have laughed, but they were interrupted.

"Jesus fuckin' Christ, Cameron!"

Oh, shit. The chief was striding toward him and looked none too happy. Bliss ducked back inside, probably remembering the last time she got him into trouble.

"Nice of you to join us," Chief Tate shouted. "Nobody knew where the hell you were."

Drake checked his radio. "Sorry, chief. I think this thing might not be working."

"Check it later. Right now we need to figure out if anyone's still inside."

"Everyone's out," Drake answered.

"And how do you know that?"

Drake pointed upward to the window where Adolf was still leaning out. "They're all up there."

The chief looked up. "Is that true, kid?"

"Yes," Adolf called. "We're all accounted for."

"Thank God for small favors," the chief mumbled.

One of the female residents Drake had helped to evacuate walked up to the chief and pointed over her shoulder with her thumb. "That man there helped us get down the fire escape. He deserves a medal."

The chief shook his head at the ground and muttered, "Of course, he does." Drake was probably the only one who knew the guy was being sarcastic.

Bliss and Angie stood on the sidewalk the following morning, scanning the devastation to their home and jobs.

Bliss hugged herself. "I had just printed all my cards to proof them before sending everything to the professional printer. I guess losing those isn't a big deal when you consider no one lost their lives."

"You lost all your hard work? Again?"

"No. Just the proofs and my cheap-ass printer. I still have the designs and my laptop."

"Whew." After a long pause, Angie shook her head. "I can't believe it. Ruxandra may have inadvertently saved my life. If it weren't for her, I'd have been in the apartment with you and not on my friend's couch, hiding under a blanket."

Bliss took a step away and gazed at her roommate. "Seriously? You were hiding under a blanket."

"Only for a few minutes. Brandee finally made me believe that Nick wouldn't let anything happen to me… and I had to come up for wine."

Bliss chuckled because she'd have done anything for a glass of wine last night. She stared again at the total destruction in front of them. *Fat chance of getting one here.*

"So… do you remember what set off Ruxandra?" Bliss had been hoping and praying that Anthony was able to hypnotize her roommate before they were interrupted. So far Angie hadn't said anything about the damning "diary" or dragons, or indicated that Bliss might have lost her mind.

"It's funny, but I really don't. I was about to ask Anthony something… and I can't even remember what it was now. Ruxandra screamed about us staring into each other's eyes like she thought we were lovers. It must have been her usual paranoia about Anthony hooking up with one of his staff."

Hiding the relieved smile that must have made a brief

appearance on her face, Bliss shook her head. "That's one thing I won't miss."

Angie looked at her, surprised. "You mean there's something you *will* miss about this place?"

"Of course there is!" Bliss put her arm around her roommate's shoulder. "I'll miss you, for sure. You've been the best, most considerate roommate I've ever had."

Angie laid her head on Bliss's shoulder. "Awww… you're just saying that."

"Not at all. It's true." Other things she would miss were more nebulous. She'd miss the friendly camaraderie of the regulars, Sophie's White Russians, Claudia… but most of all, she'd miss her independence.

"So, where will you go now?" Angie asked.

Bliss groaned. "The only place I can afford that won't resent my presence after a day or two. My parents' house."

Angie gasped and stared at her with an expression of horrified sympathy. "Oh, no. I know how much you hate it there. Couldn't you move in with Drake?"

Bliss would have loved that, but picturing the two of them in that one cramped room was impossible. "I stayed there last night, but he was at the station. It's too early in our relationship to be on top of each other—well, you know what I mean…"

Angie laughed. Bliss was glad to hear her laugh about something, even if it was her own Freudian slip. "Anyway, that's one good way to kill a romance."

"I suppose." Then as if something just occurred to her, Angie gasped. "The competition! Are you still able to participate? I mean, they were coming the day after tomorrow, right?"

"Yes. I called the producer this morning. They'll

meet with me at my parents' house, and I'll just have to insist my mother behave herself."

"What are you afraid she'll do?"

Bliss pinched the bridge of her nose. "She'll announce that I'm single and probably look right into the camera and claim any man would be lucky to have a woman who can cook and clean like she taught me."

Angie covered her mouth and tried, unsuccessfully, to hide a smile.

Bliss didn't give her a chance to pursue that conversation further. "You should have heard the glee in the producer's voice when I told her I had been in not one, but *two* fires and had to recreate all my designs."

"I guess that'll make for good TV."

"Exactly. I don't know why I expected she'd react differently, but she never asked, 'Wow, are you hurt?' or 'Is there anything we can do to help?' You know what she said?"

"What?"

"She said, 'Holy shit, the viewers will *love* that!' Apparently I'm already the fan favorite, but when the show with the finalists and their families airs, and everyone hears about the catastrophes I had..." Bliss rolled her eyes.

"Hey, you should get *something* out of all this." Angie rubbed Bliss's back. "Did you call your mother to tell her you're coming home?"

Remembering how her mother reacted the last time she'd heard her precious daughter had barely escaped death, Bliss sighed. "No."

"I have my cell phone if you want to use it."

"Thanks, but no. I figured I'd be better off telling her

in person this time. As long as she can see me standing, walking, and talking, she might react a little better than last time. And that's just a maybe."

"I'm sure she'll be relieved to know you're all right."

Bliss snorted. "Yeah, after she rails at the ceiling, asking God what I've done to deserve this. Then, assuming I know the answer to that, she'll insist I go to confession and follow whatever edict the priest gives me to save my tarnished soul."

"Or maybe she'll just pray for you."

Bliss chuckled. "You don't know my mother."

Drake sat in the chair opposite Chief Tate's desk. *What did I do now?*

When the chief finally walked into his office, he didn't even sit down. "You're going to the EAP, Drake."

"The Employee Assistance Program? Why?"

"Because I think you should."

"I don't need…"

Chief Tate held up one hand to silence him. "I didn't say you had a choice."

"But I'm fine." Drake turned his chair to face him. "I don't understand. I had on my protective gear, I'm not coughing…"

"I'm not sending you for smoke inhalation… although that might be a good thing to look at and see if it's clouding your brain."

"Huh?"

"I *could order* you to get a psych eval. I could say you have a death wish and are not only endangering your own life, but the lives of other firefighters."

Drake shot to his feet. "*What?*"

The chief folded his arms and set his jaw, as if accepting Drake's challenge. "You're going. It'll look better if you ask for the appointment yourself and talk to someone confidentially. I need to know if you have a death wish. If not, I'll be glad to keep you on."

"What the hell are you talking about?"

"From what I've seen and heard over the past few weeks, you've been taking too many chances and tempting fate. I thought you were in the bar when it collapsed, and that's when I made my decision."

"You thought you'd send my dead body for a psych eval?"

"No, dimwit. I promised myself if you got out alive, I'd send you for some kind of help *before* you wound up dead… and God knows how many more I might lose, trying to rescue you. I hate attending firefighters' funerals."

"That makes two of us."

Drake didn't like what he was hearing, but he had to admit the chief had cause. Anyone paying attention would eventually realize he was always the first one in and the last one out. It might look bad to those who didn't know he was fireproof… in other words, everyone.

"Chief," Drake tried to relax. "I understand how it might look, but I assure you I'm very happy with my life. I don't have a death wish."

"Fine. Tell it to the shrink, or whoever the EAP hooks you up with. If he thinks you need help, you'll do what he tells you. Understood?"

Drake rubbed his eyes and muttered, "I don't believe this."

"Oh, you can believe it, all right."

"You're not *committing* me or anything… There's still a chance the EAP will send me home with a warning to be more careful, isn't there?"

The chief shrugged. "I have no idea what he'll decide, but whatever that is, you'll do it."

Drake felt like a two-year-old who'd been scolded for running with scissors. "So when do I need to go?"

"How's now for you?"

"I guess now works."

"Great. Dismissed."

Chapter 18

"MOM, I NEED YOU TO PROMISE ME, WHEN THE PRO-
ducer and camera crew get here you'll be on your
best behavior."

Malinda Russo bristled. "What on earth are you talking about? Why would you think I'd be anything less
than gracious?"

"I don't think you'd be rude or anything… at least
not on purpose."

Bliss's mother jammed her hands on her hips.
"What's that supposed to mean?"

"This is very important to me," Bliss peeked through
the lace curtain and saw the truck pull up with the camera crew. "And to them."

Malinda waved away her daughter's concern. "Oh,
for heaven's sake. I may have thought it was just a silly
competition before, but now that I see how much it
means to you, I'll be nothing but supportive."

Bliss hugged her. "Thank you, Mom." As soon as she
let go, she had to add, "And no trying to fix me up with
the cameraman or lighting crew. Got it?"

Malinda rolled her eyes. "Why would you think I'd
do that?"

Bliss hesitated. Sometimes honesty wasn't the best
policy. "No reason."

"Are they Italian?"

Bliss blew the bangs out of her eyes. "That's why!

For heaven's sake, Mom. I don't know and I don't care if they're Italian, Polish, or space aliens… You *will not* mention that I need a husband—or put across the idea in any other grouping of words. *Capiche*?"

"Fine, fine." Her mother waved her hands and left the room, insisting, "I get it, Miss Independent," on her way into the kitchen.

Bliss prayed her mother really did understand and would leave the unmarried men alone. One of the judges was male but as gay as they came. Her mother's gaydar might go on the fritz because he was a handsome guy and might look like a good father for Malinda's future grandchildren.

The doorbell rang and Bliss sucked in a deep breath. Then she forced herself to relax and answered the door, while her mother looked on.

A cameraman stood on their front stoop. "You're Bliss Russo, right?"

"Yes. Come in."

He waved to someone behind him and called out, "This is the place."

In minutes, people, lighting, cameras, and cords invaded the small living room. Mrs. Russo peeked out from the kitchen and her jaw dropped. Bliss offered her mother a comforting smile, which she returned while seeming to relax a smidge.

Maybe this will go all right after all.

"We're going to set up out there to catch your expression when the host arrives," the cameraman said, pointing to the stoop, "and here to see hers when you greet her." He set his marks and the lighting guys set their professional light panels.

"Then, I'd suggest you lead her into your kitchen and introduce her to your big Italian family."

Oh shit. "You want the whole family here?"

"Well, yeah. That's what the producers were expecting."

"I thought it was usually just a roommate or friend…"

"Nope. They want the whole shebang. Let me see the kitchen." He strode into the kitchen without Bliss showing him the way.

"Um… Would you like some coffee?" Mrs. Russo offered.

"No. Just checking out how many people you can get around the table. Maybe you can whip up a big Italian meal and invite the host to sit down with you. She'll take a bite, tell you how good it is, then talk about Bliss's childhood and…"

"My childhood! Oh, my freakin' God. Don't you mean the greeting card company my sister started and how I took it over, and… and…"

"Naw. The viewers know all that. They want to get to know the finalists the way their family and friends know them."

"Oh, how exciting! I'll call your brothers right now… oh, and we'll need to use the dining room. I'll set it with the nice tablecloth and our wedding china…"

Bliss dropped her head into her hands. "Calgon, take me away."

The cameraman snapped his fingers. "Oh yeah. Do you have a makeup person coming?"

"No. I usually do my own makeup."

"Yeah, but you learned how to do it for the camera. Your family didn't."

"I didn't expect this big Italian family dinner."

"Do you want the producers to find someone to help? It's kind of last minute. I thought you got all this info beforehand."

Bliss sighed. "Maybe I did. Maybe it was in my apartment that burned down a month ago, or maybe it was in the pile of mail I didn't get to open Friday night, because *that* building burned down too."

The cameraman stared at her wide-eyed. "Jesus. Are you cursed or some kind of firebug?"

Bliss's mother quickly crossed herself. "Bite your tongue. It has nothing to do with either of those things. It was just bad luck… or maybe good luck since the firefighter who saved her life is now her boyfriend."

"Seriously?" The cameraman grinned. "Fantastic! That's a great angle. Can you get him over here too?"

Oh, dear God. Please don't make me put Drake through this.

Mrs. Russo clapped her hands. "Oh, yes! Bliss, invite Drake."

Bliss wanted to hang herself. Instead, she saw an opportunity to escape some of the sibling teasing she knew would be in store for her. She rested a hand on her hip. "Tell you what. I'll call him if I don't have to invite my brothers, but there are no guarantees Drake will be free."

"I'll call the producers," he said. "You just get that boyfriend of yours to come."

Bliss smirked. *I wish I could take that another way.*

Drake was sitting in the EAP's office when his phone rang. He grabbed it and glanced at the screen. *Bliss.*

"Sorry, I've got to take this."

The gentleman nodded.

Drake strode to the waiting room before he answered. "Bliss? What's up?"

"I—uh. I was wondering if you're free… now."

Drake glanced back at the inner office. He'd tried to convince the EAP he was not in need of an appointment and the chief had overreacted, but he wasn't off the hook yet.

"I should be free in a few. Why?"

"The show's producers really want you here when they interview me."

"Me? Why?"

"Because it's some kind of great angle for the TV show—me dating the firefighter who saved my life. They just love this human-interest shit."

Drake chuckled. "So, what you're saying is, I get fifteen minutes of fame and you have a better chance of winning the competition."

"Exactly."

Hmmm… that might be a great way to remind the chief that I'm doing my job and doing it well… not trying to kill myself and take as many guys with me as I can.

"Sure. I should be there in about an hour."

"Thanks. I love you for that."

"Only that?"

Bliss whispered, "I'd tell you all the other great stuff I love about you, but I'm not alone."

Drake heard her mother's voice. "I knew it! They're in love."

"Mom! Get off the damn phone."

One hearty giggle later, Drake heard a click.

Bliss let out an audible sigh. "Jesus, Drake, I'm sorry

about that. If you want to skip it, I'll understand. I'm
afraid she might try to measure you for a tux."

He chuckled. "Let her. You never know... See you
in an hour."

Drake hung up and marched into the EAP's office.

"I'm not suicidal. I don't need to talk to anyone, and
I've got a girlfriend who needs me at the moment. I'm
out of here."

Bliss hung up the phone with myriad emotions swirling
through her. What should she do first? Give her mother
hell for picking up the other phone and listening in?
Chastise herself for letting it happen? Or contemplate
what Drake meant when he said, "You never know..."?

Bliss chose to contemplate, and a tiny smile spread
across her face as she did. If she were twelve, she'd be
writing Mrs. Drake Cameron in a notebook. Fortunately
she was an adult now and knew it was too soon. She
simply gave herself a mental high five and opened her
mind to the future possibility.

"I'm sorry I overheard your conversation, Bliss,"
her mother said sheepishly as she entered the upstairs
master bedroom.

"No you're not."

Her mom grinned. "You're right. I'm not." She strode
over to her daughter and enveloped her in a warm hug.
"I'm happy for you."

If anyone would be happy for me, it's my mother.

Bliss hugged her back. "Thanks, Mom, but please
don't get carried away."

"I'd be offended by that, but you're right. I'm afraid

I've jumped the gun in the past, and maybe that's what put you off marriage."

Gee, ya think? "Mom, I know you just want me to be happy, but I'm afraid your enthusiasm could scare away any potential future I might have with a guy."

"Not if it's the *right* guy." Her mother's smile returned.

Bliss had to think about that. How easy would it have been for Drake to walk away when Zina started causing trouble? She didn't think he was protecting her out of a sense of duty. Well, *not only* for that reason. He was a good man with an ethical code, and he wouldn't say he loved her if he didn't mean it.

Bliss was just about to forgive her mother for years of pushiness when Mrs. Russo said, "Now, aren't you glad that old building burned down?"

What? Is she kidding? Oh, for the love of… "Sheesh. I wouldn't go that far, Mom. A lot of people lost everything they owned. Myself included."

Her mother looped an arm around Bliss's waist. "Oh, but look what you gained."

Bliss let out a long sigh. Her mom was her mom, and trying to change her would be an exercise in frustration.

The director, Bliss, and Malinda sat at the kitchen table, waiting for the host to show up. "So, tell us what Bliss was like as a child."

Bliss cringed but knew Malinda Russo could talk about her children all afternoon. Hopefully, this dry run would help guide her mother so she'd know what to say before they filmed it. Of course, if the director thought something was particularly cute or funny, he might ask her to repeat it for the camera. Bliss crossed her fingers under the table.

Malinda smiled sweetly and sighed. "My youngest was the perfect child. So kind and selfless. Always helping around the house…"

To say Bliss was stunned was an understatement. *Who is her mother talking about? I am her youngest… at least I thought I was. So why isn't she telling the world what a hellion I was and how I gave her three-quarters of her gray hairs… like she usually does.*

The doorbell rang at that moment, and Bliss practically jumped out of her chair. "That must be Drake. I'll get it."

Malinda followed her. "Or it could be your brothers…"

Bliss stopped in her tracks and whirled on her mother. "Are you kidding me? I thought the deal was if I called Drake, you *wouldn't* call Emilio and Ricky, and since when do they knock?"

Malinda pointed to the director. "Well, this nice man here said I should. I'm sorry. I've forgotten your name."

He rose and buttoned his suit jacket. "Boguchwal Mickolajczyk."

"Hmmm… I may forget again. Do you have a nickname?"

He smiled indulgently. "Yes. You can call me Bo."

Malinda followed Bliss to the door, mumbling something about long, difficult Polish names. Bliss almost said something about long Italian names, but Malinda wouldn't equate the two—ever. Bliss made sure she reached the door first and opened it, only to have her brothers push past her.

Ricky ruffled her hair. "Hey, squirt."

"Christ, Ricky! Do you know how long it took me to do my hair and makeup today?"

Emilio snorted. "Oh, that's right. You're a big movie star now, huh?"

"Oh, for frig's sake, it's TV and you know it. Ma, did you *have to* invite them?"

Malinda threw her hands in the air. "As I said before, your producer told me to. I'm just trying to cooperate... like you asked."

Bliss almost swallowed her tongue when she realized the cameras were rolling. That must be why the guys rang the bell. To warn the cameraman to start rolling.

The boys made a beeline for the kitchen.

Ricky said, "I smell Ma's chicken parmigiano-reggiano."

"Don't you touch that," Malinda called out as she followed her sons. "I want it to look perfect on television."

Bliss rolled her eyes. *Like her dinner is going to be the center of attention.* Though she had to admit, it usually was.

She looked directly at the cameraman. "Can you possibly roll that back and erase it?"

He smiled and kept filming. "You know I can't. If Bo wants to edit it out, he will."

She blew the bangs out of her eyes, then strolled to the mirror to check how badly Ricky had ruined her hair.

The door opened and a cameraman poked his head in. "Judith is here, Bliss. It's showtime." He closed the door again and the second cameraman focused on the front door, ready to capture the big moment.

Butterflies used to invade her stomach in the beginning of filming the show, but Bliss thought she had gotten used to it. Apparently that wasn't true, because moths were flapping around in there now.

The doorbell rang and Bliss quickly finger-combed her hair into place. She tried to look natural as she strode to the door and opened it.

"Hi, Judith," she tried to say enthusiastically upon seeing the tall blond who had cruelly trashed someone's work in every episode.

To her shock, Judith kissed her on both cheeks.

"Bliss! How marvelous to see you again. I can't wait to hear all about your hard work over the last six weeks. I understand it was even more difficult because of some unusual circumstances."

Bliss groaned inwardly while keeping a pleasant smile plastered on her face. She knew exactly what the attention grabber was talking about. Judith wanted her to elaborate on the near disasters—not the work she'd done creating her Hall-Snark cards.

As she'd been coached, Bliss said, "It's wonderful to see you too, Judith. Come in. I'd like you to meet my family." *Yeah, right. I'd like to hide them in the bushes in the backyard.*

She led the woman into her mother's kitchen where Malinda stirred an empty pot on the stove. Her brothers were sitting at the kitchen table along with her father, who'd apparently decided to leave his man-cave in the basement and make an appearance.

The three men rose and waited to be introduced, almost as if they'd developed manners in the last three minutes. Malinda wiped her perfectly clean hands on her apron and joined the family ticking time-bomb.

"Judith Applebottom, these are my parents, Malinda and Romeo Russo, and my brothers, Ricky and Emilio."

The host stuck out her hand and shook those of each

family member. "Yes. I can see the resemblance," she said.

Oh, puuulease. We all have dark brown hair and brown eyes. That's about it. But to their credit, at least none of them look like deer in the headlights or psychotic killers.

"Please have a seat," Malinda said. "We're just waiting for one more family member, and then we can eat."

Oh. My. God. She couldn't possibly be referring to Drake as family already, could she?

The director yelled, "Cut."

"What's the matter?" Malinda said, anxiously. "Did I do something wrong?"

"No, that was fine. I'd just like to get everyone together in the living room to talk. The kitchen is a little crowded already and if another relative arrives…"

"He's not a relative." Bliss glared at her mother.

She looked sheepish. "Not yet."

"Oh, God, Ma. Do *not* blow this out of proportion!"

Bliss's father blustered, "Malinda, what the hell are you talking about?"

"Bliss's boyfriend, of course."

Ricky's and Emilio's eyes lit up. Ricky laughed evilly. "The squirt's got a boyfriend? Oh, I can't wait…"

"So help me, God, if any of you…" Bliss trailed off when she noticed a camera aimed at her with the red light on.

Everyone was seated in the living room. Bliss fidgeted in the middle of the old-fashioned blue velvet sofa with her parents on either side. Brothers Emilio and Ricky slid the armchairs from beside the fireplace to a spot on each end of the sofa for easy camera viewing.

The host looked for a place to sit until Malinda said, "Ricky. Get up and give our guest your chair. You can take the ottoman."

"Oh, Ma…"

She silenced him with a severe look.

"Sheesh." Ricky got up and made a sweeping gesture toward the chair. "Please have a seat, Miss…"

"You can just call me Judith." She smiled and took the vacated chair. "Is everyone ready?"

"As ready as we'll ever be," Bliss muttered.

"Great."

The director told the cameramen to resume filming. The host had just commented on the delicious dinner, which of course they hadn't eaten yet. Anticipating her mother's reaction, Bliss took her hand and gave it a slight squeeze. She'd set up the signal ahead of time. It meant, "shut the hell up," but naturally she didn't explain it that way to her mother. "Let me do the talking" is what Bliss had told her it meant.

"So, tell me what Bliss was like growing up, Mr. Russo."

He laughed. Before he could tell the truth, his wife interjected, "Bliss was a perfect child."

She was probably going to continue her "sweet and selfless" speech, but her father and two brothers roared with laughter.

The host grinned. "I take it that means she wasn't so perfect after all?"

The three men grinned at each other, as if daring each other to go first.

Finally, Ricky said, "She was a little pest. She wanted to do whatever we were doing, and we couldn't get rid of her no matter how hard we tried."

Emilio chimed in, "Remember the time we put her in the rowboat with no oars and shoved her out to sea?"

Mrs. Russo looked horror stricken. "When did you do that? Why didn't I know about it?"

"Because you'd have tanned our hides, Ma," Ricky said.

Judith seemed delighted with the anecdote. "I take it Bliss didn't tattle on the two of you?"

"Of course not," Emilio said.

"Well, that's quite something, isn't it?"

Ricky laughed again. "Not really. If she'd said anything to our parents, we'd have made her life a living hell."

"Hmmm." Judith turned to Bliss. "So what *did* you do?"

Bliss rolled her eyes. "I dog-paddled my way to shore, then jumped on Emilio and pummeled the life out of him while Ricky laughed his ass off."

Judith raised her eyebrows. "It sounds as if you learned to take care of yourself at an early age."

"Oh, yeah. Having two older brothers was all kinds of fun, but at least they prepared me for whatever the rest of the world could throw my way."

"That explains why you were so cool, calm, and collected throughout the show."

Bliss snorted. *In comparison to the drama queens.* "Probably. It also explains why my cards are so snarky."

Judith chuckled. "I imagine verbally is one way a youngest child could fight back. But your sister started the business. And I believe you said she moved to India. Is she in India right now?"

"Yes. I wish she could be here. She deserves a lot of the credit."

"But you had no help at all in the past few weeks... in fact, I understand there was a major complication that hindered your progress."

Bliss took a deep breath. *Here it comes.* "Yes. One night I was sound asleep in my apartment when the fire alarm went off."

The host let out a little gasp and looked properly shocked. "The fire alarm?"

As if she doesn't know this story backward and forward by now. "Yes," Bliss continued. "The building was on fire and I had to get out. My computer melted in the fire, so I had to buy a new one and recreate all my designs."

"My goodness!" Judith exclaimed. "How frightening."

At that moment the doorbell rang. Malinda jumped up. "Oh, let me get that. It's probably Drake. Bliss, stay right where you are." Dodging cords and lighting, Mrs. Russo rushed to the front door.

"Cut," the director yelled. "Mrs. Russo. Wait until the cameras are ready before you open the door."

She jammed her hands on her hips. "I will not make our guest stand on the stoop and wait while you rearrange your precious cameras."

If only Bliss could reach across the room and squeeze her mother's hand—or her throat.

Malinda threw open the door and exclaimed, "Drake! I'm so glad you could make it."

Fortunately or not, the cameraman managed to get the shot.

"Hello, Mrs. Russo. Nice to see you again."

She grabbed his hand. "Come in. I can't wait to introduce you to everyone."

Not realizing what chaos he was walking into, Drake seemed relaxed and let Mrs. Russo pull him across the room.

"Sit right here next to Bliss."

"Oh, I don't want to be on camera. I'll just wait until you're all finished."

The host jumped up and said, "Please. It will help Bliss tremendously if we tell the *whole* story." She winked. "And I hear you're a big part of that story."

It'll help the show tremendously. They couldn't care less if it helps me or not.

Drake smiled at Bliss. "Okay, then. If it'll help Bliss, I'll do my best." He settled in next to her and took her hand. Malinda perched on the arm of the sofa next to Drake. She patted his shoulder and said, "This is the fireman who saved our daughter's life." She sniffed and dabbed at fake tears. "When I think about what could have happened…"

"Hold that thought," the director interjected. He checked to see that the cameras were ready and said, "Roll 'em."

Judith jumped up, strode over to Drake, and shook his hand. "We have a real, live hero in our midst! It's an honor to meet you, sir. Bliss, do you want to tell us who this special guy is?"

"Sure. This is my boyfriend, Drake. He's the firefighter who saved my life."

"Really? How incredible! Did you know each other before the fire?"

"No. We met in the middle of the smoke. I couldn't see to find my way out; so he picked me up and carried me to safety."

The host slapped a hand over her heart. "How romantic."

Bliss couldn't imagine the embarrassment Drake must be feeling, but to his credit he didn't blush. She hoped no one commented on his strange red and yellow streaks, but just in case, she shot her brothers a pointed glare.

Instead her father piped up and said, "You've got some punk rock hairdo there, son."

"Romeo! Don't be rude. This is the man who saved Blissy's life!"

Oh, shit. I forgot Dad didn't see him when he came to help me move… and Mom used my nickname. Bliss pinched the bridge of her nose.

Drake just laughed. "It's weird, I know."

Mr. Russo humphed but thankfully let it drop.

The hostess returned to her seat and begged Drake to tell his side of the story.

"You don't have to do that." Bliss implored him with her eyes. She hoped he wouldn't tell them about going in after her computer and getting suspended for it.

"It was just another job," he said, and shrugged. Then he looked directly into Bliss's eyes. "Until I met this beautiful lady."

"Awww… Tell us about that," Judith urged.

"Oh, don't make him go through it all again," Bliss said.

The director yelled, "Cut."

Judith's eyes narrowed. "Why not? Do you have something to hide?"

"Of course not! I just don't want Drake to feel like he's being cross-examined."

"It's okay, Bliss. I mean, there's not much to tell. It was a typical job." He winked at her and she breathed a sigh. He seemed to know she didn't want him to tell the world what an idiot she had been over her stupid computer—especially when it was too late to save it.

"Okay, then. Maybe we'll talk more about that later. Right now I'll get back to how it impacted Bliss in the competition."

Whew.

The director called for the cameras to roll again, and the host acted as if she hadn't missed a beat. "So, you saw her through the smoke and knew she was in trouble. Tell us about that."

Drake draped an arm around Bliss's shoulder. "We help anyone we come across in a fire. We have protective gear, so we—"

The host rolled her eyes and the director yelled, "Cut."

Judith looked at Drake as if he were an errant child. "People don't want to hear about what you do for everyone. They want to know about Bliss... and the romance. Can't you elaborate on how she felt in your arms or something?"

"Uh... I guess so."

Bliss jumped up. "Look. My family and friends aren't used to being directed for TV. How about if you cut them a break. Let them say whatever the hell they want. If you don't like it, you can edit it later."

Judith and the director exchanged stares. Finally Bo nodded. "That's fine. We want them to seem as natural as possible."

"Good." Bliss sat down again.

Malinda wrung her hands. "We should probably eat dinner soon. I turned off the oven, but the chicken could dry out if it's left too long."

Judith waved away the comment. "Oh, I won't really be eating with you. I'm on a very strict diet and it doesn't include Italian food. We'll just smear some sauce on a plate and make it look like I did."

Malinda rose and crossed her arms. "Are you saying my dinner isn't good enough for you?"

Uh-oh. Them's fightin' words!

"Ma, I'm sure she doesn't mean it that way."

"Then why should we waste my excellent gravy on a plate if she doesn't want to eat it?"

Judith rose and looked as if she was going to stroll over to Malinda but thought better of it. "Mrs. Russo, this is TV. I can't take the chance of smearing my lipstick or having a spot of red sauce on my chin."

Ricky spoke up. "Ma, nothing on reality TV is real. Didn't you know that?"

Malinda huffed. "No, I did *not* know that. Why would I? If it's not real, why do they call it reality TV?"

"You know what?" Judith said to Bo. "I think we should just finish up the interview with Bliss and her boyfriend. Then we can be on our way."

Malinda lifted her nose in the air. "I think that's a good idea. Everyone else… let's eat."

Chapter 19

THE CAMERAMEN, HOSTESS, AND DIRECTOR FOLLOWED the couple into the backyard, which gently sloped down to a private dock. They strolled toward some deck furniture casually grouped together on the grass.

As soon as they were all seated, Judith said, "So, where are your designs? I'm excited to see them."

"They're still on my computer." Bliss knew what was coming. This was the part where the host would pretend to be shocked by the news of the second fire.

Judith halted and faced Bliss head-on. "Still on your computer! But your entire line is due soon. Don't you have any finished that you can show us?"

Drake squeezed Bliss's hand, giving her some much-needed empathy.

"I know you expected to see some finished products, but I don't have any."

"Well? Why are you so behind?"

"I had nearly all of them redone a couple weeks after the fire. I even saved the designs on a disk and locked it in a safe-deposit box—that time."

"Okay…"

Judith had said to drag it out for dramatic effect, but Bliss really didn't feel like reliving the past few weeks in gory detail. Still… when had she ever had a choice when it came to this damn show?

She took a deep breath and continued. "Well, as you

know, I had to relocate, so I moved to an apartment over a bar where my friend worked. She gave me a job there so I could pay the rent without dipping into the money you gave me to create the line."

Judith raised her perfect eyebrows. "You were working as a cocktail waitress the whole time you had to recreate your designs?"

Bliss had to give herself a mental warning not to roll her eyes. "Yes. But it was okay. I was back on track until Friday night. I had printed out all the initial samples and made sure they were ready for the professional company I use to make a beautiful finished product. Even so, it would have had to be a rush job, but before I could get over to their shop in the North End…"

Judith pressed a hand over her heart as if she were so nervous she might have a coronary. "What happened? Tell us."

"The bar burned down, and with it, my apartment, the CD, and all my samples. I was lucky to get out alive with my computer."

Judith gasped. "Another fire? You were burned out of not one, but *two* apartments in the last few weeks?"

"Yes, but at least this time I managed to save my computer. It had all my designs on it, and since the bank burned…"

"What? The bank where you had the safe-deposit box burned too? What the…" Judith looked as if she was about to lose it, then she quickly pulled herself back from the non-scripted edge. She chuckled. "Thank goodness you had everything in two places. They used to say, if you could only grab one thing on your way out of a fire to take your photo albums. Now, everyone's photos are on their computers along with a host of other things."

"Yeah." Bliss didn't quite know what to say to that, so she just waited for Judith to talk again.

"So, it sounds like Boston has had more than its share of fires recently."

"Yes," Drake interjected. "It's not usually like this."

Psychotic, jealous dragon in town and everything...

"And were you there to save your girlfriend's life again?"

The cameras both focused in on Drake.

He chuckled. "I was there, but Bliss saved herself that time. I was helping other people."

"Oh my. You must have been worried about her..." Judith prompted. "I'll bet you wanted to leave those people to the other firefighters and run right to Bliss. Didn't you?"

"Well, of course I was worried about her and called out to her as soon as I was inside—but leaving people in trouble isn't what we do. I was cut off from my fellow firefighters when the ceiling caved in."

Judith sucked in another deep breath. "The ceiling caved in? And you knew Bliss was living on the second floor of that very building?"

She's just loving this.

"Yeah. And there was a family on the third floor too. They all got out together. Until I saw my girl and knew she'd made it out okay, I was a little frantic." He squeezed Bliss's hand and they smiled at each other.

Yup, that's the bit they were looking for.

"I can't imagine what that must be like. To put your-self in harm's way for people you don't even know...

the whole time realizing your own loved one could be in peril…"

Judith leaned back in her chair as if stunned. Meanwhile, something big and dark swooped over them.

"Cut," the director yelled. "Where the hell did that shadow come from?"

Drake scanned the sky and muttered, "Oh, crap. It couldn't be…"

A horrible feeling of dread made the hairs on Bliss's arms stand up. *No way…Zina?* Had she found them somehow? What kind of exposure would she risk to cause trouble?

Drake rose from his chair and excused himself. He jogged toward the front of the house, despite the protests of Judith and the director.

"How can he just get up and leave?" Judith shouted. "How are we going to make a sensible segue out of a sudden exit like that?"

The director shrugged. "Say he got called to a fire. Maybe we can get him to film the call as soon as he gets back."

"Nice save," Judith said. "What an exciting moment that would make."

Bliss jumped to her feet. "There won't be any more filming. We all need to get inside and lock the doors."

"What the hell are you talking about, Bliss?" Judith demanded.

"Roll 'em," the director called as he fled.

"Trust me… and run!" She grabbed Judith's arm and dashed to the house with the cameramen on her heels, capturing every second.

As soon as they were inside and the dead bolt was locked, Judith exclaimed, "This is insane!"

"No," said Ricky's voice from the living room. "What's insane is Bliss's boyfriend running down the street yelling, 'Taxi!'"

"This isn't the city," Mr. Russo said. "We don't have taxis trolling the streets looking for a fare."

Oh, no. Bliss led the others into the living room to see her brothers peering out the side window, while her parents parted the lace curtains and stared out the little window on the front door.

"What did you do to scare him off, Bliss?" her mother asked tearfully.

How am I going to explain this one?

Emilio chuckled. "She probably mentioned the *M* word... marriage."

Vulcan gauged the right moment to appear without being detected by humans. He snapped his fingers, and his white robe turned into a business suit. Drake had just rounded the corner out of sight of the Russo residence and halted, letting out a huge sigh of relief when he spotted him.

"Thank *God*, you heard me."

Vulcan chuckled. *If you only knew how true your words are.* "Yes. I assume you've located the delinquent paranormal?"

"She just swooped over the area. I don't know precisely where she is at this moment."

Vulcan sniffed the air. A faint sour scent tinged the fresh ocean breeze.

"You can smell her?"

"No. I've never been close enough to catch her scent. What I'm detecting is smoke."

Drake's eyes widened in shock. "No... not again! I should have picked up the familiar smell. Are you sure?"

"There." Vulcan pointed back toward Pleasant Street. A gray spiral rose into the air.

"Shit." Drake dashed back toward the Russo home while Vulcan tried to keep up. He wasn't used to running since he could transport himself just about anywhere with a thought.

The house didn't seem to be burning, but smoke was billowing from a short distance behind it.

"Around the back," Drake shouted.

Sure enough. The dock was on fire. *If no one's watching, I can put that out with one wave of my hand.*

But at that very moment, several people rushed out the back door. Even a camera crew!

"Stay back," Drake yelled. "I've got this."

Two young men stood with their hands in their pockets, looking on and wisecracking. "I thought he ran off. Now he's back?"

"Bliss has that effect on some people," her father said.

Mrs. Russo elbowed her husband in the ribs. "And you wonder why she never brings her friends home."

A metal bucket sat on the dock, enveloped in flames. Drake dashed into the blaze and grabbed the handle. The heat of the aluminum would have burned a human hand, but a dragon's skin was so thick, it wouldn't even make a mark.

Drake leaped over the flames to the part of the dock closest to shore. He filled the bucket and tossed the water where fire met dry wood.

Bliss appeared in the doorway, waving frantically

to catch Vulcan's attention. He started toward her, but then she pointed to the shed in the next yard. Apparently she'd spotted Zina.

Bliss started dashing toward the neighbor's shed at a flat run.

Vulcan sprinted across the lawn and tried to catch up with her.

As he rounded the shed, he saw the female dragon zipping up her leather jacket. Her surprised gaze snapped to Bliss's face, but before she could do or say anything, Bliss opened the shed door, shoved Zina inside, and leaned against it.

"Can you zap her out of here quick? Maybe to outer space?"

Vulcan chuckled. "I know just what to do with her."

He transported himself inside the shed, grabbed Zina before she could get away again, and in a flash they arrived on the top floor of the office building that housed the Council. Zina gazed at the glass-bubble dome, open-mouthed but silent.

His god cronies looked up from their poker game, but where was Gaia?

"Is she here?"

He didn't have to tell the other gods who he meant. Apollo pointed to the forest in the corner. "She's been in there all day... chanting."

"Chanting?" *That's new*. "Should I disturb her?"

"At your own peril."

Zina ripped her arm out of Vulcan's grasp. "Where the hell are we? And how did we get here? Who are you anyway?"

"I'm out." Apollo tossed his cards into the middle

of the table, rose, and strolled over to them. "Is this the dragon she's after?"

"And who are you, pretty boy?" Zina gave the sun god a grin that was probably supposed to be alluring. Instead it made her look like the predator she was.

"This is she," Vulcan answered. "Zina."

"I think Gaia would want to know. I'll get her." Apollo strode off to the forest and spoke softly. He made a reverent apology for disturbing her and stepped away.

A few moments later, a bleary-eyed Mother Nature emerged. "Who dares disturb me when I'm deep in meditation?"

Vulcan appeared before her quickly so she wouldn't blame Apollo. "That would be me. Meditation? I've never known you to meditate before." He immediately wondered if he should have said that out loud.

"I understand it might make me a little calmer. Believe me, I could use some serenity."

Oh, I believe you.

She glanced over at Zina and frowned. "Is that who I think it is?"

"Yes, Gaia. Zina is the dragon who's been setting fires to your beloved city."

"And risking exposure of her kind... not that I'm fond of dragons, but the human population really can't handle the knowledge that they exist—or ever existed. We've finally managed to convince them that the whole race was a myth. She almost single-handedly undid all that work."

"Yes, Gaia."

She reached out and touched his arm. "You did well, Vulcan. Now, leave her to me."

"Can I watch?" he asked impulsively.

Mother Nature paused, and he wondered if she was going to tell him to mind his own business, but to his surprise, she simply nodded. The two of them approached Zina together.

The usually cocky dragon took a few steps backward as they came closer.

"Not so confident now, are you?" Gaia said.

"Only because I don't know who you are." Then she puffed herself up. "Not that it matters. There's nothing you can do to me."

A sinister smile spread slowly across Gaia's lips. "Oh, no?"

"Nope. I'm immortal."

Mother Nature grinned. "I know. Which makes my punishment for you even richer."

"Punishment? Who are you to punish me? I don't see a judge or jury anywhere."

Chuckling, Gaia strolled around her. "I'm neither judge nor jury… I am your mother—the mother of all, and you've been very naughty."

"Mother of all?" Suddenly Zina's eyes grew wide. "Me remember now. Mother Nature?"

"The one and only."

"Oh shit."

"Indeed."

Zina looked all around her, probably hoping for an escape route. She saw the bank of elevators and began to inch toward them.

"It's too late," Gaia said. "I've already done most of what I plan to do to you."

"Most of… what are you talking about?" Zina asked.

Vulcan couldn't help echoing the question in his head too.

Mother Nature held herself regally as she pronounced, "Zina, you have abused your gift of flight. You can no longer fly. You have abused your power of fire. You can no longer breathe fire."

Zina opened her mouth and huffed. Nothing came out. Not so much as a smoke curl.

Gaia strolled around her. "And now I need to know why. Did all of this stem from trying to make someone love you and create the gift of life inside you?"

"It started that way, but my cycle ended three days ago. Thanks to that harlot, I won't get another chance for five years."

Mother Nature's brows rose. "Excuse me? Did you say your cycle ended three days ago?"

"Yes. What of it?"

"Isn't that when you set fire to the bar in which she and several other people worked? The building that was previously home to five people?"

Zina held her head high. "I was upset. I don't like being rejected."

"Nobody likes to be rejected… just like it's not nice to fool Mother Nature. Believe me, I understand. But do I burn down every company that makes butter taste good with half the calories? Or smite every sixty-year-old who tries Botox? Hmmm… do I?"

"No."

"Of course not. Only spoiled children expect to get their own way all of the time. Which isn't to say it's not natural to want what you want… It's just not okay to get revenge when things don't go your way."

Zina crossed her arms and looked like she was pouting.

Gaia paced back and forth, hands clasped behind her back, muttering, "What am I going to do with you?"

At last she stopped in front of Zina and pointed at her. "Because you have abused your fertility, I'm taking that away from you until you can handle it."

"You can't do that!" Zina screamed.

"Yes, I can. In fact, I can do a little more. Have fun in Siberia." Mother Nature waved her hand in a wide arc, and Zina disappeared from sight.

<hr />

Drake had finished putting out the dock fire and rested on the shore. Bliss was arguing with her family, but he didn't know why. He figured he should probably stay out of the way... until he heard one of the male voices saying, "Hey, it happens all the time. Firemen like to play hero. He probably made us think he left when he ran off looking for a taxi, then his accomplice snuck back there and set the fire."

"Then he ran back to save the day," said the other brother.

"What are you, nuts?" Bliss was obviously getting agitated, but it was her family. She could handle them.

"I don't know, Blissy. It makes a certain kind of sense," Mrs. Russo said.

"No, it doesn't! It doesn't make any sense at all. Why would he make more work for himself?"

"It's not logical, Sis. I think there's a name for that type of thing, but I don't know what it is. Some kind of mental disorder."

"Are you saying he's deranged? How dare you? He

was in the station when most of those fires broke out, and then he risked his life to answer the calls. Don't you think his buddies would notice if he was missing?"

Uh-oh. Bliss's voice is loud enough to alert the media—in New York.

Drake rose and checked the area behind the arguing family. There stood the director and cameramen—with their little red lights indicating they were still filming.

Shit. Now what?

He strolled slowly toward the family. A noise like "pssst" from the corner of the house caught his attention. When he glanced over, he saw Vulcan in his white robe, waving him over.

Oh, great. He looks like Father Time, and of all the imperfect timing... Drake altered his route, planning to ask Vulcan to change back into his street clothes. Then they'd need to come up with a reason for his presence so the family didn't suspect Vulcan of being an accomplice. They had to figure out some way to fix this so Bliss didn't have to defend them.

Unfortunately, as soon as Drake rounded the corner, he disappeared into the brightest white light he'd ever seen, and a moment later he found himself standing under a clear bubble.

"Oh, crap. Not again."

Gaia strolled over to him. "I took care of your problem, and this is the thanks I get?"

Drake stared at the all-powerful woman who looked like an aging beauty queen. "You took care of... what problem?"

"Your dragon, Zina. She won't be bothering you or this city anymore."

Drake glanced at Vulcan. "Is this true?"

Vulcan nodded. "I wish you could have been here to see it."

"Seriously, Vulcan?" Mother Nature cocked her head like she was talking to a foolish child. "If you want him to see what happened, just show him."

"If you don't mind…" Vulcan seemed reluctant. "You don't usually like us to show anyone your reactions."

"I'll make an exception."

Vulcan gave a slight bow, and then with extended arm and index finger, he drew a circle in the air. Appearing in the circle were tiny exact replicas of himself, Mother Nature, and Zina. He snapped his fingers, and the picture came to life.

Drake watched the whole interaction with alarming clarity. *The whole thing really was my fault. If only I had told Zina up front I wasn't interested, maybe I'd still have had a couple broken ribs, but none of this would have happened to Bliss.*

He brought his attention back to the movie playing in front of him. Mother Nature had punished the dragon for her crimes, and it sounded as if Zina wouldn't be bothering him or Bliss again.

The picture stopped with only Gaia and Vulcan in the frame. Then the vision and circle dissipated as if it had never been there.

"You sent her to Siberia? And made her infertile?"

Gaia crossed her arms. "Yes, and I took away her fire and flight. Why? Do you disapprove?"

Drake let out a sigh of relief. "No. I approve wholeheartedly."

"Good. I like you, Drake. You're not like some

dragons who think they're above the laws of nature. I'm giving you back your immortality."

He placed a hand over his heart. "Thank you. I couldn't be more grateful, but…"

Mother Nature raised her eyebrows. "But? There's a but?"

"I–I have a mortal girlfriend. Actually, I plan to make her my wife, and I can't see going through eternity without her."

Gaia smiled. "Good to know. Because I actually have a favor to ask of you."

Uh-oh. It's never good when a deity wants a favor. "What is it?"

"Your girlfriend…" Mother Nature began.

"Bliss? You want Bliss?"

Gaia rolled her eyes. "Everyone wants bliss, stupid. I just want to know more about your girlfriend."

"Well, for starters, her name is Bliss."

Mother Nature burst out laughing. "Oops. Who'd have thought… well, never mind. What kind of person is she?"

"Honest, loyal, she's one of the bravest women I know. She's been under incredible pressure and didn't crumble once. She even saw my alternate form and didn't faint or run."

"She saw you as a dragon?"

"Yes. She didn't believe me and I really needed her to. I wouldn't have been able to warn her about Zina if she didn't take me seriously. If something happened to her because I hadn't warned her properly, I'd never forgive myself."

Mother Nature clasped her hands behind her back and

started to pace again. "So, she doesn't believe in things she hasn't seen with her own eyes?"

"I don't know about that," Vulcan interjected. "She seemed to accept my help without protesting my nonexistence."

Gaia narrowed her eyes at him. "Cute." She pointed to a spot on the floor until a small sofa and armchair appeared.

"Have a seat, Drake. I think your Bliss might be just the kind of woman I'm looking for."

Crap. Drake lowered himself onto the couch slowly. He sat on the edge in case he needed to jump up and run. *Run where?* That was a good question, and hopefully he wouldn't need to answer it.

"Relax, dragon. I'm not going to do anything to your human... that is, if she doesn't want me to..."

"Can we make this conversation a little less ambiguous?" Drake asked bravely. He didn't want to upset the goddess, but she was upsetting the heck out of him.

"Here's the thing... I need a few new muses. The world's population has grown and evolved over the centuries. Some of my current muses are complaining that they can't handle all the challenges, especially when it comes to new technology. Your girl seems pretty savvy and modern. Isn't she?"

Drake nodded slowly. "She is."

"Do you think she'd make a good muse?"

Drake couldn't believe what he was hearing. Bliss... a muse? "That would make her immortal. Wouldn't it?"

"Yes. I know you didn't want to go on alone after she died, but are you worried about being with the same woman for eternity?"

"Not at all. I'd love to be with Bliss forever. She never fails to surprise me. I doubt very much I'd ever get bored."

"Good. Then I don't see any reason not to make the offer. Do you?"

Drake wished he had more time to think about it, but inevitably this would be Bliss's decision, not his. "I can't think of anything. She'll tell you if she's not up for it."

"Good. So now that we have that cleared up, go back to your nice, normal life, and I'll contact her."

"You might want to wait a few days. She's in the middle of a big competition right now, and her focus needs to be in one place."

"And you think me making her a minor goddess might be a distraction?"

"Just a bit."

"Fine. I'll wait. But not long."

Chapter 20

BLISS NERVOUSLY CHEWED ON HER FINGERNAIL, A nasty habit she thought she'd beaten, but the competition was bringing out the worst in everyone. Candy, one of the other finalists, was twirling her hair, and Dick, the third, was tapping the tabletop. If he didn't stop it, Bliss was going to strangle him.

"What's taking so long?" the other female finalist asked in her soft, little girl voice.

No wonder she designs inspirational cards.

"I don't know, Candy. Why don't you go ask?" Dick had earned his name during the competition. Every reality show seems to have one.

"Well, whatever happens"—Candy reached out to grasp the hands of the other finalists—"it's been a privilege, y'all."

Dick yanked his hand away.

She giggled. "Why, bless your heart. You must be more nervous than you look."

The door to the windowless room in the New York TV station opened, and Judith poked her head in.

"Is everyone ready?"

Candy clapped her hands rapidly. "Oh, goody! This is it."

Dick rolled his eyes. "Are you kidding? We've been ready for hours."

"Sorry. The judges wanted to meet your families."

Bliss leaped up. "Our families are here?"

"Of course. It's part of the show and the viewers love it. They want to see the winner's family react with pride. Unfortunately, we had to tell a few of them how to do that."

Bliss pinched the bridge of her nose. "Probably mine. I didn't invite them for a reason."

"Your family seems to be behaving themselves, Bliss. Don't be too hard on them for speaking their minds. Families show their love and support in different ways. It's obvious your parents are thrilled for you."

Bliss slapped the side of her head. "Oh, no. My boyfriend is coming and doesn't know how angry they are with him. He'll be walking into an ambush."

"They're still angry that he disappeared? I thought it was obvious why he left."

Dick leaned forward. "This sounds interesting. What happened?"

Bliss tried to wave the incident off like it was nothing. "Oh, they were just being their usual overly talkative selves and they accidentally insulted him."

"Really? What did they say?"

She turned on Dick and spat out, "Nothing. Forget it!"

He rubbed his hands together. "It doesn't sound like nothing to me. Better get those cameras rolling, Judith."

"Shit. At this stage of the show, it's not the kind of thing we want happening. Bliss, maybe you should come out here and explain…"

"What is *he* doing here?" a male voice cried out.

Oh, crap. Too late. Bliss rose and dashed from the room into the hallway, which was clogged with people.

Some of them stepped back and cleared a path so she could see what was going on. *Yup. Just as I thought.*

Drake stood still while her father poked him in the chest. "You're not good enough for my daughter. If you want to be part of this family, you have to know how to stand and defend yourself."

Wow, that's for sure. "Dad!" Bliss elbowed her way to her father. "Leave my boyfriend alone."

"But he ran away. One little insult and he was gone." Romeo Russo was using his hands to talk in grand gestures destined to whack someone in the face.

"I wasn't insulted," Drake said.

Bliss reached him and whispered in his ear. "Yes, you were. It was the only way to explain your disappearance."

"I've got this, honey." Drake put his arm around her shoulder and addressed her parents. "Mr. and Mrs. Russo. I'm sure you must know how unnerving it can be to meet your future bride's family, and then when you think they dislike you for some reason—"

"Bride?" Mrs. Russo's hand covered her heart.

"Now, wait just a—"

Mrs. Russo's other hand covered her husband's mouth. "Blissy, did you know about this?"

Bliss stared at Drake's face, looking for a clue. He seemed perfectly calm and happy. Then he winked at her.

What is he up to? "Uh, no, Mom, I didn't."

"I wasn't planning on doing this until after the winner's announced, but maybe you should know that win or lose, I want you in my life, Bliss."

The hallway fell silent and all eyes were on her. She tried to whisper in his ear so they wouldn't be overheard. "Are you sure? Even with the amount of insanity in my family?"

Drake chuckled. "I'm sure. And your family's insanity isn't that bad."

They smiled at each other until Mrs. Russo burst out with, "Say something, Bliss!"

"Like what? I don't think he proposed. He just said he wanted me in his life. I want him in mine too."

"Even if your father doesn't approve?" Mr. Russo asked and crossed his arms over his big barrel chest.

Bliss rolled her eyes. "Even if my father posted attack ads in the *Boston Globe*." She palmed Drake's cheek and kissed him.

Mrs. Russo tried to put her arm around her husband's considerable waist and laid her head on his shoulder. "I'd say that no matter what happens in a few minutes, Bliss won the biggest prize of all. Love."

Mr. Russo humphed. "There was a time when a girl had to have her father's permission."

Bliss broke the lip-lock to give her father an annoyed glare. "Yeah, and there was a time when you'd have had to pay him in goats to take me."

Mr. Russo sighed. "Fine. How many goats would you like, Drake?"

"No goats. Just your beautiful daughter." He swept a stray lock of hair behind Bliss's ear and kissed it. "Does that mean you approve?"

"And start World War III with my wife if I don't?"

Romeo Russo extended his hand and Drake shook it.

Just then, Judith reappeared and clapped her hands to get everyone's attention. "It's time to take your seats."

The double doors to the auditorium opened, and as people filed through, the hallway emptied. Drake dropped Bliss's hand and said, "Lead the way, honey."

"I have to sit up on stage, but I'll find you in the audience."

"I'll sit with your folks."

Bliss chuckled. "You're a glutton for punishment, aren't you?"

Five hours of film later, the three finalists all sat on the edge of their seats. The jumbotrons set up on either side of the stage were used to showcase their work for a large audience. The giant screens made something as small as a greeting card or as flexible as an animated, online card look great.

Bliss had to admit the competitors' designs were fantastic. Some of them. And some of hers were home runs too. It was really anybody's contest.

At last the judges returned from their backstage deliberations and presented Judith with an envelope.

This is it. Either fifty grand in my hand or back to the drawing board.

She thought about how she and Drake might use the money. A down payment on a house, maybe? A magazine ad campaign to kick-start her business? There were no stipulations on how the money was to be spent. Bliss had previously only thought about winning it to pay off a small mountain of debt and maybe lengthen the vacation the winner got as part of the prize. She needed a long one.

Judith waved the envelope. "Now, which of our terrific designers is going to win? Will it be Dick for his rock-and-roll lyrics? Or Candy for her inspirational poetry? Or Bliss for her sense of humor?"

The audience began chanting, "Bliss, Bliss, Bliss..."

Judith opened the envelope and smiled at the contents. When she held up her hand, the audience quieted. "I have a check here in the amount of fifty thousand dollars, and it's made out to…"

She paused so long Bliss thought half the audience might pass out from holding their collective breaths.

"Bliss Russo for Hall-Snark Cards!"

The roar of applause and shock to her system drowned out any thoughts that might have been going through her head. Bliss rose and walked woodenly toward Judith. Before she reached her, she remembered to smile and echoed Judith's giant grin with one of her own.

When the applause finally died down, Judith clasped her shoulder. "Now, before I can give this to you, Bliss. I'm afraid there's a stipulation."

There is? What the heck could that be?

"The judges heard about your wonderful news and want to be invited to the wedding."

Another roar of applause began but died out when Bliss muttered, "Um… we haven't even discussed the details yet."

"Well, we have. As you know, the winner also receives a vacation. We'd like to throw you a destination wedding in…" Again the pause was far too long. Then confetti fell from the rafters and Judith shouted, "Hawaii! Congratulations."

Bliss almost groaned aloud. She searched the audience and saw cameras focused on her parents' proud faces. Her mother was openly crying, and her father's beaming eyes seemed to be a bit watery too.

But where was Drake? The seat next to them was empty.

Oh, no.

"She's speechless, folks. Go on," Judith said as she gave Bliss a shove. "Go share this moment with your family."

Bliss trotted down the side stairs, and cameras followed her up the aisle to her parents' seats. They jumped up and each gave her long hugs and kisses. At last she saw Drake. He had just reentered the room through the double doors at the back.

He smiled when he saw her and jogged down the aisle. "What did I miss?"

Mr. Russo slapped himself on the forehead. "Oh, for the love of God."

"Hey, I'm sorry. I couldn't hold it any longer."

"My future son-in-law will probably disappear from his own Hawaiian wedding."

"What?"

"Never mind, Drake." Bliss placed the check in his hand. "We won!"

"You did?"

"*We* did! This couldn't have happened without you."

He picked her up, whooped, and whirled her around in a wide arc. "That's fantastic. But I didn't do anything, honey. It was all you. Your hard work and talent."

"No. You just saved my life. That's all."

He shrugged one shoulder. "All in a day's work." He whispered in her ear, "Speaking of work, there's a job offer I need to talk to you about when we're alone."

Bliss glanced all around at the cameras and the swell of people coming closer to offer congratulations.

"That may have to wait a while. Can you give me a hint?"

He laughed. "No hints. You'll just have to wait."

Hmmm... Bliss was intrigued and could hardly wait to hear what her cryptic boyfriend had in mind, but by then, she was being embraced and jostled by one person after another, including her fellow finalists.

Candy hugged her and said sweetly, "I knew you'd win. Your cards are so funny."

When Dick hugged her, he said, "I'm just glad the little sweetie pie didn't win. Her cards give me cavities."

A couple days later, the hoopla had finally died down and Bliss returned from New York by train. Transporting all her stuff was much easier without air travel's inconvenience of weight restrictions, luggage searches, and pat downs that made her feel like a criminal.

This time when she arrived "home," she wasn't quite sure where to go. Her parents' house? *Ugh.* Drake's tiny place? *It may be cozy, but at least it's calm.*

She called Drake at the fire station. After she chatted briefly with Mike Kelly, he put Drake on the phone. It was so good to hear his voice. She took a chance and said, "Hi, honey, I'm home."

"Great! I'm off soon. Where are you? Winthrop?"

Bliss snorted. "No. I'm still at South Station. I'm not sure where to go from here. My mother will make a big deal out of everything. The neighbors want to come over and congratulate me on the win my parents weren't supposed to tell people about yet."

Drake chuckled. "When does it air?"

"Not until next week. That gives me about a week of relative peace. I don't want to squander it."

"Come to my place."

"I was hoping you'd say that."

"Terrific. I'll come and get you."

"Aren't you at work?"

"Yeah, but my shift is almost over. The guys can cover for me for a little while."

"No. I don't want to take you away from your job, and I'm a big girl. I can take care of myself."

"Are you sure?"

"What… that I can take care of myself?"

He chuckled. "No. I'm completely sure of that. I meant are you sure you don't want me to come and get you? I have something to tell you, and we'll need complete privacy."

"Oh yeah? I have something to say to you in private too—or rather, my body does."

"I like the sound of that. So, I'll see you at my place soon?"

"Can't wait."

"Me neither."

They hung up and she hailed a cab. She'd had no time to think for so long. First there was the fire, then Zina, then the other fire, then the competition… It was good to have a little breathing room.

Drake had said Zina was no longer a problem, but he said he'd explain later. His evasive tone left her uneasy, despite assurances that the she-dragon was really out of the picture.

Don't waste your time thinking about her, she told herself. You have much better things to focus on.

One of those things was Drake's sort-of proposal. He said he wanted her in his life. That didn't mean marriage. Bliss didn't dare ask for clarification with her mother standing there. If he'd meant simply living together, Malinda Russo would have had a fit and her father—good God. Who knew what Romeo Russo would have blurted out?

The judges would have looked like fools too. Why did they have to turn her vacation into a wedding? And why, oh why, did it have to be Hawaii? It was beautiful and everything, but the air travel from Boston was brutal. She had been hoping for the Caribbean or Europe.

Ah, well. It was probably too late to do anything about what the show would air. That didn't mean she and Drake couldn't just turn her prize back into a vacation and quietly ask her mother to put away the guest list for a few years.

All the way to Drake's place, she ruminated over the little things she hadn't been able to focus on for the past day and a half. Her prize money was going to be eaten up by a new apartment, new furniture, and a new wardrobe. Sheesh. On the other hand, what would she have done without it?

She thought about the stores that catered to her eclectic taste. When her sister had made her weekly phone call from India, of course her mother talked about the "engagement." Her sister wanted to know if Bliss would like some beautiful bed linens she could buy over there. Next time Bliss spoke to her sister, maybe she'd know what size her bed was and if she was engaged or not.

Bliss finally arrived at Drake's front door and rang the bell. She didn't even have a key yet. Their relationship had moved so far, so fast, some basic milestones had fallen by the wayside.

She was just about to ring the bell a second time

when Drake opened the door and pulled her into a tight hug. "I just got home. If I'd had more time, I'd have met you with roses."

Drake inhaled her fragrance and detected the faint scent of lilacs. It was wonderful to hold her in his arms again. She had been either off limits or surrounded by hoopla lately, and this was the moment he'd been looking forward to for days.

"No roses needed. I just want to curl up with you and talk."

"Just talk? Damn."

She chuckled. "Of course I want to shag you silly, but there are a few details I need to clarify for my own peace of mind first—*then* I'll shag you silly."

He stepped back and made a sweeping gesture. "Please, come in."

Drake had a few things he needed to clarify for peace of mind too. During his visit with Gaia, he'd told the goddess he was in love with a human. She seemed strangely okay with that and wanted to meet her. How and when the meeting would happen was anyone's guess.

His major dilemma now was how he could prepare Bliss for it. If he didn't, she might get upset and cope by saying something snarky... something she'd regret. On the other hand, maybe Gaia would get a kick out of their shared attitude. *Probably not.*

"Can I get you a glass of wine?"

"Oh, yes please. That would be perfect." She fumbled with a small piece of paper, stuffing it in her purse, and mumbled, "Jeez, I have receipts up the wazoo."

Drake pulled the chilled bottle from the refrigerator. "Don't worry. I'll help you check your wazoo. Have you eaten?"

She grinned and took a seat in one of the Lucite chairs at his tiny kitchen table. "I had a snack. I'm all set for a couple hours."

"Good. I wouldn't want you to starve while I'm making sweet passionate love to you."

Bliss grinned.

He handed her the glass of Chardonnay and took the other chair. "It seems we both have some things to say, but you can go first."

"Are you sure?"

"Positive." *I still have to think about the right way to say, "You might be meeting a real, live goddess at any moment."*

"Okay, let's start with an easy one. How do you know Zina is no longer a problem, and is that going to last?"

Drake almost groaned. *That's not an easy one.* "Why don't we come back to that? The explanation is a bit—confusing."

"Oh." Bliss took a sip of her wine and seemed to be thinking something over.

"Don't worry. I'll tell you everything."

She smiled and seemed satisfied with that. "Okay. In that case, I think we'd better talk about our so-called engagement."

"So-called?" He didn't like the sound of that. Was she having second thoughts?

"I mean… you didn't actually propose. You just said you wanted me in your life. My mother was the one who took that as a proposal and just assumed I'd say yes."

"Now I'm confused. Did you want to slow down or something?"

She took another sip of wine. *Maybe she needs courage?*

"Please, Bliss. Just say whatever you have to say. We can figure this out if we talk and stop assuming things."

She set her glass down. "Okay. Did you or did you not mean to propose marriage?"

"I didn't mean to at that moment... surrounded by mostly strangers in the middle of a noisy hallway. I'm not taking it back, though."

She smiled and looked down at her hand. *Ah, she must be wondering about the ring.* "I didn't buy a ring yet, so if you want to help me pick it out..."

"Oh, yes please. I have kind of picky taste in jewelry—especially something I'm going to wear for the rest of my life."

Whew. Drake grinned, but he still had to ask... "So, is that a 'yes'?"

"It's kind of fast, but... *hell*, yes."

He chuckled and rose enough to lean across the table and kiss her. "There's more where that came from, but I don't think we're done talking yet."

"Not by a long shot."

"Okay. What else did you want to know?"

"Would you be heartbroken if we didn't go to Hawaii?"

"No. But that's part of the prize you won, isn't it?"

"I'm not afraid of flying, but I'm not in love with it, either. I'm sure they'll understand if I say, 'No, thanks. Fourteen hours in the sky is just too much.'"

"The judges will be disappointed."

"That was just for TV. They've all got busy schedules and weren't planning to attend a wedding anywhere, much less in Hawaii. Besides, if any of them really want to go, they can arrange their own vacation."

"Boy. You're a hard ass, aren't you?"

She chuckled. "You'd better believe it. Still want me?"

He reached for her hand. "Very much."

She glanced over at his bed, which he'd just made before she arrived. "So, can that explanation about Zina wait for a bit?"

"Why? What did you have in mind?" *Please be too turned on to wait…*

"I'm too horny to wait."

Close enough. Drake got out of the chair so fast that he almost tipped it over. Still holding her hand, he strode to the bed and kissed her as they fell onto it.

Lying beside her again felt so right. Finally together with no threat of Zina, no cameras, and no fires to put out, it was time they stoked the fire between them.

"I love you, Bliss."

She sighed. "I love you too."

She stroked his jaw and then began placing little nibbling kisses along the path where her fingers had trailed.

"Bliss… I have to touch you. More of you. *All* of you."

She giggled and began unbuttoning her blouse.

"I'll do that," he said.

She smiled and let him undress her. As soon as he'd revealed her beautiful breasts, he dove for one and sucked while he unzipped her jeans. She arched into his mouth and moaned.

"Not fair. I want you naked too."

"I'll get there. Don't worry."

"Get there now," she demanded and pulled his T-shirt out of his pants.

He chuckled, jerked his shirt off in one quick move, and tossed it on the floor. His pants soon followed. Bliss didn't wait for his help and discarded the rest of her clothes too. At last they were skin to skin, in bed and in love.

Bliss gazed at him. His chest rippled with muscles. A light thatch of chest hair arrowed down his tight abdomen. And his cock. *My God*, the man was impressive. She vividly remembered how it felt when he thrust into her, so hard and so deep.

He kissed her tenderly, then leaned over to do the same to each of her breasts. A soft moan escaped from her lips as her nipples tightened.

"Wait. I want to do something for you first."

When he looked up at her, his eyes glowed gold. "And what would that be?"

"Lie back, and I'll show you."

Drake grinned and did as she asked.

I love a man who doesn't balk when I want to do something nice for him.

His gaze seemed to glow even more. It was a bit distracting, but where Bliss was going, she wouldn't see his eyes anyway.

She scooted down and took his thick cock in her hand. He let out a moan and she thought she saw a tiny curl of smoke out of the corner of her eye.

"Are you about to spontaneously combust?"

"Honey, it's been a few days, and, hey… I need you, bad."

She stared at his pecs. His strong, muscled chest rose and fell rapidly.

"Is this a good idea? I mean, can you handle the… attention I was planning to give you?"

"If I can't, I'll let you know." He propped his head up on his arm so he could watch. His lips rose on one side in a smug smile.

Her fingers didn't meet as she gripped his cock, but she stroked up and down as best she could. Meanwhile, she kissed the reddened tip and tongued the slit. His groan of pleasure meant the world to her.

Then she moved so she could lick the length of him, finally taking the head into her mouth. He sucked in a deep breath through his teeth.

She let her tongue swirl around his cock. He tasted salty. She drew him into her mouth deeper, loving the way he arched slightly and groaned. She took him as deep as she could, then applied suction and withdrew.

"Playtime's over," he said, grabbing her and pulling her up his body. His mouth crashed down on hers, and his tongue plunged into her mouth.

The room spun and she found herself on her back, her legs spread with Drake over her. His legs were between hers and his cock was poised at her opening.

"I'm sorry about the lack of foreplay. I promise I'll take care of you better next time." She noticed his heavy breathing as he spoke.

"Hey, it was entirely my fault."

He grinned. "Yes, it was." He dipped two fingers into her channel and said, "You seem ready for me…"

"Oh, I am. Go for it, dragon boy."

"Not just yet. There's a little something I can do for you first." His slick fingers found her clit and rubbed slow circles around it. She arched and moaned.

"That's my good girl." He sped up the motion and zeroed in on her most sensitive spot. "I'm going to make you come for me," he almost growled.

Like she could resist…

He leaned down and sucked her breast as he continued his love massage. She couldn't hold back the noises emanating from her throat if she wanted to. He lifted his head and latched on to her other nipple. As he sucked, she began to erupt.

Oh, God… Oh, God… Oh, God… Ripples of sheer joy burst through her. She bucked and screamed out her release.

Her eyes teared up. When her thighs stopped quivering, she was spent, but she *so* wanted to give him the same pleasure. She reached for him. "Come to me. Come *in* me. I love you."

"I love you too." He positioned himself so that his cock was pushing at her sex, and then he thrust, filling her.

"Oh, God. That feels so good," she murmured.

He answered with a groan, then found his rhythm and rode her hard.

"You're so tight. So hot…" His breaths came in short gasps as he angled his pelvis and slammed into her.

It felt incredible. She could only lie there, riding the waves of pleasure and moaning in joy as he thrust in and out.

She couldn't believe it. A second climax was building. *Dear Lord.*

The familiar rippling built to a peak and she cried out. He did too. She spasmed as her body shot into heaven again. His body jerked with wild abandon, both of them crashing over the same wave at the same time.

He rode her to the last aftershock and then collapsed on top of her. Taking his heat and weight was no hardship. She felt protected, covered with his love. Their chests heaved for another few seconds, and when he rolled off her, he gathered her in his arms.

"That was incredible," he said, panting. "I didn't hurt you, did I?"

"Hell, no. Every bit of it felt fantastic. I've never... well, let's just leave it at fantastic."

He chuckled. "Okay, then. If that will hold you for a while, I'll make something for dinner. I'm starving."

She was too but hadn't noticed until he said something. "Can I help?"

He rolled out of bed and pulled on his pants. "No. You stay right there and rest."

That sounded perfect to her. She didn't want to move. She could lie there and bask in the afterglow all night... or until dinner was ready.

"I'll tell you the rest after we eat."

The rest? "The rest of what?"

"Zina. I thought you wanted to know."

"Oh, I do." Bliss couldn't believe she'd almost forgotten about her nemesis. *Good sex will do that to a person, I guess.*

Drake chuckled. "Practice those words."

"What words?"

"I do."

Chapter 21

DRAKE AND BLISS SAT AT HIS TINY TABLE AND BUMPED knees. Fortunately, when bumping knees with the love of his life, Drake didn't mind at all.

"So, tell me. What happened to Zina?" Bliss took a bite of her chili dog—Drake's specialty—and chewed politely.

"Well, it's a long story."

She nodded, swallowed, and said, "I'm not going anywhere."

Unless you react badly to the truth, and then you might run out of here screaming.

"Well, it's like this… I need to tell you more about my supernatural world before what happened to Zina makes any sense to you."

Bliss groaned. "Oh, no. There's more? Is this it? Because I'm really getting sick of learning all this crap nobody knows and being sworn to secrecy."

"This is it. In fact, this is such a big secret, most paranormals don't even know about it."

"Fabulous," Bliss muttered.

"It's not too late if you really don't want to know. I don't have to—"

"Oh, yes you do. Otherwise I'll wonder and project and drive myself crazy. Please, tell me everything. Whatever it is, it can't be worse than finding out you're a dragon."

Hold that thought.

Drake bought some time by taking a bite of his own hot dog. Someone else did most of the cooking at the firehouse, and his kitchen was so tiny he'd never learned much more than how to open a can of chili and microwave a ready meal.

Bliss crossed her arms and waited for him to swallow. Apparently she wasn't going to eat until he told her the story. *Just as well… when she learns about Mother Nature and all the rest of the pantheon, she might choke on her hot dog.*

"Okay, here goes… Do you remember the Greek pantheon of gods and goddesses from your mythology books?"

Bliss turned her head without breaking eye contact. "Yeah…" she said slowly, as if preparing to be skeptical.

"Well, they're real. Case in point—Vulcan."

Her eyes narrowed. "But Vulcan is a Roman god."

"You're right. His name in Greek is Hephaestus, but he prefers Vulcan. It reminds him of his blacksmith shop inside a volcano. I don't think he gets to spend a lot of time there anymore, and he misses it." *Shut up, Drake. You're babbling.*

Bliss leaned forward. "Let me get this straight. You're saying the reason Vulcan was able to walk through a wall and transport me out of Zina's clutches was because he's a god?"

"Correct." *Whew, this is going better than I thought.*

And then Bliss burst out laughing. When her laughter disintegrated into giggles, she swiped at her eyes and said, "I suppose that's one explanation for a majorly cool magic trick."

Damn. If she didn't believe Vulcan was a god, how would he explain Gaia and all the rest?

She held up her index finger as if she'd just remembered something. "Okay, so let's say he's a god. When he took me somewhere with a blinding white light, was that supposed to be Heaven?"

"Ah, I don't think so. I wasn't with you so I can't say for sure, but he may have tried to blind you so you couldn't see the rest of the Council."

"Council? What Council?"

"It's called the Gods and Immortals Association."

"Wait a minute… we weren't alone. I *did* hear a woman chewing him out for taking me there."

Here we go… "That would be Gaia, also known as Mother Nature. She's the head of the Council."

Bliss's jaw dropped and the conversation took a long, awkward pause.

"She's the one who took Zina out."

Bliss gasped. "She killed her?"

"Well, no. I said that wrong. Actually, she took away her fire, her flight, and her fertility, then dumped her in Siberia.

At last, Bliss closed her mouth and gulped.

"She wants to meet you."

"Me? Are you saying Mother Nature is real and she wants to meet me?" Bliss's eyes opened so wide, he could see the white all around her pretty brown irises.

Drake took a deep breath. "Yes. She's very powerful, so I don't blame you for being afraid."

"I'm not…" Bliss took a deep breath and blew it out slowly. "Hell. I'm lying. I'm terrified. I can't forget that blinding light and her anger at Vulcan for bringing me… *wherever* it was."

"The Council is headquartered in a downtown office building."

"In Boston?"

"Yes. They can go anywhere they want to with a snap of their fingers, but they seem to like it here. At least Gaia does."

Bliss started with the giggles this time and worked herself into laughter. "Of all places… Boston? Why not Tahiti or Rio?"

"She likes the change of seasons."

"Well, she's freakin' got it here."

Drake chuckled, not only because Bliss entertained him, but also because he was relieved. His lover seemed to believe him. He smiled as he realized that was major evidence of her trust.

"So, why does she want to meet me?"

"She has a job offer for you."

Bliss's eyebrows shot up. "A job offer? What kind of job can I do for Mother Nature? Weed the public gardens? I'm pretty sure there are city workers already doing that."

Now Bliss was babbling. He had to quickly explain the situation before she panicked.

"Bliss, honey, listen carefully. When I helped capture Zina, Mother Nature rewarded me by giving me back my immortality. I respectfully declined unless she could do the same for you. I couldn't imagine going through eternity without the woman I love. As it turns out, she needs more muses. The original nine aren't able to keep up with all the technological advances." He waited for her to digest that much information before he continued… only Bliss filled in the blanks herself.

"And she wants me to be a muse?"

"Yes."

"But what about my greeting card career?"

"You can still do that. In fact, she wants you to use your expertise in that area."

"Huh?"

He reached across the table and took her hand. "You're talented. You're modern. You understand contemporary communication. She wants you to be the muse of social media."

"You're kidding. Like Twitter? What would I be? The head twit?"

"No, sweetheart. You'd be what you are—a goddess."

"Awww…" Her eyes softened and she gave his hand a squeeze. "But no. I really don't want a job outside of my card business. It's about to take off, and it'll be all I can do to keep up with that."

Drake reared back. "You don't want to be a goddess? Why not?"

"Well, for one thing, you know how I feel about the Internet. If I didn't trust it for my cards, how can I trust social media? I'll bet the pay and benefits suck too."

He laughed but couldn't help being a little disappointed.

"Way to go, Dragon Breath."

Bliss whirled around to see a woman standing behind her. She wore a flowing white gown and had long, white hair, crowned by a ring of blue cornflowers that matched her eyes.

It can't be…

The woman jammed her hands on her hips. "I wanted to be the one to tell her, blabbermouth. Now you've gone and ruined the surprise."

Drake cringed. "Sorry, Gaia, I thought I ought to prepare her for your arrival."

"Why? Because she might faint at the sight of me?"

He shrugged one shoulder. "Well, you never know… She's been incredibly understanding up to now, but everyone has their limits."

"Hey, people." Bliss waved. "I'm right here."

Mother Nature grinned. "She's feisty. I like that. Vulcan vouched for her, so I was pretty sure she could handle my glorious presence."

Drake smiled at Bliss and let go of her hand as he rose. "Gaia, I'd like to formally introduce you to Bliss Russo."

Bliss rose and offered Mother Nature her hand. "Pleased to meet you, Gaia."

"Odd little custom," Gaia muttered, but she shook hands with Bliss.

"Please… have a seat," Drake said and offered her his chair.

Mother Nature glanced around the room and finally pointed to a spot by the table where an extra chair appeared. "Sure. But first, I'd like a glass of water. Do you have any on tap?"

Drake moved quickly to the refrigerator. "I can do better than that. I have bottled water."

"Ack!" Gaia turned her head and shielded her eyes as if just seeing the item might offend her delicate sensibilities. "Don't tell me you buy water in those damn plastic bottles. It'll take centuries for them to decompose."

"Oh. I'm sorry. I didn't… never mind. I can get you a glass of tap water."

Still frowning, Gaia sat in the chair, then popped back up. She pointed to the seat and a cushion appeared. When she sat again, she wiggled a bit as if getting comfortable. "There. That's better. I don't mind a few modern conveniences as long as they don't muck up my world."

She tapped the chair next to her, inviting Bliss to sit down.

"Can you make one of those cushions for me too?" Bliss asked.

Gaia leaned back and studied her for a moment. "If you took the muse position, you could make it yourself." She sighed. "Let me give you a taste of what it would be like to be a goddess—even a minor one. Just point to the seat and think 'cushion.'"

Bliss could hardly believe this was happening. Did she have the power to make things appear and disappear at will now? She took a deep breath, closed her eyes, and thought, "Cushion."

Something soft landed on her head. Opening her eyes, she noticed a matching cushion to the one Mother Nature had conjured tumbling onto the floor.

Gaia reared back and laughed.

Bliss glanced at Drake, who appeared to be trying hard not to smile. He set the glass of water in front of Gaia.

"See? I'm not cut out for this," Bliss said.

"I've heard you're a quick study," Gaia said. "I won't have the time or patience to train you."

Bliss's eyes rounded. "Then how would I know what to do? I might transport myself into the middle of a tree or accidentally blow up the Internet."

Gaia smirked. "Don't worry. I wouldn't let you loose on the world without supervision." She snapped her fingers and another young woman appeared. She looked exotic and was wearing colorful silks in the style of a belly-dancing costume. "Where were you, Thalia?"

"Just having a bit of fun," the young woman said and chuckled. "Some kid found a beer can on the beach and rubbed it, wishing for a genie."

Mother Nature rolled her eyes. "Oh, yes… you'd get along just fine. Bliss, this is Thalia, the muse of comedy. *If* you take the offer, she'd show you how to be a muse. And, Thalia…" Gaia pointed to Bliss. "This one doesn't need you putting crazy ideas in her head. She has enough of those already. I'd just need you to teach her to be a well-behaved minor goddess."

"Of course." Thalia bowed to Mother Nature and rested a hand on Bliss's shoulder. "You can count on me. What will she be the muse of?"

Mother Nature pointed to the middle of the room where a desk and computer appeared. "Keeping electronic communication healthy. Not poetry readings like the rest of you ninnies. She'll be in charge of the Internet."

"Whoa." Bliss held up one hand. "Don't I get a vote? Because if I still have a shred of free will, I don't want the job."

Thalia muttered, "Damn! Me and my sisters would love to be rid of *that* responsibility."

Bliss shrugged. "Sorry."

Mother Nature folded her arms. "Are you sure?"

Thalia draped an arm around her shoulder. "We could have so much fun! Think of the video bloopers. You should at least try it." Thalia pointed directly at her. "Don't touch the politically incorrect jokes, though. The jokes are mine."

Bliss was tempted to back away. "Watch where you point that thing."

Thalia leaned back and laughed.

"Look, you make it sound like fun," Bliss said. "But I'll bet there's a whole lot of unfun stuff you're not telling me about."

Gaia straightened to her full height. Actually higher than her full height. She appeared to be hovering a few inches off the ground. Thunderclouds appeared in her eyes.

Oh, shit. Now I'm in for it.

Just as unexpectedly, Gaia floated to the floor and her whole demeanor changed. "How about a bribe? If you live in this little hovel, you can't be making that much. Here's a money tree." Gaia pointed to the spot where she'd put the desk, and it disappeared. A second later a tree with rectangular leaves replaced it.

Are you kidding me? Bliss strolled over to the tree and plucked a crisp hundred-dollar bill from a low branch. With her mouth hanging open, she swiveled toward Gaia. "You can do that?"

"Of course I can. I'm Mother-freakin'-Nature. If I want a tree to grow puppies, I can make one."

Bliss was too blown away to speak. Drake ambled over to her and put his arm around her waist. "I have some money saved up to buy us a bigger place. We don't need to rely on Mother Nature to provide for us."

Her gaze swept over the tree. It was firmly rooted in the floor. The ceiling was high enough to accommodate several branches, and there must have been thousands of dollars on it.

"I reward my muses. The last one wanted her own

gallery on Newbury Street. That wasn't cheap, either. Believe me."

Thalia chuckled. "Actually, I think the tree is kind of brilliant. Unless there's something else you want..."

Bliss stared at Drake and thought hard. At last she said, "I can't think of anything I want that I don't already have."

Drake pulled her into a long, warm hug.

"Aw... that's so sweet. I'd better go before you attract flies."

"Wait," Drake said. "Before you go. If Bliss doesn't want to be a muse, I don't want to be immortal."

Gaia's jaw dropped.

"I can't imagine facing eternity without her."

The powerful goddess threw her hands in the air. "You two are impossible to please."

"Sorry," Bliss said. "But thank you for the generous offer."

"We're happy just the way we are," Drake added. He wrapped an arm around Bliss's waist and gave her a side squeeze.

"Your loss." Mother Nature folded her arms and disappeared.

Thalia stayed behind.

Bliss leaned in and lowered her voice. "Can she hear us?"

"Only if she wants to, and I doubt she does."

"Whew. I can't imagine working for her. She seems so..." Bliss couldn't come up with the right word.

"Cynical? Snarky? Scoffing? Mocking?" Thalia supplied plenty of appropriate options to choose from.

"Yeah. All of that."

Thalia shrugged. "You get used to it."

"Well, I'm used to working for myself, and I like it that way."

"Are you sure you won't change your mind? There are so many cool things you could do. Do you like Paris?"

"I've never been there."

One finger snap later, Bliss and Thalia were sitting atop the Eiffel Tower. It lit up the night in multiple colors. Bliss panicked and grabbed on to a steel beam. "What the… ? How did you do that?"

"Simple." Thalia snapped her fingers and they returned to Drake's apartment.

He was glancing all around as if wondering where they went. "Sheesh. I was afraid I'd lost you."

"You'll never lose me." Bliss walked into Drake's open arms. Thalia smiled and said, "I guess you really do have what you want."

"I really do."

Thalia winked and disappeared.

"Well, that was… enlightening," Bliss said.

"Once again, you amaze me."

"How is that?"

"You stuck to your guns. Even the most powerful goddess on earth can't beg or bribe you out of your integrity."

Bliss smiled. "And you impressed me too, lover. Giving up your immortality? For me? Are you sure you want to do that?"

He caressed her arms and gazed into her eyes. "Positive."

They shared a long, languorous kiss. Their lips parted at the same time, and their tongues sought each other and swirled in perfect synchronization. Bliss's heart was full.

"I have to go to my parents' house tonight," Bliss said. "If I don't get there soon, they'll send out a Saint Bernard to find me."

"I imagine they already have the red carpet rolled out for you," Drake said.

"Uh… maybe. But the party might be over as soon as I deliver some bad news."

"Bad news? What is it, honey? Maybe I can help."

"No. I'm afraid you *are* the bad news."

"Huh?"

"I have to let my mother know I won't be producing grandchildren."

"Oh. I can be there to support you. Maybe if she knows how much I love you… and I'd be fine with adoption."

Bliss held up one hand. "Stop. That's why I can't have you there. You might say something to get her hopes up. I'm not sure if *I* want kids. *We* haven't discussed it yet. All I want to do is tell her not to fix up the nursery. I can do that on my own."

"Are you sure?"

"I'm sure. In fact, I should get going. Seriously. I've put this off for too long as it is, but it's time."

Drake nodded and let her go.

Bliss strolled up to her parents' front door and knocked.

When her mother opened the door she blinked. "Bliss. Why did you knock? Don't you have your keys?"

"No. I forgot them at Drake's place, but we were half-way here and I didn't want him to turn around and go back."

Her mother stuck her head out the door and glanced up and down the front porch. "Where's Drake? And for that matter, where's your luggage? Your purse?"

"Ma. I forgot everything in Drake's truck. I was a little—distracted. I have something important to discuss with you."

"Oh, no. You two didn't have a fight, did you?"

"No. We're fine."

Mrs. Russo wiped her forehead dramatically. "Whew!"

"So, can I come in or what?"

"Oh. Of course." Her mother giggled and stepped aside.

Bliss headed to the kitchen where they always had their talks. Serious talks or just chitchat. It happened more easily in the kitchen. She started to open the refrigerator for a bottle of water. Suddenly, Mother Nature's reaction replayed in her head and she grabbed a glass from the cabinet and drew her water from the tap instead.

"Tap water? We have some of the good stuff in the fridge."

"No, thanks. I want to lessen my carbon footprint."

"Whatever that means," her mother mumbled.

I won't bother to explain it now. "Where's Dad?"

"He's in the basement, of course. Is this serious, Blissy?" Malinda Russo's pretty forehead had few wrinkles unless she was worried. At that moment new wrinkles seemed to make an appearance. Bliss wondered how many of those were her fault. Chances were that Ricky and Emilio had contributed plenty.

"It's not terrible… at least not to me. You might be disappointed, though."

"Did they take the prize away from you? Were

you mugged? Drugged?" She gasped. "Were you in another fire—"

"Ma, stop! I'm fine."

At last her mother said, "I'll get Daddy," and she strode to the cellar door.

Oh, no. Her mother didn't call him "Daddy" unless she was preparing to make Bliss feel like a little girl again. No doubt her mother was already planning to make Bliss move back in so she could take care of her.

"Romeo," her mother bellowed. "Bliss is home, and she has something bad to tell us."

"Oh crap," she heard her father say from below.

Bliss groaned. "Don't make a big deal out of it, Mom. It's really not that bad." *I hope.*

When all three of them were seated at the kitchen table, Bliss began. "I don't know any way to say this tactfully, so I'll just say it."

"Why should this be different from any other conversation?" her father mumbled.

Bliss held her tongue until the urge to retaliate had passed. "Look. I know you were counting on grandchildren…"

Her mother's hand flew to her chest. She looked like she was holding her breath, so Bliss thought she'd better get to the point before her mother passed out.

"Drake's sterile. We won't be having kids."

Her mother sagged back in her chair, and her hand dropped to dangle by her side.

"That's it?" her father asked. "That's the big, bad news?"

"Yeah. That's it."

Mrs. Russo closed her eyes and swallowed. She

looked as if she were counting to ten. At last, she opened her glistening eyes and said, "Honey, it's not the end of the world."

Bliss almost fell off her chair. "It's not?"

"No. It's not. There are alternatives these days. There are sperm banks and—"

"Oh, for the love of… Look. We aren't even married yet. We don't know if we want to pursue other options or not. I just wanted you to know so you wouldn't be hinting to Drake or asking me every month if I'd missed my period."

"That's it for me," her father said. He rose and went back to the basement.

Her mother put on a brave smile. "I understand, Blissy. I'll let you two figure it out on your own. Lord, I was afraid you were going to tell me the wedding was off."

Bliss chuckled. "Well, we haven't set a date or anything. I figure you guys will understand if we just elope to Las Vegas."

Mrs. Russo shot to her feet. "How dare you! Your father and I have been saving money for your wedding since you were born."

Bliss laughed. "Relax, Ma. I was kidding."

Her mother plopped onto her chair and gazed at the ceiling. "You'll be the death of me, young lady."

"So, is it a deal? No pressure on me to have kids? And you won't hold it against Drake?"

Her mother leaned over and smoothed Bliss's hair like when she was little. "As long as he makes you happy, honey, that's the most important thing."

"He does, Ma. He really does."

Chapter 22

"WE NEED TO PICK A DATE SOON. EVEN IF WE NARROW it down to a month, that should satisfy your parents for a while."

"Yeah, in other words, before my mother has a chance to bug us about it."

Drake chuckled. He was getting to know the Russos fairly well. As much as they all complained about Malinda's nagging, they loved her dearly. In fact, Drake and Bliss were strolling through the Russos' neighborhood, having come for a visit—voluntarily.

"So, what are you thinking of in terms of a good month?" Bliss asked. "Is there a fire season or anything we should avoid?"

"The city doesn't have to worry about that as much as rural areas do. High summer when the vegetation is dry can be a problem out in the country—or even the suburbs. But we shouldn't need to worry about it."

"Yeah, now that Zina is gone, the city doesn't have to worry at all." Bliss bit her lip. "She *is* gone, isn't she?"

"She really is. And I don't think she'll be bothering us anymore after the dressing-down she got from Gaia."

Bliss seemed to relax. "Autumn is nice. Does that sound okay to you?"

Drake draped an arm around her shoulder. "Anything you want is fine with me."

"Maybe we should get married sooner. Like as soon

as we can book a church and fake you a birth certificate. Then they wouldn't have time to put together a full-blown carnival. I know my mother will be relieved that she's not the only one who rushed into a June wedding."

"Can you handle the pressure of coordinating something quickly?"

Bliss laughed. "I think you know I can handle pressure. Hell, I work best under pressure."

"You're amazing. You deserve to have the wedding you want. I'm still impressed by how well you handled Zina's threats to you at the time."

Bliss snorted. "I was scared, but I didn't have time to fall apart. And I didn't want her to get the better of me and run my life. Not even for a little while."

Drake kissed her cheek. "That's the woman I love."

"Come to think of it, you must be afraid sometimes when you run into a fire—but you do it anyway."

"I'm more afraid for the guys with me. I'm fireproof. They're not."

"True." After a few moments of quiet contemplation, she brightened. "We're getting off the subject. So, when do you want to get married?"

"Now."

Bliss chuckled. "Right this minute?"

"Yup. Right here, right now."

"You know my parents would have a fit."

"I know. We'll give them the whole three-ring circus later, but right now—while it's just you and me…" Drake stopped walking and took both of Bliss's hands in his. He faced her and said, "Bliss Russo, will you take this sorry-ass dragon to be your lawfully wedded husband for as long as you can tolerate me?"

Bliss laughed. "In other words, forever?"

Her smile warmed his heart. "If forever exists, then yes."

"Yes, Drake Cameron. I will. Do you think you can put up with my sarcasm and impatience for the rest of eternity?"

"I do."

"I now pronounce us officially crazy," Bliss said, and they kissed.

Epilogue

BLISS OPENED HER EYES AND FOUND HERSELF NOSE TO snout with a dragon in her bed. She shrieked and jumped out from under the covers, knowing but not caring that she was naked.

Drake shifted into his human form, laughing.

"Don't *do* that!" Bliss shouted.

He wiped a tear from the corner of his eye as he struggled to get his laughter under control. "I'm sorry, honey. I got so hot watching my beautiful wife sleeping beside me that I shifted."

"Oh. Well, in that case…" Bliss returned to bed and scooted into his waiting arms.

"Have I told you I love you?" he asked.

"About a million times, but you can tell me again if you want to."

Drake rolled up onto his elbow and stared down at her. "I love you, Bliss Cameron. I never thought I'd find a woman like you."

"What do you mean, like me?"

"Beautiful, intelligent, fun, *and* dragon tolerant."

She snorted. "Just don't make a habit of testing that tolerance like you did this morning."

"Good morning, Mr. and Mrs. Dragon!"

Bliss startled, then rolled toward the female voice in their spacious new bedroom. She began to sputter, "What is with you people and knock—"

Mother Nature stood there, crossed her arms, and frowned.

"Oh, it's you," Bliss said sheepishly. "Sorry."

Gaia rolled her eyes. "I suppose I can forgive you. I'm here to update you on the Zina fiasco."

"Zina!" Bliss grasped the sheet to her chest as she sat up. "Is she back?"

"No. And don't bother covering your breasts. I've seen them before."

Bliss raised her eyebrows. "You have?"

"Well, not specifically yours, but millions of others. Let's get to that update, shall we?"

Drake pulled himself up and rested against the headboard next to his wife. "Please tell me she's not in our hemisphere. You warned her not to come back."

"I realize that. Now be a good dragon and shut up while I talk."

Bliss opened her mouth to address the way Gaia spoke to her husband, but as soon as she noticed Mother Nature's intense glare, she quickly shut it. No use poking the beehive. A metaphor inspired by Gaia's current hairdo.

Mother Nature relaxed and smiled at Bliss. "As you may or may not know, I sent her off with a specific set of circumstances and a warning. I told her she wouldn't be fertile again until she learned how to handle it. In other words, she'd have to attract a voluntary mate, create a safe and loving environment to bring a child into the world, and try to be the best mother she can be."

Bliss blew out a deep breath. "Do you think she can do all that?"

Gaia shrugged. "I don't know, but at least she has a chance."

"More of a chance than we have," Bliss muttered.

Gaia waved away her complaint and continued. "I haven't discussed your reward for trapping her so Vulcan could bring her to me yet. Wouldn't you like to know what it is?"

Bliss's eyes popped open. "There's a reward?"

"Indeed. Now, I understand you two would like to have a family someday, but as we all know, dragons and humans can mate until the sun and moon collide, but no child will come of it."

Drake hung his head, apparently blaming himself for dashing their hopes and dreams. Bliss reached over and took his hand. "That's okay. We're making peace with it."

A sly smile raised one side of the goddess's lips and her eyes twinkled. "What if I could change that?"

Bliss gaped. "Can you?"

"Remember who you're talking to."

Drake squeezed her hand but didn't say anything.

"Of course." Bliss nodded, reverently—at least she hoped she conveyed reverence. "If anyone could change that, it would be you."

"Exactly. Keep creating the loving, child-friendly environment you have here—and begin using birth control."

With that, Gaia disappeared. Bliss didn't know if Mother Nature heard her gasp, but she gasped loudly.

"Drake. Do you know what that means?"

He was grinning. "I think we can have kids."

"She must have altered your DNA or something. I wish she'd stuck around to explain it. Holy moly, we didn't even get a chance to thank her."

Drake chuckled. "You know she's all business. I get the feeling that was her way of thanking *you*."

"Oh, my God! Or goddess. We should celebrate. Tell our friends…"

"Slow down, sweetheart. Let's take a shower together first."

Bliss grinned, then remembered their new status. "Shoot. We need some kind of birth control. We don't even have condoms."

Drake rolled out of bed and strode over to her. He took her in his arms and said in a low voice, "Or we could take our chances. Either way, I'm okay with the consequences. Are you?"

Bliss didn't have to think it over very long. Giving birth, taking care of, and loving Drake's baby would make her happier than ever. Her mother would be insanely happy to babysit if Bliss couldn't take the little tyke with her when she was needed elsewhere. And she could still make her cards during nap time.

"Yes. I'm fine with whatever happens too. Let's take that shower together."

"I'll race you."

Acknowledgments

I need to give a big, big thank-you to Massachusetts firefighter Tom Madigan. He proofread all my scenes having to do with Drake's job and gave me some terrific suggestions. Did I mention he has a great sense of humor too?

And it wouldn't be right to thank Tom without thanking Sherry Ingalls, the fan who loaned me her hottie fireman for research. Not *that* kind of research! Jeez, people. I have a husband for that.

And speaking of my husband, I am soooooo lucky to be married to my best friend, love of my life, Renaissance man, and sugar daddy. There's nothing he can't do—except write novels. We all owe him a big thank-you for letting me do the one thing I'm sort of good at.

And finally, I want to thank the people who looked at the bearable first draft and helped me make it better. Mia Marlowe, Aubrey Poole, Nicole Resciniti, and Virginia Ettel, and last but not least, my fabulous editor Leah Hultenschmidt.

In case you missed it, read on for an excerpt from

Flirting Under a Full Moon

Now available from Ashlyn Chase
and Sourcebooks Casablanca

OVER THE DIN OF CLINKING ICE AND LIVELY CONVERSA-
tion, the entire bar heard waitress Brandee Hanson wail,
"Dumped in a text message? *Really?*"

Suddenly the place quieted. Heat crept up her neck,
and she dropped her BlackBerry into her apron pocket.
She was about to slink off to the ladies' room when
Sadie Maven, the owner's eccentric aunt, waved her
over to the booth she regularly occupied.

"Have a seat, dear. Let me do a quick reading for
you—on the house." Sadie was already shuffling her
tarot cards.

Brandee slumped onto the opposite bench and set
down her tray.

"I had a premonition about you just now." Sadie
winked. "It might make you feel better."

Brandee sighed. "I'm all for feeling better. Just don't
talk about my love life. I've sworn off men."

"Since when?"

"Since just now."

Sadie spread the cards across the table. "Pick one."

Brandee pulled one card from the middle and turned
it over. On it was a picture of a couple entwined in a
passionate embrace, and the text beneath proclaimed:
The Lovers.

"Ah. I was right. You'll meet your true love soon. In
fact, he could be the next man to walk through that door."

Psychic Sadie nodded toward Boston Uncommon's Charles Street entrance.

Brandee gazed at the door expectantly. It swung open and a tall, blond, broad-shouldered hunk of a man breezed in.

Oh no. It couldn't be. "One-Night Nick? Are you kidding me?" She burst out laughing.

Sadie shrugged one shoulder. "You never know…"

Brandee picked up her tray and returned to work, still chuckling and shaking her head.

"What put that smile on your face, beautiful? Besides seeing me, of course." Nick Wolfensen grabbed a stool and sat on it backward. Even with the stool's height, his big feet hit the floor. His powerful thighs bulged under his blue jeans. That wasn't the only bulge she thought she saw.

Brandee knew her regulars and Nick was a good tipper. She'd play nice, even though Sadie's omen sat uncomfortably in the back of her mind. "Just something Sadie said. I think I've served her one too many White Russians."

"Well, you haven't served me at all, girl. I'm parched."

"What can I get you?"

"Whatever Sam Adams you have on tap."

"Coming right up."

Usually Angie would get Nick's beer, but the bartender looked engrossed in a conversation. Brandee lifted the part of the bar that flipped up and strode in. "It must be your evening off. You're not in uniform, and you're ordering a brew."

Nick frowned. "Yeah, kind of."

His set jaw and the twitch in his cheek told her she shouldn't pursue the subject. She simply grabbed a frosted mug and held it at an angle under the tap like Angie had shown her. It created less froth and made room for more beer.

When she set it in front of him, his cocky smile returned. "Ah, you're a good girl. I'd sing 'Brandy' but you've probably heard it a few thousand times."

"Yeah, thanks for not doing that." Brandee played the song in her head, and when the words pointed out what a good wife she would be, she scurried away, mumbling, "Well, I gotta get back to work."

She grabbed a clean rag and wiped down a table that didn't need it. Over her shoulder she caught Nick unabashedly admiring her rear end. She quickly moved on to another empty table and made sure she was facing him. As soon as she bent over to reach the surface, her V-neck dipped. Now he was gazing at her cleavage like he might drool. She bolted upright.

Oh, my Fruity Pebbles. Why can't he turn around?

Nick rose, left his beer on the bar, and strolled over to her. He leaned down so he could whisper in her ear. "When, Brandee?"

She tried to look casual. "When what?"

"When are you going to let me show you the time of your life?"

She smiled, thinking what that might entail, but quickly schooled her expression. "I'm not that kind of girl."

He tried to look innocent, but she knew it was an act. Players like Nick scared her. Not that it stopped her from fantasizing about him. Handsome, charming, intelligent, and dangerous. Whether she had just been dumped or not, he wasn't the kind of guy she needed right now—or maybe ever.

Nick backed up a step. "What are you talking about?"

Brandee rested a hand on her hip and tried to look uncompromising. "I know your reputation. They don't call you 'One-Night Nick' for nothing."

"At least I'm honest about it. I never lead girls on by saying, 'I'll call you,' then leave them to wonder why I didn't. A lot of guys do. I treat a woman to an awesome night she'll never forget. I'm just not interested in getting tied down right now."

She lowered her voice. "Look, I'm not saying I want to get married either. But casual sex isn't my style."

He feigned shock, then boomed in his baritone, "Who said anything about sex? Of course if that's what *you* want, I'd be happy to oblige."

"Oh, my Playboy penthouse… Lower your voice, dammit." She glanced around, but people seemed to have lost interest in her. They continued their own conversations or preoccupation with the football game. *Thank you, Tom Brady.*

"What's your penthouse got to do with anything?"

She chuckled. "I don't live in a penthouse, I live over the bar. That's just something I do when I'm shocked. Instead of saying, "Oh my God—I substitute some other word or words for God."

"Are you religious? Don't want to take the Lord's name in vain or something?"

"Heck no. It's just way overused. I don't want to wear it out." She faced Sadie, who she knew took an interest in all the waitresses' love lives. Sadie shuffled her tarot cards with a knowing smile on her face.

He chuckled. "I'm not going to lie to you, Brandee. I think you're sexy as hell, and redheads are my weakness, but if you can't allow yourself a night of fun without some damn commitment…"

She sighed. "It's not like that."

"Then what is it?"

She couldn't put her feelings into words. Sure she'd like to have a good time, but was one night worth the trouble and expense of getting a full body wax and a mani-pedi and buying a new outfit? She needed her tips to pay for her photography supplies. A night with the handsome cop would probably steal her breath away, but she didn't want to risk losing her heart too.

He waved and walked away. "Forget it."

By the time he had retaken his stool and started watching the game, Brandee regretted her hesitancy. Damn it all, Nick was hot. His blond hair was growing out just enough to curl around his ears, and his sapphire blue eyes were impossible to ignore. A suspect wouldn't stand a chance against that intense stare. Hell. *She* didn't stand a chance when he looked at her with those gorgeous eyes.

Still, "No casual sex, no matter how tempting the guy might be" was a good policy. She *did* want to fall in love and get married some day. Even a protected one-night stand could result in a life-altering "accident." And if that happened, it would *not* be with a playboy like Nick Wolfensen.

A man who only dated to have a night of fun with a different woman each time must be extremely superficial. How satisfying could that be? What would make someone do that? Had he been hurt so badly he didn't want to risk it again? She couldn't think of any other reason.

Sadie caught her attention and held up her empty glass, calling for another.

Oh my pickled herring…that woman can put them away. But her nephew owned the bar and he'd told the staff to keep her happy. Not only did Anthony seem genuinely fond of his aunt, but she was good for business. To sit at her booth and have a tarot card reading, the patron had to meet the one-drink minimum.

When Brandee delivered Sadie's fourth White Russian, the fortune-teller said, "You know, my Dmitri was like that once."

"Like what?"

She smirked. "You should know better than to feign innocence with a psychic."

Brandee rolled her eyes. "Fine. So, you had a commitment-phobic boyfriend."

Sadie shuffled the cards again. "It wasn't that as much as he wanted to be free when the right woman came along. He really didn't like the idea of hurting anyone." She flipped over a card. "I think your Nick is doing the same thing."

"First of all, he's not *my* Nick."

Sadie pushed the card across the table toward her. "If you say so."

Brandee glanced at the card, then stared more closely. It was the same one. A man and a woman entwined in a passionate embrace. The Lovers.

Oh, my heartbreak…I'm toast.

―◆◆◆―

"What's got your jockstrap in a twist?" Konrad asked.

Nick sat across from his twin brother, with a big mahogany desk between them. "It's nothing." He reached out and ran his hand over the polished surface, glancing at the gleaming brass plate that read Dean Konrad Wolfensen. "Jeez, I can't visit you without feeling like I've been sent to the principal's office."

Konrad laughed. "Maybe you were there too many times when we were kids. What's going on?"

"I quit."

Konrad's jaw dropped. "The force?"

"Yeah, what else do I have to quit?"

"Why?"

Nick fidgeted in his seat. He couldn't very well say his brother's high-profile court case had damaged his credibility, could he? Just because they looked exactly alike and Konrad had incurred public wrath and humiliation, Nick couldn't be absolutely sure that was the only reason his honor had been questioned—more than once—even though he had done nothing to deserve it. He hated the idea that it might be his brother's fault.

"I was butting heads with some of the guys."

"What about?"

Nick shrugged. "Nothing in particular. John Q. Public has been pissing me off too."

"Are you sleeping?"

"Not well."

"You look like you've lost weight."

Nick glanced down at his baggy Dockers. "Yeah, maybe a little."

"Sorry, Bro. I hate to say it, but it sounds like symptoms of depression."

Nick laughed. "Me? What do I have to be depressed about?"

Konrad gave him a sympathetic smile. "You just

stood up for me as my best man. Maybe without realizing it..."

"You think I'm jealous? Of you?" Nick was about to let out another bellowing laugh, but he thought better of it. He didn't want to insult his brother—or his new sister-in-law. Roz was a great girl and Konrad had found his true mate. Marriage was right for him. Nick didn't want to settle for less than that, and he didn't have to. He just had to be patient—correction—*more* patient, but it better not take much longer. At one hundred and one years old, Nick's secret wish was to find the *right* one without being attached to the wrong one.

"So tell me about quitting the force after nine years. It can't be over a few personality clashes."

Nick shifted uncomfortably. "What are you, my shrink now?"

"No, of course not, but you called and said you wanted to see me."

"I was bored."

Konrad leaned back in his big, oak armchair. "You were bored? You interrupted my workday because you were bored?"

"Hey, sorry I bothered you." Nick rose, ready to walk out.

"Stop. I didn't mean to run you off. You're here now, and I'm sure you weren't in the neighborhood. Newton isn't exactly around the corner."

"Nah, you're right. I should let you get back to work."

"Not if you need me. Look, I know you're not telling me everything. What's going on?"

Nick let out a long sigh. Konrad was right. There was more to it than just quitting his job. His lifestyle didn't hold the same glamour it once had, but he didn't dare voice that thought. Everyone was quick to tell him he needed to find a nice girl and settle down. Better to blame his boredom on job dissatisfaction. "I need to work for myself. I'm tired of taking orders, but I don't want to give them either."

"Then you're kind of fucked."

"Not necessarily. I thought of a way to work for myself without taking on a bunch of pesky employees. I'm getting my PI license."

"Private investigator?"

"No, public idiot. Of course private investigator. I'd be perfect for it. With my experience as a cop, I know the law—and how to get around it. As a paranormal PI, I can corner a niche market. There aren't any others in Boston."

"I don't know," Konrad said. "Public idiot sounds a lot more fun."

Nick snorted. "Well, I've made up my mind. I'm going to be a paranormal PI. There's only one thing left to do. I need three upstanding citizens to vouch for me."

"So that's why you're here?"

"That and to see my brother and his lovely wife."

"Stay for dinner. I'll give Roz a call." Konrad picked up the phone.

"If it's no trouble. Since she's an attorney, I was hoping to ask her to be one of my three upstanding citizens."

"I'm sure she'd be honored."

"I'll get out of your hair and see who might be hanging around the teachers' lounge. Is it okay if I stop back later to see what she says about dinner?"

"Why don't you wait a minute? Then you won't have to interrupt me twice."

After a brief conversation, Konrad ended the call with a whispered endearment. He grinned and hung up.

A pang of envy took Nick by surprise. *Damn it, maybe he and everyone else is right. All I need is the right girl…wherever she is. So why is it taking so long?*

"Roz said she'll thaw another steak. Not to worry. You're always welcome."

"Thanks. Well, I'll let you get back to work. What time should I show up at your apartment?"

"Six would be good."

"I'll be there. Meanwhile, I'll see if I can find two more upstanding citizens who will vouch for me."

Konrad rose. "What about me?"

Good God. How can I turn down my brother's generous offer without offending the hell out of him? My identical twin brother, who got busted for the biggest art heist in history, won't go a long way toward credibility. Even though he was proven innocent, people will believe what they want to believe.

"I think you're too close. I mean, really…it's like getting your mom to say what a good boy you are."

"Yeah. I can see that. Well, good luck finding any of the fifty pack members who love you to attest to your character."

Nick smiled. *Yeah, there are advantages to being in good stead with one's werewolf pack—at last. I'm glad I wasn't the only one who believed in my brother's innocence.*

Chapter 2

"ONE-NIGHT NICK? WAS SADIE SOBER?" BRANDEE'S bartender-roommate stretched the kinks out of her shoulders after a long shift.

"I think so. I can usually tell when Sadie's had enough." Brandee dropped onto the soft sectional in their living room, removed her shoes, and massaged her aching feet.

"Do you think she was dealing from the bottom of the deck?"

"Nope. She was shuffling the cards as she always does."

It was nice of Angie to attempt to discredit the psychic to make Brandee feel better, but Sadie was never wrong. *Never*.

"Did she come right out and say it was a prediction?"

"Kinda, sorta, not really."

"What exactly did she say?"

"Something about having a premonition that I'd be meeting Mr. Right soon. Then she said the next man through the door could be the love of my life…and Nick walked in."

"She said 'could.' That means she *could be wrong*."

"Have you ever known Sadie to be wrong? I think she just says 'could' because she doesn't want to imply a person has no free will. Maybe she's afraid of being wrong if a person is determined to prove her wrong."

Angie gave her a sympathetic look. "Maybe. Or

maybe there really aren't any guarantees. I know she's constantly been right before, but there's always a first time to mess up, right?"

"Let's hope so. I need my heart broken like a nunnery needs a condom dispenser." Brandee rested her elbows on her knees and dropped her head in her hands. "I thought maybe the jerk-face who dumped me was my ticket out of Boringsville."

Angie scrutinized her. "What do you mean?"

"You know. Living above the place I work. Struggling to make ends meet and hopefully save a little money for a rainy day. Hell, I thought I might even be able to afford my dream of owning a gallery if he and I..." She let out a long sigh. "Forget it."

"You're kidding. You really expect some guy to swoop in and rescue you from a life you don't like?"

"No! Oh, my female gigolo...no." Brandee shook her head emphatically. "It's just damn hard to make it as an artist and support myself at the same time."

"Did you think he was Mr. Right?"

She shrugged. "Mr. Possible, maybe." *Time to change the subject.* "By the way, as soon as you're ready for bed, can I commandeer the bathroom for the rest of the night?"

"Oh, crap. Did you forget you're lactose intolerant again?"

Brandee snorted. "No. Do you hear me burping up a lung? And for your information, I don't *forget* my condition. I just forget to take my medication with me sometimes and then can't resist a special treat.

"I want to set up a temporary darkroom in the bathroom. I *have* to begin selling my work, not just to get a few dollars ahead, but also to build a name for myself."

"I get that. So what do you have to do to sell your photographs?"

"Create a look or product no one else has. Make my name synonymous with that product. Capitalize on opportunities for publicity, and make everyone who can afford my work want to collect it."

"That's all, huh?" Angie gave her a sympathetic look. "I'll get you a glass of wine."

"I'll get it. You do that all day."

Angie was already walking toward the kitchen. "It's how I show I care."

Brandee chuckled. "It's how you support yourself. Besides, I know you care. Otherwise I wouldn't have told you what I'm going through."

"Yes you would," Angie called from the next room. The refrigerator door opened and clunked shut. A few moments later she strolled back into the living room, holding two glasses of white wine. "You tell me everything."

"Do you ever get tired of it?"

"Tired of what? Your train wreck of a life?"

"Not just mine. Lots of people tell you more than you want to hear. It looked as if someone was talking your ear off when I was getting Nick his beer."

"Nah. That was just a tourist wanting recommendations for cheap hotels. Like fifty bucks a night."

Angie handed her a glass of Chardonnay, and Brandee took a welcome sip. "Fifty dollars? In this city?"

"Yeah, that's a hoot, huh? I tried to recommend the hostel I'd heard about, but they weren't interested."

Brandee leaned back against the loose pillows. "So, getting back to me…if you were in my knockoff shoes, would you accept a date with Nick Wolfensen?"

"Not unless he changed his policy."

"That's what I was thinking. But how do you tell a guy to completely change his lifestyle?"

"Just come right out and say it. Someone needs to." Angie sipped her wine.

"I guess so. I've got nothing to lose if there's nothing to gain."

Angie scratched her head. "I think that made sense."

Brandee thumped her feet onto the coffee table and crossed them at the ankles. "Okay, I'll confront him."

"Good. Do it where I can watch."

"Pervert."

"Nick, I know this is your first case, but we're desperate. The mayor's stepdaughter has been kidnapped."

"*Desperate?*" *That's hardly a vote of confidence*. "If you're so desperate, why use a brand-new PI? There are plenty of options for a kidnapping case." *Nick wanted the job, but his cop instincts told him something didn't sound right*. Captain Hunter had arranged this meeting fifteen minutes ago. They met at Boston Uncommon but left the bar immediately so they could talk in private.

"There are paranormal circumstances, and we don't have time for lengthy explanations."

"I see. What are these 'circumstances'?"

"She's a fire mage."

Nick's eyebrows shot up. "Shit." He stopped at a bench and glanced around. No one was within earshot, so he and Hunter sat down. "Do you think the kidnappers know this?"

"Don't know. No ransom demands have been made. There's been no contact at all."

"Any witnesses?"

"A neighbor thought she heard something like a muffled yelp of surprise, but when she looked out her window she didn't see anything."

"Where were her parents?"

"The mayor was at City Hall and her mother was in the house. She didn't think she needed to supervise a twelve-year-old in her own backyard. Now she's sick with guilt."

Nick felt for the poor woman. The best way to help her was to find her daughter. "So they may have kidnapped her for her power." Nick rubbed his chin. "The criminal who's not looking for money is usually looking for some kind of power."

"It gets worse. The girl doesn't know what she can do yet. A female fire mage won't realize her power until the first solar eclipse after she hits puberty. Her mother kept putting off telling her."

"Shit. She's untrained and unprepared. Her parents must be frantic."

"To put it mildly." The captain rested his hand on Nick's shoulder. "This case could make or break your career. I wouldn't blame you if you decline, but I hope you won't. I think you're our only hope."

How could he refuse? Not only would he feel responsible if anything happened to the girl, but she could burn the city to the ground if the kidnappers couldn't teach her how to control the power she didn't even know she had—the power to set fires with no more than a thought.

"I'll do my best."

The captain let out a long breath, as if he'd been holding it for a while. "You'd better do better than your best. The next solar eclipse is in nine days."

Strange Neighbors

by Ashlyn Chase

—✦—

He's looking for peace, quiet, and a little romance...

There's never a dull moment when hunky all-star pitcher and shapeshifter Jason Falco invests in an old Boston brownstone apartment building full of supernatural creatures. But when Merry MacKenzie moves into the ground floor apartment, the playboy pitcher decides he might just be done playing the field...

A girl just wants to have fun...

Sexy Jason seems like the perfect fling, but newly independent nurse Merry's not sure she's ready to trust him with her heart...especially when the tabloids start trumpeting his playboy lifestyle.

Then pandemonium breaks loose and Merry and Jason will never get it together without a little help from the vampire who lives in the basement and the werewolf from upstairs...

—✦—

"The good-natured fun never stops. Chase
brings on plenty of laughs along with steamy
sex scenes."—*Publishers Weekly*

For more Ashlyn Chase, visit:

www.sourcebooks.com

The Werewolf Upstairs

by Ashlyn Chase

Petty crime never looked so good…

Alpha werewolf Konrad Wolfensen sees it as his duty to protect the citizens of Boston, even if it means breaking into their businesses just to prove their security systems don't work. But when his unsolicited services land him in trouble with the law, he'll have to turn to his sexy new neighbor for help.

She should know better…

Attorney Roz Wells is bored. She used to have such a knack for attracting the weird and unexpected, but ever since she took a job as a Boston public defender, the quirky quotient in her life has taken a serious hit. Until her sexy werewolf neighbor starts coming around…

"Original and full of laughs, steamy sex, and madcap mayhem."—*Night Owl Romance*

"Beyond funny, extremely sexy, and jam-packed full of eccentric character-driven chaotic fun from cover to cover."—*Bitten by Books*

For more Ashlyn Chase, visit:

www.sourcebooks.com

The Vampire
Next Door

by Ashlyn Chase

———

Room for Rent: Normal need not apply

This old Boston brownstone is not known for quiet living…
first the shapeshifter meets his nurse, then the werewolf falls
for his sassy lawyer, but now the vampire is looking for love
with a witch who's afraid of the dark…and you thought your
neighbors had issues!

Undead Sly is content playing vigilante vampire, keeping the
neighborhood safe from human criminals, until Morgaine
moves in upstairs. Suddenly he finds himself weak with desire,
which isn't a good place for a vampire to be. And Morgaine
isn't exactly without her own issues—will the two of them
be able to get past their deepest fears before their chance at
"normal" slips away…

———

Praise for The Werewolf Upstairs:

"Witty and wonderful…the entertaining plot,
humor, sizzling sensual scenes, and romance make
this story unforgettable." —*Romance Junkies*

For more Ashlyn Chase books, visit:

www.sourcebooks.com

USA Today Bestselling Author

Jaguar Fever

by Terry Spear

———

She's a material girl…

Being the only jaguar shape-shifter in town was getting tiresome for Maya Anderson. She's finally found a hangout in a nearby city where she can go on the prowl with her own kind—and she intends to make the most of it.

In a feline world…

Wade Patterson knew he could love her the moment he looked into Maya's piercing eyes, but he thinks she's in over her head with the big city cats. Wade's playing a deadly game of cat and mouse with a different sort of predator, and if Maya gets in the middle, they're all going to find out just how wild a jungle cat can be.

———

Praise for **Savage Hunger***:*

"Spear paints a colorful, vivid portrait of the lush jungle and deadly beauty… of jaguars."—*Publishers Weekly*

"A sizzling page turner."—*Night Owl Romance* Reviewer Top Pick, 5 Stars

For more Terry Spear, visit:

www.sourcebooks.com

Tall, Dark, and Vampire

by Sara Humphreys

—✺—

She always knew Fate was cruel...

The last person Olivia expected to turn up at her club was her one true love. It would normally be great to see him, *except he's been dead for centuries*. Olivia really thought she had moved on with her immortal life, but as soon as she sees Doug Paxton, she knows she'd rather die than lose him again. And that's a real problem...

But this is beyond the pale...

Doug is a no-nonsense cop by day, but his nights are tormented by dreams of a gorgeous redhead who's so much a part of him, she seems to be in his blood. When he meets Olivia face-to-face, long-buried memories begin to surface. She might be the answer to his prayers...or she might be the death of him.

—✺—

Praise for Untamed:

"The characters are well-developed, the twists and turns of the plot are well-crafted, and the situations are alternately funny, action-packed, and sensual."—*Fresh Fiction*

"An excellent paranormal romance with awesome world-building and strong leads."—*The Romance Reviews*

For more Sara Humphreys, visit:

www.sourcebooks.com

About the Author

Ashlyn Chase describes herself as an Almond Joy bar. A little nutty, a little flaky, but basically sweet, wanting only to give her readers a satisfying reading experience.

She holds a degree in behavioral sciences, worked as a psychiatric RN for several years, and spent a few more years working for the American Red Cross. She credits her sense of humor to her former careers since comedy helped preserve whatever was left of her sanity. She is a multipublished, award-winning author of humorous erotic and paranormal romances, represented by the Seymour Agency.

She lives in beautiful New Hampshire with her true-life hot, hero husband (who looks like Hugh Jackman if you squint), and they're owned by a spoiled brat cat.

Where there's fire, there's Ash.
Check out my news, contest, videos, and reviews: www.ashlynchase.com
Join my Facebook fan page: www.facebook.com /AuthorAshlynChase
Chat with me: groups.yahoo.com/group/ashlynsnew bestfriends/
Tweet with me: @GoddessAsh
Ask me to sign your ebook at www.authorgraph.com